SMOKE IN THE MIRROR

Aimee Nicole Walker

Smoke in the Mirror (Road to Blissville, #5)
Copyright © 2018 Aimee Nicole Walker

ISBN: 978-1-948273-06-0

aimeenicolewalker@blogspot.com

Cover photograph © Wander Aguiar—www.wanderaguiar.com
Cover art © Jay Aheer of Simply Defined Art—www.simplydefinedart.com

Editing provided by Miranda Vescio of V8 Editing and Proofreading—www.facebook.com/V8Editing/

Proofreading provided by Judy Zweifel of Judy's Proofreading—www.judysproofreading.com

Interior Design and Formatting provided by Stacey Ryan Blake of Champagne Book Design—www.champagnebookdesign.com

DEDICATION

To Wyatt,

You're my teddy bear of a kid who would give the shirt off his back to a total stranger. Don't let the world harden your generous and kind heart. I am so very proud to be your mother.

CHAPTER ONE

Memphis Sullivan

I DON'T KNOW WHAT THE HELL PROMPTED ME TO OPEN MY MOUTH and door to Lyric Willows, psychic medium, host of the popular show *The Paranormal Whisperer* and the star of my early-morning, mid-day, and late-night fantasies. I'd had several opportunities to meet Lyric over the years because my cousin, Emory Jackson, was a psychic guest on the show many times. Emory knew how hard I crushed on that raspy-voiced, tattooed, leather-wearing God of a man and had offered to introduce us many times. I, of course, declined because I was afraid the reality of Lyric would ruin the fantasy of him. Well, that's the excuse I gave Emory anyway. The truth is I became extremely tongue-tied just thinking about him. I nearly swallowed my tongue during Lyric-induced orgasms and was terrified how I'd behave if we were ever in the same room.

Then a situation arose where avoiding him would've seemed rude. Lyric was in the area scouting potential locations for an up-coming season of his show and called Emory to see if they could meet up. My dear cousin didn't bother telling me Lyric called him or stopped in Blissville, but I couldn't be upset with Emory. I might've made up bullshit excuses in the past, but he knew I was at a comic book convention and wouldn't return home until almost midnight.

I learned about Lyric's appearance over Sunday brunch the next morning with Milo and Maegan, the Miracle twins, and their significant others. Jackie Miracle, their mother, had stopped by their café and bookstore, Books and Brew, the previous evening to pick up her paperback book order and noticed Lyric looking through books on the history of Blissville, particularly the mystery of Bliss House which Maegan had recently purchased. I suspected I couldn't avoid meeting Lyric if he returned to town, a feeling that was confirmed when I stopped by my comic book and record store, Vinyl and Villains, after brunch to add my newly purchased items to the inventory. Someone had slipped a note inside the mail slot in the door, and it landed on top of the mail on the floor. My heart skipped several beats when I read the masculine scrawl.

Memphis,

I was in town to see Emory and thought I'd stop by to introduce myself even though it seems like I already know you through Em. Maybe next time.

Lyric

BTW, love the name of your store.

The fact that Lyric sought me out changed everything. It would've been a total dick move if I'd ignored him, but honestly, I figured his interest in Maegan's house would fade. Of all the small towns in America with haunted houses, why pick Blissville? It turned out I underestimated Bliss House's appeal because Lyric informed Maegan he was definitely interested. Then he fell off the face of the earth when his show went on a sudden hiatus with no one talking about why. Out of the blue a month or so later, Lyric reached out to Maegan and arranged to tour Bliss House in mid-June. Of course, she turned it into a barbecue and invited me, his number one fan.

Lyric asked if there was a place he could rent while he stayed in town to investigate and film. Finding landlords willing to rent you a house or apartment short-term was unlikely, and we didn't have a bed and breakfast. He could've stayed at a hotel in the neighboring town of Goodville, but it didn't feel right to me, especially considering the sadness that clung to him. One second, I'm pondering places he could stay, and the next, I'm opening my mouth and offering him the spare bedroom in the house I rent. I didn't panic over my surprising boldness because there was no way he would accept the offer to bunk with a stranger, regardless of how well he knew my cousin.

Lyric slightly narrowed his eyes as he studied my face like he was trying to determine if I was serious. *Was I?* Yes, I was, but I didn't so much as blink, let alone speak, while he decided. Or maybe he wanted to shoot me down but worried about offending Emory. I was about to assure Lyric he could refuse without hurting my feelings when he answered.

"Okay."

What? I had no idea at the time just how much one word would change my life. I wasn't the only one at the table surprised by both my offer and his acceptance, and I could feel everyone's regard focused on me. It made me feel uncomfortable as I imagined what was going through their brains. Some of them would be thinking things that would make me blush if I allowed my mind to go there, and the rest were worried I'd get my heart broken. Then I glanced over at Milo who winked playfully. My friend looked neither lecherous nor worried; he looked smug because he put a great significance on Lyric's appearance in town. Milo acted like it was meant to be while I believed it was pure circumstance.

After dinner, the strain got to be too much, and I announced I needed to head home to get ready for my work week. I scooped up Gigi, my tiny white Chihuahua who loved playing in the big back yard at Bliss House with my friends' dogs. It felt awkward approaching Lyric, but I couldn't offer him a place to stay without giving him the address or a way to contact me.

"Cute dog," Lyric said, reaching out to scratch behind Gigi's ears. I'd never been so jealous of an animal in my entire life. "That was one of the things I wanted to talk to you about before you left."

"Her name is Gigi. One of the things?" I teased. "Are you going to grill me to make sure I don't have a collection of severed fingers under my bed or something."

"Um, I hadn't planned to ask that, but maybe I should," Lyric said then chuckled. "I was thinking along the lines of asking if you were allergic to dogs or had pet restrictions at your house. I think Gigi answers those questions."

"How do you know I don't own the home?"

"I was pretty sure Emory mentioned you rented a house from..." His words trailed off as he tried to recall the conversation. "It was something cutesy."

"The Matrons of Maple Lane."

"That's it."

"I'm a little worried about what Emory has said about me," I told the man who stood at least six to seven inches taller than my five-eight height. "I can't imagine how the subject of my landlord, her mother, and her sister came up."

"It had more to do with my remarks on this quaint but quirky town," Lyric replied in a tone I found soothing and seductive at the same time. "Em used the Matrons as an example of the best, but quirkiest, parts of living in Blissville."

I was so happy to hear Emory got a kick out of the Matrons trying to set me up with all the eligible bachelors in town and the surrounding county. Was that what Em had told Lyric? If not, I debated on telling him what he was subjecting himself to by moving in with me, even if temporarily. Instead, I said. "I have no allergies and pets are welcome."

"Good," Lyric replied, sounding relieved. "I can't stay anyplace Daisy isn't welcome, and I won't leave her behind longer than necessary."

Beneath his tatted, tough-guy exterior lived a dog lover. Could he be any sexier? Could he make my dick any harder? Well, maybe if he had a piercing, or two. I halted my thoughts before I sprung wood in Maegan's back yard.

"I don't want to hold you up, so here's my business card. You can send your address to my email." I took the offered card and slid it in my front pocket.

"What other things did you want to discuss aside from pets and allergies?"

"It's not important," Lyric replied. "Daisy was my biggest concern and everything else will work itself out."

"Fair enough," I agreed. "Talk to you soon."

"Yeah, we'll talk soon."

Three weeks passed with no word from Lyric. I would've taken it personally if he was communicating with Maegan during that timeframe, but she hadn't heard from him either. I'd shamefully looked online for answers, but he had pulled another disappearing act. I accepted he'd changed his mind and moved on to a different town and haunted house. I'd kept my house spotless during the first month of waiting because I wanted to make a good impression on the man when he arrived, but I gave up on tidiness at the same time I gave up on him showing up on my doorstep.

That's why I was masturbating at eleven o'clock on a Saturday night instead of scrubbing the bathroom and kitchen when his truck rumbled into my driveway. I didn't realize he arrived right away of course because I was fingering my ass with two fingers from my left hand while stroking my dick with my right. What else would I be doing on a Saturday night? I was about to shoot my load when I heard Gigi growling low in her throat in the hallway. At first, I thought she was pissed because I locked her out of the bedroom since I couldn't jerk off with her judgmental eyes watching me. Then the growl became a full-out squeaking bark about the same time I heard voices downstairs. My stroking hand stilled as panic flooded my body.

"What the fuck are they doing here?" I whispered out loud. The Matrons were nosy as fuck, but they'd never unlocked the door and let themselves in. Then I heard a fourth voice join them, one so deep and raspy with the perfect amount of southern drawl, and it sent electric thrills coursing through my body. The slightest jerk with my right hand made me come hard enough for my toes to curl and my eyes roll back in my head.

"Memphis is probably sleeping," Gertie said loudly from the bottom of the steps. She was the oldest, and mother of Sandra and Clara. Sandra was the one who owned the house I rented, and it was mostly furnished with her belongings. The only things I moved in were my clothes and my bed. Sandra moved in with Gertie after her husband's sudden death a few years prior. Up until that moment, I felt exceedingly lucky to find such a nurturing landlord and two additional ladies to fuss over me.

"Fuck!" I whisper-yelled, jackknifing off the bed and grabbing the closest pair of sweats off the floor. I grabbed a T-shirt too, but instead of pulling it over my head, I wiped the cum off my chest and tossed it in the direction of the dirty clothes basket.

"Surely not," Sandra said. "It's a Saturday night. He's most likely busy doing something else." *Fuck me!* "We were all young and single once."

"Who needs to be young or single to masturbate?" Gertie asked her oldest daughter.

"Mom!" Clara admonished. She was the softest spoken and most demure of the three, but that wasn't saying much.

"We love your show," Gertie said, changing the subject. "Memphis is a big fan too."

"Is he now?" I heard Lyric ask. It sounded like he was trying hard not to laugh at the exchange he'd just witnessed.

I threw on the first shirt I could find because I couldn't go down there bare-chested in case my cum smears were still wet. The first thing I noticed when I stepped off the bottom step was the size of Daisy. When Lyric mentioned his dog, I imagined something little and cute like the name implied. Daisy was a black and white Great

Dane whose head came up past my waist. Gigi wasn't intimidated though and ran right up to the big dog to greet her. Daisy lay on her belly and lowered her head for Gigi to sniff her instead of intimidating my dog with their size difference. Gigi barked and spun in circles while Daisy wagged her tail.

"At least the dogs will get along well," Lyric said.

I looked away from the dogs to meet Lyric's eyes for the first time and nearly gasped when I saw how exhausted he looked. His mouth tilted up into a crooked half smile.

"I'm sorry I didn't call to let you know I was on the way. I don't know what the hell I was thinking. I could've stayed at the pet-friendly hotel in Goodville tonight and let you sleep." Gertie snorted at the suggestion I was sleeping, but I couldn't tear my eyes away from Lyric Willows. There was something more than exhaustion wearing on him, but I didn't know the man well enough to comment, especially not in front of the ladies.

"Nonsense," I assured him. "I'm glad you're here." I almost said I was glad he came, but I knew it would make Sandra and Gertie giggle. "Are you hungry?"

"Nah," he said, shaking his head. "I hit a drive-thru in Goodville." It was a good thing he stopped, more than a week had passed since the last time I bought groceries.

"How long were you on the road?" Gertie asked. "You look like you've been ridden hard and put away wet."

I grew up around horses in West Virginia, so I'd heard variations of that phrase practically my entire life. It sounded so dirty though when I stood there looking into Lyric's eyes. His cheeks turned pink, and he cleared his throat but didn't look away from me.

"I was on the road for the better part of twelve hours. I only stopped for gas, food, and to let Daisy stretch her legs. I'm feeling pretty rough," Lyric admitted. "If it's okay with you, I'd like to take a quick shower to wash away the road dirt and crash for the night."

"Sure, let me show you where you can find the bathroom and

your bedroom." I turned and faced the Matrons who all looked at me with various smiles on their faces.

"Nice shirt," Sandra finally said.

I looked down and saw that I'd pulled on my Powerpuff Girls T-shirt. My mother always said I needed to dress like I was thirty and not thirteen. I'd never agreed with her until I tried to envision what I might look like to Lyric.

"I need to do laundry," I said defensively. Gertie raised her brow because she knew damn well I wore the shirt weekly.

"And tidy up a bit," Sandra added, looking around. "What happened? I was just over here last week, and it was spotless. A person could've eaten off the floors."

"Things got a little busy at the store," I said calmly. "The days just seemed to slip away from me." If Gertie's brow got any higher, it would merge into her hairline. Okay, fine. I pouted like a spoiled child because Lyric hadn't emailed or called to let me know when he was coming or even if he changed his mind

"Don't worry about trying to make me happy," Lyric said. "Pretend I'm not here." *Yeah, right.*

"Let's head on upstairs, and you," I pointed to all three ladies, "need to get on home so I can show Lyric to his room."

"Goodnight," all three of them said, waving at us before they disappeared.

I faced Lyric once more and smiled sheepishly. "I probably should've warned you about them. It's not too late to run for your life, you know. I promise I won't be offended."

"Nah," Lyric replied for the second time that night. "I'm sure they only mean well."

"Mostly. Follow me, and I'll give you the tour of the upstairs. It's pretty obvious where everything is down here."

Hearing the heavy sounds of his boots trudging up the steps set my nerves to tingling. It was really happening. How was I going to sleep with him down the hallway from me? The bathroom was between our bedrooms, and I'd be able to lie in bed and hear the shower running and imagine water cascading down his long, hot body. I was so lost in thought I missed the next step in front of me and tripped *up* the stairs.

"Shit!" Lyric exclaimed. "Are you okay?"

"My dignity is the only thing hurt," I said, getting back up to my feet. *Dumbass.*

I pointed to my room as we walked by, grateful I'd thought to shut the door so Lyric didn't see the hideous mess inside. "This is the bathroom we'll share, and the next door down is your bedroom. There's a third bedroom downstairs if you'd like more privacy, but it's so small only a twin bed fits inside it.

"This is fine. It's a decent size and tidy." Lyric walked into the room with Daisy and Gigi following behind him. I had no intention of walking in there too until I realized Gigi wasn't coming out of the room willingly.

"Come on, girl," I cooed. "It's bedtime. You can see Daisy in the morning."

Gigi's answer was to dart beneath the bed and bark like it was playtime. I dropped to my knees, lifted the dust ruffle, and lowered my upper body so I could glare at my dog. "Young lady, I'm not playing." I reached beneath the bed, but she darted away from my hand before I could grab her. Behind me, Lyric made a strangled noise in his throat, and I worried he was good and pissed. I turned to look over my shoulder and caught him staring at my ass before he jerked his eyes back up to meet mine.

"I'm so damn sorry," I told him. "Why don't you go ahead and take a shower while I drag Gigi out from under your bed. Surprisingly enough, there are clean towels in the closet." *At least I'd done something right that week.*

"Yeah, okay," Lyric said, rubbing the back of his neck. "Um, I'll see you in the morning."

As soon as I heard the bathroom door shut, I looked back under the bed. "Listen here; you better come out of there right now."

Gigi just barked again and wagged her tail. Daisy walked over and lay beside me. Gigi came running right to her, so I snagged my dog before she could dart back under the bed.

"You're a very good girl, Daisy," I said, stroking a soft, floppy ear. "Thank you."

I returned to my room where, as predicted, I lay awake most of the night. It was sometime around four in the morning when I finally nodded off, and I jerked awake around seven. I quickly dressed and brushed my teeth before heading downstairs to clean the kitchen and living room as quietly as I could. I knew Lyric was exhausted and wanted him to sleep as long as he needed. He wasn't awake by the time I finished the first floor, and I debated if I should do brunch with my friends or go grocery shopping. I decided to do the right thing and buy food, so I texted Milo to let him know I wouldn't make it to brunch then took my ass to the grocery store.

I had no idea what the hell the man liked to eat, so I focused on the basics for the moment. When I returned home forty-five minutes later, Lyric still hadn't risen. My dick sure was alert from remembering he was asleep upstairs, probably naked. I ignored my growing erection and tiptoed as quietly as I could up the stairs to tackle the bathroom and my bedroom, not that I expected Lyric to visit me there.

A mortifying realization hit me as soon as I walked into the bathroom. I'd been too rattled to think about it the night before and too anxious that morning to remember what I'd left in my shower. I was pretty sure Milo thought it was a gag gift when he gave it to me for my birthday, but I had taken many a ride on the lifelike dildo. I didn't normally leave it suctioned to the bathroom wall for people to see when they came over or moved in temporarily in this case. I slowly approached the shower curtain like there was a knife-wielding psycho on the other side, praying I hadn't left Big Bob in the shower. I gripped the shower curtain and jerked it open fast just like a person did when removing a Band-Aid. Big Bob was indeed still suctioned to the shower wall. If that wasn't bad enough, Lyric had hung his washcloth over the thick, long dildo. How was I ever going to look him in the eyes again? "Oh my God," I mumbled.

"Yeah, I bet you say that a lot," said a deep voice from behind me. "I'm impressed."

CHAPTER TWO

Lyric Willows

MEMPHIS'S ENTIRE BODY TENSED, BUT HE DIDN'T TURN around. "Oh my God," he said for the second time. His head fell forward and hung like he was ashamed, and I felt horrible for saying anything.

"Don't be embarrassed," I said, trying to smooth things over. "We all need to come." Memphis released a strangled groan-sigh combo, letting me know I failed to ease his worry. "At first, I thought it was part of the amenities at Casa de Memphis, but then I remembered you weren't expecting me last night." Memphis's shoulders began to shake, and I worried that he was crying. "Fuck, I really know how to screw things up." I placed my hand on his shoulder and turned him around to look at me. I got lost in his big brown eyes and forgot what I was going to say.

"I should be humiliated but remarks like 'we all need to come' and 'amenities at Casa de Memphis' just won't let me." I relaxed a little when I saw the tears in his eyes were from laughter and not humiliation. "Thank you for that."

"Don't thank me," I replied dryly. "If I were a good person, I would've pretended not to see it, not hung my washcloth over it and cracked jokes the next morning."

"Afternoon," Memphis corrected.

"Oh yeah," I replied, still in disbelief I'd slept until noon.

"About the washcloth," Memphis said. "Um, were you disgusted about the toy or unsure what to do with your washcloth after you used it?"

"I wasn't disgusted, but it was a bit intimidating, and I felt like it was watching me." This remark earned me a deep belly laugh, making me want to whip off his adorable, black-rimmed glasses and taste the laughter on his lips. It had been so long since I laughed, or even wanted to, but Memphis stirred the desire, among many others, inside me.

"Big Bob is harmless," Memphis said.

"Big Bob?" I asked. "He's way too intimidating for such a tame name."

"That's what Milo named him."

"Um, your best friend named your dildo?" They had a closer relationship than I realized. For reasons unfathomable to me, I didn't like it.

"Oh my God!" Memphis shook his head and covered his mouth as more laughter bubbled out of him.

I wanted to take his hand away so his joy could echo around the room, and maybe infuse my soul. Then I wanted to drag him to my room where I could make him forget all about Big Bob while he chanted "Oh my God!" over and over and over in my ear. Leaning against the doorframe, I casually crossed my right leg over my left and hoped it looked like I was settling in for a delightful story instead of hiding my growing erection.

"Milo bought it for me as a gag gift for my latest birthday. Big Bob was the name on the box it came in, and I didn't think about changing it. I guess I still don't know much about its personality, so Big Bob works for now." His face turned pink like he worried he'd said too much.

I knew he was cute from pictures on Emory's phone and social media sites, and I told the truth in the note I left at his store several weeks ago. I felt like I knew Memphis from the stories Emory told me about him. Until Memphis, I never really knew it was possible to like someone I'd never met or even spoke to. He intrigued me in ways usually only restless spirits of the paranormal variety did, and that was *before* I met him. At Maegan's house, he seemed quiet and a little reserved until he offered up his guestroom out of the blue. At the time, I didn't see a problem accepting his offer.

Everything changed the moment Memphis came down the steps the previous night. His curly dark hair looked tousled from sleep, or something else, and his glasses sat slightly crooked on his face. The Powerpuff Girls T-shirt and sweatpants hanging low on his hips just took the adorability level up a hundred points. It was obvious he'd just thrown on his clothes, and I couldn't help wondering if he was naked beneath his sweats. Memphis looked and smelled like someone who'd just come, and it drove me wild. My eyes zeroed in on his fine ass when I followed him up the steps, and I nearly fell on top of him when he stumbled. I so wanted to high-five Gigi when she ran under my bed and Memphis dropped to his knees and stuck his delectable ass in the air. He caught me staring, but I wasn't thinking clearly enough to regret it.

My dick had started to twitch to life while looking at the way the cotton molded to his ass. I readily accepted his suggestion that I hit the shower, certain hot water would ease my tension from traveling all day and allow me to sleep. Then I pulled back the shower curtain and saw Big Bob suctioned to the wall, and I got tense for entirely different reasons. I couldn't stop myself from picturing Memphis fucking the dildo and wondering what sounds he made when he was turned on. I couldn't walk out of the bathroom with my dick sticking out from my body like a sword. The only logical thing to do was take myself in hand while the hot water eased my aching body and let my fantasy play out. It worked like a charm too because I fell into the deepest sleep I'd experienced in years, maybe even a decade, after I stumbled to my room.

Looking at his flushed cheeks and laughing eyes made the need and want return ten times stronger than the night before. I knew I should pack my bags and get the hell out of there before I fucked up and did something I'd regret, but I didn't move from my spot in the doorway.

"Well, I'll just be taking Big Bob out of here so you can get on with your day," Memphis said, breaking eye contact when he turned and faced the shower.

"Big Bob doesn't have to leave on my account," I told him. "This is your home, and I meant it when I said I didn't want you going to any trouble."

"I don't usually keep Big Bob in the shower," Memphis said, reaching for his sex toy. I don't know why it felt so important, but I shifted to the other side of the doorway to watch him remove the dildo from the shower wall. Memphis casually wrapped his hand around the base of the lifelike cock with one hand and gave it a sharp tug. Big Bob didn't budge. He jerked two more times, and I swear I could almost feel his hands wrapped around my dick, jacking me. Memphis fisted the shaft with his second hand, but the dildo was so big the crown remained uncovered. He tugged and pulled, making the tip bounce up and down like it was mocking him.

I bit my lip to keep from laughing hysterically. "I don't think Bob wants to leave."

Memphis gave the dildo one last yank at the same time he looked over his shoulder at me with a crooked grin on his face. That's when Big Bob gave up the fight. Memphis wasn't prepared for the sudden release and started falling backward, which sent Big Bob flying through the air. It hit me in the chest and dropped to the bathroom floor with a solid *thud*. Memphis cracked his head on the tile floor, and the situation became anything but funny.

"Are you okay?" I asked dropping to my knees beside Memphis where he lay on the floor blinking his big brown eyes. I reached over and adjusted his crooked glasses, and he looked at me.

"No."

15

"You hit your head pretty hard," I told him. "Are you experiencing any dizziness or nausea? Are the bright lights hurting your eyes?" I gently placed my hands beneath his head and slid my fingers through his silky curls to look for lumps.

"I don't have a concussion," Memphis said, closing his eyes when I looked back at him. "I'm mortified. Could this have gone any worse?"

"It could've gone much worse," I replied calmly. I noticed my fingers in his hair had turned from seeking to comforting, so I removed them. The best way not to disappoint him was to not give in to the electricity arcing between us. Memphis was surrounded by people pairing up with their soul mates which was something I could never be for him or anyone. I couldn't allow myself to forget it because, in addition to hurting Memphis, I'd lose a wonderful friend in Emory. I vowed to stand strong and resist his charms.

"How could it possibly have gone worse?"

"I could've discovered this house was possessed by an evil spirit biding its time to attack you," I replied, thinking fast on my feet.

"True," Memphis said as he sat up. "But Big Bob..." He turned and gestured to where the dildo should've been lying on the floor.

"Made a *big* impression," I suggested.

Memphis shook his head. "Oh no. It's missing."

"What?" I tore my eyes off him long enough to see Big Bob was indeed gone.

I knew damn well who'd stolen it when I heard Daisy growling and Gigi barking playfully. I scrambled to my feet and ran down the hall. Sure enough, Daisy had Big Bob pinned to the floor by his balls and was gnawing on the shaft.

"Oh fuck! Drop it, Daisy!" I said firmly. My dog obediently let the shaft fall to the floor between her huge paws. "My dog ate your dildo," I said when Memphis came up behind me. There were huge gouges from Daisy's teeth all up and down the sex toy.

Memphis collapsed against the wall in a fit of laughter, clutching his stomach as tears rolled down his face. "Oh my God! Laughter is the best ab workout." I wanted to lift his shirt and press my hand against his stomach to feel the muscles working beneath the skin as he laughed over our dogs' shenanigans.

Gigi tried to get her mouth around it and barked when she was unsuccessful. "Don't feel bad, Gigi," I said supportively. "Not many could get one so big in their mouths." That only made Memphis laugh harder, and I wanted to see his lips stretched around my cock. I didn't want to seem like a braggart, but Big Bob had nothing on me. "Looks like I owe you a replacement."

That made Memphis stop laughing. His eyebrow rose high on his forehead like one of the Matrons last night. I thought her name was Gertie, but I had a difficult time recalling anything beyond the interactions I had with Memphis. What was the cause for his surprise? Could he tell how much I wanted to replace his lifelike dildo with my flesh-and-blood cock?

"Please don't buy me a replacement dildo," Memphis implored.

"Do you already have a backup on standby?" I asked without thinking. "Wait! Don't answer that highly inappropriate question. I've made a big enough mess of things as it is."

"You didn't," Memphis said walking toward me. I thought he was going to stop in front of me, but he kept walking until he reached the dogs. Gigi growled possessively when he bent to retrieve Big Bitten Bob off the floor. "Great, she thinks it's a treasure."

"Some would agree with her," I quipped. "Why don't I distract the dogs by taking them outside while you deal with the carnage?"

"Deal," Memphis said in relief.

I walked past him and gave a sharp whistle for Daisy to follow me, knowing Gigi would most likely shadow her. I sat on the back deck for about fifteen minutes while the girls did their business. When we went back inside, I noticed the kitchen and living room were sparkling clean. I wondered what time Memphis got up to accomplish it all. I hated that he went to any trouble on my behalf and wanted to do something nice to make it up to him. Sucking his dick would be especially nice for both of us, but it pissed in the face of my determination to resist temptation. My stomach growled to remind me how long it had been since I'd last eaten, so I looked through the cabinets and refrigerator to see what he had on hand to eat.

It took Memphis longer to come down than I expected, which made me wonder what he was doing upstairs. I heard him moving around up there but couldn't tell exactly what was going on until I heard him fire up a vacuum. By the time he came downstairs, the blueberry peach muffins I'd made were cooling on the counter.

"Whoa," he said in awe, sniffing the air. "I didn't hear the Matrons stop by with fresh baked goods."

"They didn't," I answered smugly.

"You baked these?" Memphis asked. "I didn't even know I had the stuff to make muffins here."

"It's a pretty basic recipe. I just had to allow for the extra moisture in the frozen fruit since I normally work with fresh fruit."

"I don't even remember buying frozen fruit." Memphis tipped his head to the side. "Oh, now I do. I made margaritas a few months ago when the gang came over to watch…" His words trailed off, and a flush of pink crept up his neck.

I suspected I knew what he was about to say before he caught himself. I didn't find it weird or creepy that he liked my show. I wasn't sure if I should try to assure him, or let it go. My last attempt at putting him at ease was an epic fail. Then I remembered the way he leaned against the wall in the hallway to laugh over Daisy destroying Bob. Maybe my attempt didn't turn out too bad after all. But what if I told him it didn't weird me out only to discover he was talking about something else? For all I knew, they gathered once a week to watch the latest porn releases.

A light knock sounded on the kitchen door. Memphis mumbled something about meddling Matrons on his way across the room, but not before he snagged a muffin off the cooling rack.

"Uh oh." I couldn't imagine what made him sound so hesitant, so I turned around.

Maegan, Elijah, Milo, and Andy all stood on his deck making faces at him through the glass door. I crossed my arms over my chest and watched the friends interact without them knowing I was there. They would've had to turn their heads sharply to the left to see me, and they obviously weren't expecting Memphis to have an overnight guest. I hated how much I liked knowing that.

"Open up," Milo demanded.

"Go away."

Milo wasn't discouraged in the least. "Not until you tell us why your text was so vague this morning."

"And explain why you ignored our follow-up texts," Maegan added.

"Is everything okay in there?" Elijah, the police detective, asked. He pivoted his body so he could see into the kitchen to make sure someone wasn't holding Memphis hostage or something. His eyes widened when they met mine. "There's nothing to see here, folks," Elijah said. "You can see Memphis is fine. He can call you all later."

"As if we don't understand that's cop talk for something big is happening," Maegan told her boyfriend.

"I'm fine, Mae," Memphis assured her. "I just had a late night and didn't sleep well. There's nothing more sinister going on than that."

"What old codger is visiting the Matrons?" Andy asked. "I've never seen that truck around here." I knew he was talking about my 1959 Chevy Apache parked in the driveway Memphis's house shared with Gertie's. *Hey, he's a classic!* People weren't used to seeing them on the road other than in parades or at car shows. They were expecting the owner to be a much older guy than me, but that beauty was my everyday truck, and I loved him.

"They're not going away until you let them in," I whispered.

Memphis looked over his shoulder at me, and three out of the four people on the other side of the door leaned forward and angled their heads to see who, or what, he was looking at. A big smile spread across the Miracle twins' faces, and Andy looked like he was chuckling.

"Can we go now," Elijah said, realizing the cat was out of the bag. "Memphis has a visitor."

"Let them in, Memphis," I said. "I'm going to head out to do some shopping and hopefully stop by to see Emory and Jon for a little bit."

"Are you sure?" he asked.

"Absolutely. Your house, your guests."

Memphis opened the door and stepped back for them to enter, but the foursome didn't seem as motivated to do so.

"I'm sorry," Maegan whispered then hugged Memphis when she stepped inside the house.

"Don't apologize for caring about me, Mae."

"Look, we can come back later," Milo said, looking back and forth between Memphis and me.

"Nonsense," I told them. "I was just heading out to do a bit of shopping." I looked at Memphis. "Do you mind if Daisy stays here with you to rest after the long drive yesterday?"

"Of course not," Memphis said. "Take your time; I don't have any plans."

"Yes, you do," Milo said. "Dinner at my parents. Remember? It's my dad's birthday barbecue."

"Oh yeah," Memphis said. "I'll be there."

"You are more than welcome to join us, Lyric," Maegan said. "My mom makes enough food for an army, and she'd enjoy talking to you again."

I could tell by Memphis's expression he expected me to decline, which was what I should've done. Instead, I said, "That sounds great. Your mom is hilarious."

"Glad you think so," Milo said wryly.

"I won't be gone long," I told Memphis. The newly arrived guests

20

parted like the Red Sea as I crossed the room toward the door. I'd just reached for the handle when he stopped me.

"I have an extra key for you," he said, blushing adorably as he walked to me. Memphis pulled a silver key off one of the hooks next to the door and held it up for me to see. I opened my palm, and he placed it in the center, his fingers brushing against my skin. It was such a simple touch, but I felt it in my bones. Haunted asylums scared me less than Memphis Sullivan.

CHAPTER THREE

Memphis

I KEPT MY BACK TURNED TO MY FRIENDS WHILE I TRIED TO FIND MY center, not realizing it looked like I was watching Lyric walk away like a lovesick fool.

"If these walls could talk…" Maegan said then sighed.

"We don't need the walls when Memphis can tell us exactly what the hell is going on," Milo said.

It looked like it was time to face the music, so I turned around and smiled disarmingly at them. "I'm so sorry I worried you."

"Not good enough," Milo told me.

"I mean, it's obvious you had a good reason for missing brunch, but I'm curious why you didn't mention it instead of a cryptic 'not going to make it' text message," Maegan added.

"And ignored us when we checked to make sure you were okay," Andy said.

"Guys, give him room to breathe," Elijah said softly.

"Babe, we're on the other side of the kitchen from him. You act like we're hovering around him or something," Maegan told her boyfriend.

"I meant figuratively, Freckles. I've seen cops be gentler while interrogating suspects than the three of you are treating your best friend right now," Elijah teased.

"It's okay," I said. "I wasn't thinking clearly this morning because

I was rushing around here trying to make the house nice after things got off to a rough start when Lyric showed up unexpectedly last night. I'd hoped for a better morning, but I ended up making things worse." It all poured out of me then, and I mean every single detail down to The Dildo Disaster of 2018.

When I finished, four sets of astounded eyes stared unblinkingly at me. I counted silently in my head as I waited to see who would crack first. *One, two...*

"Holy fuck!" Elijah exclaimed then doubled over laughing.

The other three joined him but were laughing too hard to speak. They just gasped for air while clutching their chests or stomachs and leaning on each other to avoid falling. Most people would've had their feelings hurt over the lack of support their *friends* showed them during a crisis. Me? I joined in and thanked the universe for shoving me into their lives.

I didn't decide one day to blindly throw a dart at a map and move to wherever it landed. Emory moved to Blissville after persistent psychic visions showed him it was where he belonged. It turned out the small town, and the people who resided there, was what Emory needed. He made incredible friends who literally introduced him to the man of his dreams, and more importantly, showed him how much they loved him when he was diagnosed with a benign brain tumor. I came to Blissville to act as Emory's medical power of attorney and help care for him after his surgery. What I found was a home I'd never looked for and friends I never knew I was missing in my life.

Milo and Maegan became more than just my friends and the people who helped me realize my dream of owning a comic book and record store. They were my snark mates, and other than Emory, the people who knew and loved me best. My adoration now extended to Andy and Elijah—the men they shared their lives with.

"I-I don't know what to say," Maegan said between gasps of air when she finally stopped laughing. "I think sorry is in order, but it would be a flat-out lie. I think Big Bob broke the awkward tension between two strangers trying to cohabitate."

"H-h-h-hung his w-w-w-washcloth on it," Milo stuttered then resumed laughing.

Andy tried to pull himself together but couldn't seem to do it.

"The sexual tension between you guys is off the fucking charts," Maegan said. "Sweet Jesus, why can't I be a fly on the wall?"

"I didn't know you were such a perv, Freckles," Elijah said, hooking his arm around her neck and pulling her close. "The dog ate my dildo is a new one for me, but oh-so-fucking hilarious."

Milo started pretending to tug on an invisible dildo, making me laugh until tears rolled down my face.

"Get this out of your systems now before he comes back," I told them. "I'm not sure Lyric will find it as funny as we do. I especially don't want to discuss this in front of your parents. We will only discuss The Dildo Disaster of 2018 in this house. Swear it."

"We swear," they all said obediently. I knew my friends were lying through their pearly white teeth.

"There will be hell to pay if I show up at brunch and find dildo-shaped pancakes or a resplendent dildo cake at your parents' barbecue some Sunday evening."

"Well, hell," Milo said. "I must be slipping because I didn't even think about it."

"Me either," Maegan agreed.

"Now you did it," Andy teased me.

"Swear you won't do those things," I insisted.

"We swear," they all said at once.

I turned my back on them to start a pot of coffee because I could tell they weren't leaving anytime soon, not until they were certain I was okay. Or maybe my friends wanted to stick around until Lyric returned. If the guy were smart, he'd circle the block until the gang left, but Lyric didn't strike me as the type who backed down from anything. Of course, I thought dealing with apparitions might be easier than well-meaning friends and neighborhood matrons.

Elijah mock-whispered, "He didn't make us pinky swear," earning a glare from me over my shoulder.

"When did you start baking?" Milo asked around a mouthful of muffin. "Mmmmmm, so good."

"Need a minute?" I asked him.

"At least ten," Andy replied for him.

I turned in time to see my friends each grab a freshly baked muffin. "Didn't you eat already?"

Andy shook his head. "We were too worried about you."

"I call bullshit. Nothing gets in between you and food, Andy."

"Okay, we ate a little, but only so we had the strength to worry about you."

"Uh huh," I replied. "Go ahead and scarf down all the muffins Lyric baked and didn't have a chance to eat before you ran him off."

Milo mumbled something that sounded like, "He baked these?" but it was hard to tell with his mouth crammed full of the muffins that made my mouth water.

"Maybe we should put these back," Elijah said, looking and sounding sad.

"Not after you've fingered them," I admonished.

"That sounds so dirty," Andy told me.

"Take your muffins and go sit down in the living room," I instructed them. "I'll bring the coffee as soon as it's finished."

"So, he showed up without warning, huh?" Maegan asked. "Did he say when he expects the rest of the film crew to arrive?"

"He didn't," I replied, "and do you know what I find strange about that?"

"Lyric didn't ask to make arrangements for them to stay someplace," she answered. "I thought it was odd when he first asked but figured he would have them stay at the hotel in Goodville. He seems like the kind of person who'd want privacy, even from his longtime friends and castmates."

"That's what I thought too, and maybe it's still the case."

"You don't sound convinced," Maegan told me.

"He's always had this sad aura around him, but it feels stronger to me. When he arrived last night, there were dark shadows under his eyes and he looked exhausted."

"I think he looked good this morning," Milo said. "He looked more shell-shocked than anything. It's probably a combination of a long day of traveling combined with the Matrons bombarding him and Memphis sexually harassing him."

"I did no such thing."

"We all saw the size of that dildo, Memphis," Elijah said. "He definitely could've felt intimidated."

"I'm impressed though," Andy spoke up.

I felt my face heating up again because as close as we were, I didn't want them to think about me riding Big Bob to mind-blowing orgasms.

"Let's get back to discussing Lyric and his crew," Maegan said, steering us back to less humiliating topics for me. She winked as if to say, "I got you."

"We haven't discussed anything besides the Matrons and the incident in the bathroom." I left off the part about the sexual tension arcing between us. I felt his fingers in my hair long after he removed them, and it took a lot of scrubbing, dusting, and vacuuming before my dick decided to go back to sleep. "I don't feel comfortable asking him. I just wanted the guy to have a peaceful place where he could rest his head each night."

Milo snorted.

"I'll talk to him about his plans tonight at Mom's barbecue," Maegan said.

They sipped coffee and ate muffins while we caught up even though I saw them the day before. One thing I learned from my friends: we never ran out of things to talk about because Blissville was the gift that kept on giving. Ken Drake got caught having an affair with his college-age nanny, someone stole Timmy Thompson's bike from his front yard, and the former mayor, Rocky Beaumont, got arrested for drunk driving after he ran up over the curb and hit a mailbox. It turned out that hitting government-owned property carried stiffer penalties than if he'd hit a parked car.

My friends continued nibbling their muffins and sipping their coffee to buy time, but Lyric still hadn't returned by the time they finished. They looked damn disappointed too when they stood up to leave until I reminded them he agreed to attend the barbecue. As soon as they left, I raced up to my bedroom with the two dogs following closely behind me. I shut the door and retrieved my laptop from the small desk tucked in the corner. Daisy jumped on my bed, and I scooped Gigi up and placed her beside her new bestie.

"Please don't tell on me, Daisy." *Get a grip, man! The dog can't read.*

I nervously chewed on my lip and tried to ignore the guilt gripping my heart as I typed my password into my MacBook. I'd joined *Willows Whisperers* many years before Emory even met the man, but I should've deactivated my user account once my cousin became his friend. Lyric trusted me enough to live under my roof while he stayed in Blissville and looking at the gossip site felt like an act of betrayal.

The fandom site started out as a fun place where fans of the show, and the cast, could chat about the episodes and even engage in harmless fan fiction writing. As the site gained popularity along with the show, the attitudes of the creators, Myla Trey and Elvie Sparks, changed drastically. Elvie became this rabid fangirl who made it her mission in life to destroy anyone who didn't worship at the Lyric Willows altar. She spent her time posting links to articles questioning if Lyric was a fraud or a legitimate medium. Her rants about the authors' ignorance felt more like a call to arms than a valid discussion about the points within the articles themselves. Often, she and her most loyal followers would wage a social media war on these authors.

Myla wasn't any better. She turned out to be nothing more than a cyber stalker who thought she was somehow entitled to know all about Lyric's life. Not only did she want to know, but she felt everyone else deserved to know too. I knew enough about Lyric's movements through Emory to realize most of the stuff she posted was absolute bullshit to make her look smarter than everyone else. She was a miserable excuse for a human being, and the two of them made me ill.

I didn't log in to chat about the show or write steamy fan fiction where Lyric fell in love with a nerdy owner of a haunted house anymore; I made sure those two shrews weren't getting too close to the truth. I had on occasion posted lies to throw them off balance. Emory told me Lyric produced and directed his show and used those roles to ensure as much privacy and secrecy as he could. The locations were never given in advance to ensure privacy during filming. Lyric made the property owners sign a non-disclosure agreement promising they wouldn't discuss the events that occurred during filming until after the show aired. Included was a clause prohibiting them from even discussing when the crew was in town. Often, the show ended up at haunted homes, hospitals, museums, and asylums in small towns. People in those communities liked to gossip, and on occasion, they would leak info to the right person who would post the details on a forum which Myla would find.

When that happened, I posted fictitious information to counter hers. If Myla said the crew was heading to a school in Georgia, I found an unknown small town in Wisconsin that boasted about a haunted house in their community. If she said New York, I argued in favor of San Francisco. Amazingly enough, she never blocked me from the site, but I figured it was because she loved to argue almost as much as she liked pretending she had inside information about the cast and crew. I would rather Myla spend her time making me out to be the villain than looking too closely at Lyric's activities.

I guess a person could say I used my membership to do good, but I doubted Lyric would see it that way. When I finally pulled the site up, two posts immediately caught my eye. The first read: Where in the World is Lyric Willows? It sounded like a cute play on the game *Where in the World is Carmen Sandiego?* which happened to be my favorite computer game as a kid. That was as far as the cuteness went because Myla threw out all kinds of lewd reasons why the show was put on hiatus again while he seemingly disappeared from public eye. The suggestions ranged from a sudden marriage to a terminal illness. Lyric did look tired, but he didn't look sick on the two occasions we were face-to-face. As for the marriage, I hoped like hell he didn't stare at my ass like he wanted to sample it or run his fingers through my hair while looking like he wanted to kiss me if he had a husband waiting for him back home.

The second post read: Network is Silencing *The Paranormal Whisperer* For Good. Compared to the previous post, this one sited credible sources and facts pointing to signs the last episodes have either aired already or would be filmed shortly.

Could Maegan's house be Lyric's final show or one of them? Was it the reason for the signs of strain I saw on his face? Or was a canceled show the reason why he didn't ask about accommodations for his crew? The idea that there would be no more new episodes or only a remaining few saddened me.

I shut my laptop and set it on the pillow beside mine. I stared up at the ceiling while turning all the information around in my mind. I discounted the husband and illness part right away but couldn't make up my mind about the show. Myla had gotten things right a time or two, which was why I had to be a hero when I tended to be attracted to villains. I must've drifted to sleep because the next thing I remember, there was a soft knock on my bedroom door.

"Yeah?" I asked sleepily.

"Sorry to wake you, but I didn't know what time we needed to leave for the barbecue."

I glanced over at my alarm clock and saw it was four thirty. "Shit!" I bolted off the bed and crossed the room to open the door. "I need to take a quick shower to wake up and brush my teeth."

Lyric's eyes roamed over me from head to toe, and I felt his gaze as strongly on my skin as I would his fingers. Definitely not a newly-wed. "I'll take the girls out while you get ready," he said finally when his gray irises locked with mine. He didn't look like he wanted to budge though; he looked like he wanted to push me into my room and do very wicked things to me. I wanted that too, but it would be a mistake. We both knew it.

"We can take them with us," I said suddenly, trying to get my mind off jumping him in the hallway. "I figured you wouldn't want to leave Daisy in a strange environment." I looked at his dog stretched across my bed. She looked pretty settled to me.

"Sounds perfect. See you downstairs in a few. Come, girls," Lyric said over his shoulder as he walked away.

Daisy waited for me to put Gigi on the floor and they obediently ran after the tall, mysterious man. I needed to come too, but unfortunately, I had to do it alone in the shower, and fast.

CHAPTER
FOUR

Lyric

WOULD THERE COME A DAY WHEN HEARING THE WORD "shower" didn't conjure an image of Memphis riding that dildo? Could I listen to the shower running in the bathroom and not want to reach for my dick while thinking of water cascading over his lean body? Probably, but I knew it wouldn't happen as long as we lived under the same roof.

I could tell Memphis returned my attraction, but I hoped he was smarter than me and would stop me before I took things too far. God, he was so fucking irresistible with his nerdy glasses, messy hair, and lips that begged me to kiss them. I wanted to blame my obsession on being hard up from going almost a year without fucking anything besides my fist or a toy, but I knew better. It was the man himself that triggered Mount Memphis in my pants. He obviously liked them big, and I certainly measured up.

Stop! Stop! Stop! I would've pounded my fists against my temples if I thought it would help shatter my attraction to the guy, but I knew better. The only person who could save Memphis from me was Memphis himself. During the time I was running errands, I thought of ways I could make myself unattractive to Memphis without being too obvious. I didn't want the guy to hate me, and I certainly didn't want to lose Emory's friendship, but I had to do something.

It occurred to me adorable, kind-hearted guys like Memphis

weren't attracted to bad boys, so I figured I could amp up that image a bit more. Which meant I probably shouldn't have bought all the ingredients to make him pancakes, pastries, and decadent desserts for the duration of my stay. Nothing screamed bad boy like serving up delicate crepes with fresh fruit for breakfast before we went off to work. It still felt like the right thing to do since he refused to accept a rent payment from me, and I was a disruption in his life. So, I'd be a nice guy in the kitchen and badass everywhere else.

I wanted to say perpetuating a bad boy image kept everyone away, but it stirred a frenzy in some. Take that fucking *Willows Whisperers* fandom site. Christ, those people needed to get a life. The two *ladies,* and I used the term loosely when discussing them, were internet trolls who didn't know when to mind their own business. Did Elvie Sparks think I got upset when people doubted my abilities? Not at all. People needed to question things; how else would they learn? And Myla Trey and her stalker tendencies were downright frightening.

I admit I loved the site when it first popped up because the fans talked about all the things they loved about the show. What creator wouldn't like that? Things started to take a twist when they allowed their members to post fan fiction stories involving the crew and me. Now, some of those were jaw droppers.

One particular story stuck out in my head for years after reading it because it pretty much involved a nearly pornographic encounter between an owner of a haunted house and me. Whoever NerdBoy88 was, he made my dick hard with his creative storytelling abilities. When I wasn't jerking off to his imagination, he had me pumping my fist victoriously in other ways by posting contradictive sightings whenever Myla got too fucking close to the truth. I owed him gratitude, and I would've suspected one of my crew members or cast mates, aka my tribe, was NerdBoy88 if it weren't for him weaving fantasies about me. I loved my tribe, and they loved me in return, but none of them were writing stories about me falling in love. They fucking knew that was never going to be in the cards for me. I didn't want or need to fall in love with anyone, and I sure as hell wouldn't wish me on my worst enemies. I would be doing Memphis a favor by discouraging his interest.

"Sorry it took me so long," Memphis said after he jogged down the stairs. "I'm so far behind on laundry. I feel much better after a nap, but I'm afraid it was another graphic T-shirt, polo shirt, or a dress shirt."

Good God, I was pretty sure I felt the fissures forming in my plan to resist Memphis as he stood there looking embarrassed over his well-worn Superman shirt. It just added to my conviction that I was looking at Hipster Clark Kent. I was seconds away from crossing the room to kiss him hard enough to knock his glasses crooked when Daisy bumped into my legs hard enough to break my stare.

"Don't act as if you missed me when you were cuddling in bed with Memphis all afternoon," I admonished playfully. I'd never been jealous of a dog before until then. I gave Daisy the adoration she sought by scratching her ears then showered Gigi with affection too. When I had my riotous emotions under control, I looked up and found Memphis biting his lip while watching me interact with the dogs.

"Is that okay?" he asked nervously. "I let Daisy on my bed without checking to see if you allowed her on furniture."

"This is Daisy's world, and I just live in it."

Memphis grinned and laughed. "I understand that completely. I didn't even know I wanted a dog until I adopted Gigi a few months ago. Andy adopted her brother, Bull, and I fell in love with him. I headed straight to the shelter when I learned from Milo that Bull's sister was still available for adoption. My life will never be the same. Thankfully, I can take her to work with me. Oh," he said suddenly. "Daisy is welcome to come too if you'd rather not leave her alone while you do your investigating."

Damn it. The fractures in my resolve were spreading. "Thank

you, Memphis. It depends on how she reacts to the ghost at Maegan's house. She's part of my team, but some spirits upset her, and I won't take her to work with me when that happens." The room went silent, and the sexual tension seemed to thicken. "Um, are you ready?"

"Ready?" Memphis asked. Did he forget what we were supposed to do while fixating on what we wanted to do?

"Dinner at the Miracles'?"

"Oh, yes! I'm ready. You guys can ride with me if you want. Oscar has more leg room than you'd expect."

"Oscar, huh?" Somehow that name fit his light-blue Volkswagen Beetle. "What year is he?"

"He's a 1969," he replied, heading toward the kitchen. Just like that, I became a randy teenager all over again. A man never outgrew the images that popped into his head when he heard the number sixty-nine.

The dogs and I followed behind him, but I bet the girls weren't noticing the way those faded jeans hung low on his hips or how certain places on his ass looked threadbare. If I looked hard enough, could I tell what color his underwear was, or if he even wore any? *Get your eyes off his ass and your mind out of the gutter, Ric.* "Did you buy him already restored or did you do the work yourself?"

"Oscar belonged to Grandpa Sullivan, and he took excellent care of him. Grandma never obtained a driver's license and had no use for the car, so she gave him to me. I know he's not the coolest of classic cars, but I love him. Luckily, the mechanic in town works on foreign and domestic cars, so I don't have to go far for maintenance work." Memphis stopped suddenly in the kitchen and looked at the cake carrier I borrowed from Gertie on the counter. "What's that?"

"While you were sleeping, I baked a dessert to take to the barbecue. My grammy would've read me the riot act if I showed up without something in my hand." Memphis rubbed the back of his neck like maybe he was anxious. I didn't mean to make him feel bad if he didn't normally take something to the barbecues. "I'm afraid my hostess gift is more basic," he said then crossed the kitchen and pulled out a bottle of red wine from a cabinet. "At least it's Jackie's favorite."

"I'm sure she appreciates it."

We went outside, and Memphis unlocked the passenger door for me then moved the seat up so the dogs could jump in the back seat. Daisy had to lie across the seat in the back to fit comfortably, but she wagged her tail happily when Gigi lay down beside her. Memphis scooted the seat back as far as it would go to reveal more leg space than I would've imagined.

"I think your truck is badass by the way. What's his name?" Memphis asked after he backed out of his driveway.

"How do you know the truck has a masculine name?"

Memphis just smirked and shrugged. "Intuition."

"Reaper."

Memphis threw his head back and laughed. "How appropriate."

Jackie and Dennis Miracle lived in a tidy one-story, brick ranch home at the opposite end of the small town from Memphis, of course that was only a few blocks and one traffic light away. The flower beds surrounding the home were immaculate and cheery which would've made my grandpa smile in appreciation.

Jackie had made quite an impression when she'd introduced herself at Books and Brew. Most of the people browsing through the books looked at me like I was about to rob the place, but not her. She marched right up to me when she saw I was looking through the books written about the history of Blissville. Emory had piqued my interest when he mentioned Bliss House which I thought was a deliberate move on his part.

He wanted me in town, but I didn't know why. The psychic abilities in one person weren't the same in another. Emory had visions of things that happened in the past or hadn't yet occurred. I never once saw a vision of a living person. My gift was communicating with the restless spirits and sometimes seeing their ethereal form.

As if fate intervened, Jackie happened to be in the right place at the right time. More importantly, her daughter would soon own Bliss House, which meant getting in to see the place would be easy. She'd given me Maegan's business card with her email address on it and directions so I could drive by the place. At the time, Maegan was still in the process of buying the home, and Andy hadn't started the renovations yet.

I felt an immediate connection to the house; the same one Maegan described having as a child. After buying it, she was determined to solve the disappearance of Anthony Bliss, a former railroad tycoon and Blissville's founder. She was convinced the ghost was his spirit and he never left the property in 1850 like was reported in the newspapers. I thought she might be right, but time would tell.

Jackie greeted us at the door wearing a summery dress that looked like the ones I saw in photos of the ladies in my family from the sixties. She even had a coordinating scarf wrapped around her head and tied so the ends hung down over one shoulder. "Oh, what's this?" she asked eyeing the cake carrier.

"I made my grammy's famous strawberries and cream cake. I hope that's okay."

"Okay?" she asked. "Honey, you can share baked goods with me anytime." Jackie stepped aside so we could enter then took the cake carrier from my hands. "Everyone else is out back." She giggled merrily. "What a pretty picture the two of you make." For a split second, I thought she was talking about Memphis and me until I noticed she was looking at the two dogs following us into the house. "You guys go on outside where Dennis is smoking brisket and a pork roast. I hope you brought your appetites with you."

My mouth watered at the mention of succulent, smoked meats. I hadn't eaten since that morning, and I wasn't sure Memphis had eaten at all even though half the muffins were gone. His unexpected guests could've devoured those.

"I have all the typical barbecue side dishes as well. I wasn't sure what you liked, so I made a little of everything."

"Mrs. Miracle, it all sounds delicious, but I hate that you went to so much trouble."

"Nonsense," she said waving me off. "I love cooking for my family and their friends."

"There they are," Maegan said when we stepped onto the covered patio. "I was starting to think you guys weren't coming after all."

"I fell asleep after you left and just woke up," Memphis said, sounding embarrassed.

I could tell by the twinkle in Milo's blue eyes he thought the reason for Memphis's exhaustion was a lot sexier than the reality. Of course, I had no idea what Memphis had gotten up to while I was gone. For all I knew, he had another shower-friendly dildo stashed away. Maybe he wore himself out on Mighty Mike while I was shopping and getting familiar with the town.

I forced my mind away from those images and introduced myself to Dennis Miracle. "I hope you brought your appetite with you."

"Yes, sir."

Dennis proceeded to ask me a series of questions. On the surface, they seemed like the typical kind people asked to get to know a stranger, but I suspected he was making sure his daughter would be safe in my presence. As if anyone with half of a brain would challenge her mammoth boyfriend who wore a gun strapped to his body for a living. I noticed Dennis's questions weren't so probing they were offensive or intrusive. He only wanted to be comfortable with me around, and I respected that. It was obvious he was a good man who loved his family and their friends.

Once Dennis was satisfied, I sought out Maegan and Elijah to make sure they were okay with my plans. "First, I want to apologize for disappearing without a trace. I realize now it made me look flakey, but I assure you that's not the case. Of course, my sudden reappearance without notice kind of flies in the face of my statement."

"It's okay, Lyric," Maegan assured me. "Anthony has been on his best behavior, so it's not like we've been living on edge this entire time or forced to stay somewhere else."

"Freckles is right, Lyric. Things are just fine at Bliss House." Out of the blue, he leaned closer, lowered his voice, and said, "There've been times in my life when I needed to disappear for a bit to regroup after some challenging times. I think I recognize the look in your eyes, friend. I own a cabin in Tennessee if you ever need to get away for a weekend while you're here. It's quiet and secluded."

"Thanks, Elijah. I appreciate it." I might have to take him up on the offer if the tension between Memphis and me became too much. "I noticed you have both a small library and a historical society in town," I said, changing the subject back to business.

"We do," Maegan said. "There are many articles on microfiche you can read, and the museum curator is my employee's husband. He's already expressed interest in speaking with you." I could tell she wanted to ask me something but worried about being too bold.

"I'm sure you're wondering where the rest of the crew is right now," I said.

"Um, a little curious," she admitted sheepishly.

"Me too," Memphis teased as he, Milo, and Andy joined us. Awareness rippled through my body stronger than I'd ever experienced with anyone else—deceased or living.

"The truth is I'm currently in talks with the network about how to move forward with *The Paranormal Whisperer*. A few of the cast and crew are getting a little restless after years on the road, and we're not sure if we want to continue shooting a series or maybe a few documentaries each year. The network couldn't be happier with the viewership the show attracts, so it's a matter of finding out what works best for everyone involved. There could be major changes or things could continue as status quo."

"Do you plan to investigate Bliss House by yourself?"

"At least for the time being. I might ask for a few volunteers to help with the equipment or hold a video camera, but as of this moment, there is no set day for my cast and crew to join me. I can understand if you're disappointed and would like to back out of the deal. I can even leave without sampling this delicious-smelling dinner."

Memphis stiffened beside me. When I glanced over, he was worrying his plump bottom lip between his teeth again. The fact that he didn't want me to leave should've been the reason I left. Instead, I also nervously waited for Maegan to decide.

"Nonsense," she said confidently. "I don't care if this appears on your show. I only want to solve Anthony's disappearance. I'm willing to compensate you for your time and experience, but I have to be honest I won't be able to match anything close to what a television network would pay you."

"I don't want or need your money," I assured her. "Like you, I want to get to the bottom of Anthony's disappearance."

"Lyric, you seem like a great guy," Milo said, "but I will not be volunteering to assist you on your ghost hunt. I do know someone who might be interested." Milo patted Memphis on the shoulder. "He's calm in a crisis and loves creeping around dark, dirty places."

I should've politely refused, and I saw Memphis expected me to do just that. Instead, I said, "Sounds like an excellent idea to me." I didn't know it then, but I sealed my fate in more ways than one with those words.

CHAPTER FIVE

Memphis

WANTED TO BLAME MY LONG AFTERNOON NAP FOR THE REASON I still wasn't tired by midnight on Lyric's second night in my house, but I knew that wasn't why I was wired. I'd seen the slight way Lyric stiffened when Milo volunteered me to help with the investigation. Of course, he didn't refuse the suggestion with me standing beside him, but was his acceptance as casual as it seemed or was he a good actor? Would he ask me to assist him or would he pretend the suggestion wasn't made? Does he sleep naked? Those were a few of the questions keeping me awake and staring at my ceiling instead of dreaming about Lyric.

I tried reading and watching Hulu to relax, but I was still wide awake when I heard Lyric quietly walk down the hallway around two in the morning. It seemed I wasn't the only one battling insomnia that night. I thought maybe he was taking Daisy out to do her business, but after thirty minutes, he still hadn't returned upstairs. I should've minded my own business and tried to get some sleep, but instead, I quietly walked down the steps to see what Lyric was up to. I had a bullshit excuse all prepared until I saw him standing shirtless in my kitchen.

It wasn't the ingredients, mixing bowls, and baking tins spread all over the counters that made me stand there in slack-jawed surprise. It was the man himself. Bare-chested, wearing nothing but a pair of sweats hanging low on his hips, I'd never seen a finer speci-men in my life. His lack of clothing allowed me to see the full sleeves of tattoos decorating his arms and the ink on his back and rib cage. I wanted to inspect the psychic symbols, skulls, and roses tatted all over his delicious skin. Would I see tattoos on his chest also if he turned around? I should've backed out of the doorway and returned upstairs, but I couldn't peel my eyes off his rounded, muscular ass and the sexy dimples above it. I wanted to cross the room and drop to my knees so I could tongue those divots.

Daisy started wagging her tail when she saw me, making a thumping noise against the tile floor and alerting her master that he wasn't alone. Lyric looked over his shoulder without turning around. I jerked my eyes up from his ass to catch him smirking.

"Did I wake you? Do I need to turn the volume down on my iPad?"

Hell, I was too enthralled by the image he made to hear the voic-es speaking on the television show he was streaming until he said something. Lyric turned his attention to whatever he was whipping by hand in a bowl. I tilted my head as I recognized the British voices.

"Are you watching *The Great British Baking Show*?"

"Guilty as charged," Lyric replied with a casual shrug. "This show is my guilty pleasure and baking is my stress reliever."

"I would never think to classify a popular baking show as a guilty pleasure," I told Lyric, stepping further into the room. "Now if you were watching a gossipy talk show, tawdry reality show, or even porn—"

"I would never classify porn as a guilty pleasure," Lyric said, sud-denly looking into my eyes again. "Who the hell doesn't watch porn?"

"Repressed people," I replied with a shrug.

"Guilty pleasure probably wasn't the proper phrase to use," Lyric said. "Guilty pleasure implies it's something you're ashamed of and don't want people to know you like. This show relaxes me and takes my mind off things that are bothering me."

"I'm sorry."

"For what?" Lyric asked, sounding bemused. "For walking into your kitchen at two in the morning? You never answered my question though. Did I wake you?"

"No, I was already awake thanks to the stupid nap this afternoon." I dropped into a kitchen chair and watched the play of muscles in his back and triceps as he worked. "What are you making?"

"I'm whisking eggs for a lemon custard filling to put with raspberry jam between layers of vanilla sponge cake."

I couldn't prevent the little moan of pleasure that escaped me. "Sounds divine."

"It's one of my favorites to make. I could practically do it blindfolded."

I moaned again because I was picturing him doing lots of things blindfolded. Lyric looked over his shoulder at me again, a wry smile firmly in place as if he knew full well where my mind had gone. I tried hard not to squirm beneath his penetrative, steel-gray stare, but I needed to shift a bit to rearrange my stiff dick.

"Who taught you how to bake?" I asked, thinking it was a safe question.

"My grammy, Jessa Rae." The sadness in his voice broke my heart. I wanted to comfort him, but his stiff posture didn't invite me to cross the room and wrap my arms around him. No matter how much I wanted to rest my forehead between his massive shoulder blades, I stayed put.

"It sounds like I'll need to step up my cardio routine," I teased.

"Probably wouldn't hurt," Lyric replied, "but I bet you're one of those guys who has a high metabolism and can eat whatever he wants and stay naturally thin."

"Yeah, I get that from my dad's side of the family. Unfortunately, my mom's side has a history of high blood pressure and cholesterol, so I try to be good."

Lyric fully turned to face me for the first time with the bowl and whisk in his hand. I felt my jaw drop and a gasp escape my mouth when I saw a golden hoop dangling from his left nipple. *Oh. My. God.* Could he get any fucking hotter? Only if he dropped his sweats and I saw he was pierced somewhere designed to make a lover scream in pleasure.

I finally allowed my eyes to roam over the rest of his perfect chest and ripped abs. Was it possible to come in your pants only from looking at someone? No touching, just looking? Could my mind create a scenario so fucking sexy I just erupted in my pants without the friction from grinding my dick against something or fingering my hole? I thought I might be capable of doing just that with a half-naked Lyric Willows standing in my kitchen.

Lyric held the large mixing bowl in front of his crotch, making it impossible to know if he had responded in kind to my attention. I knew damn well he felt the chemistry between us when I looked into his eyes. The only thing that kept me from being overjoyed about the mutual attraction was the tension in his body. I wanted him to be rigid from lust and longing, but it wasn't. Lyric wanted me, but I could tell he wasn't happy about it.

"Did that hurt?" I asked suddenly.

"The tattoos or the piercing?"

"Um, the piercing." *Ask me which one? Let there be more!*

"It did hurt, but the pain was worth it." A devilish smile slowly crept across his face at the same pace that raw desire sent a flush up my neck and face. I wanted to tug the gold hoop with my teeth and make him cry out in pleasure. "Are you going to ask if I have other piercings?"

"Do you want me to ask?"

"I do, but you shouldn't." We both knew where it would lead, and it was obvious Lyric didn't want that. "I'm not a relationship guy, Memphis. I have zero to offer you."

"Besides mind-numbing orgasms?"

"Yeah, besides that." Lyric let out a shaky sigh and set the bowl on the countertop, giving me my first look at his crotch. He was turned on in a very big way, making my mouth salivate with the possibilities. "I need you to go back upstairs now, Memphis." Lyric's voice sounded tired and strained, pulling my focus back up to his gorgeous face. As much as I loved that I could turn him on, I hated the regret I saw in his eyes.

I wanted to counter every objection he had with sound reasoning why we should give in to the passion arcing between us, but I didn't. I rose to my feet, allowing him to see how he affected me too. "I guess I'll see you in the morning." It was already morning. "Um, later?" It sounded more like a question than a statement.

"You will," Lyric assured me.

I didn't go to my room. I went straight to the bathroom to jerk off in the shower. I didn't care if Lyric heard the water running and knew exactly what I was doing. In fact, I wanted him to know I jacked my cock while wishing it was his mouth instead of my fist. My ass ached to be filled, but not by a dildo. It didn't take me long to shoot my load, dry off, and return to my room where Gigi waited for me with judgmental eyes.

"Go to sleep," I told her when I climbed into bed.

I expected my overstimulated brain to keep me awake, but I was out as soon as my head hit the pillow.

My alarm woke me too soon, and I lay there nestled comfortably in my bed until I remembered the events from the night before. Dread settled in the pit of my stomach as I jackknifed into a sitting position. Gigi growled her displeasure at being jostled, so I reached over and stroked her back. Humiliation flooded my body as I recalled the interaction with Lyric in my kitchen earlier that morning.

"He surely packed his shit and left after I fell asleep," I whispered.

The urge to creep down the hall to his room was strong, but I ignored it in favor of going through my normal morning routine. I sighed in relief when I saw his toothbrush still in the holder. He wouldn't have left without it.

He would if he was running for his life in the middle of the night.

When I went downstairs, I saw he'd finished making the cake and another dozen muffins. Next to his bounty was a folded piece of paper. I wanted to pretend it was his recipe he'd left behind, but I saw my name scrawled on it. I could pretend I didn't see it, but that didn't feel right either. I bravely picked up the sheet of paper and unfolded it.

Memphis,

I need you to know something very important. I want you. I want you so bad my teeth ache, but I won't allow myself to have you. How's that for honesty? I meant it when I said I have nothing to offer you, and I believe you deserve more than someone who will only use your body then walk away when the job is over. That's exactly what I will do, and most likely without saying goodbye.

The only thing I can offer you is baked goods and friendship. Here's an abundance of one thing in case you're repulsed by the other. I will understand if you'd like me to leave.

Lyric

I read the letter in disbelief then read it again, and then once more for good measure. I was stunned Lyric could be so candid about wanting me and disappointed he would never act on it. More than either of those things, I was saddened by how little Lyric thought of himself. I sighed as I folded the note and shoved it in my pocket. Then I picked up the pen and notebook he'd found in the drawer and wrote out a response.

Lyric,

Thank you for the delicious peace offering. I happily accept. I absolutely do not want you to leave. We're both adults here and not horny teenagers who can't control their urges. I'll be at my store for most of the day. Feel free to bring Daisy by if you're going to the library or historical society.

Memphis

I folded the note and wrote his name in big, bold letters then placed it in the same spot he'd left mine. I figured things would be awkward for a bit, but it couldn't be worse than him finding my huge dildo in the bathroom.

I grabbed a few muffins to go, and Gigi followed me out to my car. She waited like a good girl in my office at the store while I ran over to get a cup of coffee from Books and Brew. Maegan greeted me with a kiss on my cheek while Milo greeted me with an all-knowing smirk.

"Wipe that grin off your face, Milo," I said firmly. "I expected meddling from the Matrons but not my friends."

"I wasn't meddling." His grin only grew broader when I glared at him. "Call it a little shove."

"You should leave them alone, Milo. Nobody likes people interfering in their love life," Maegan said.

"Stay out of it as you did with Andy and me?" Milo asked his sister. "You looked for every excuse to push us together."

"Look how that turned out," Maegan said proudly.

"So, why can't I do the same for Memphis? The unresolved sexual tension is so thick between them." Milo faced me and narrowed his eyes. "Or have you *resolved* the sexual tension?"

"Milo," I said in a warning tone. "That's none of your business."

"I'm sorry, Memphis. I only want to see you happy." *Like I am,* he left unsaid.

"I appreciate that, Milo, but it's not going to happen with Lyric." I shrugged like it was no big deal when I wanted to throw a fit.

"I don't see why not," he replied stubbornly. "I think it's a mistake to throw away chemistry like that."

"My home and life are here in Blissville, and his life is...wherever he needs to be at the moment." There was more to it than that, but I wasn't in a position to know. Even if I were, I wouldn't share his pain and secrets with anyone else.

"Fine, I'll let it go," Milo agreed.

"I'll see you guys for lunch," I told them before I headed back to my store.

My morning routine consisted of checking my online store to see if I'd made any sales and reading my emails to see if anyone hired me to acquire items for them. I was pleasantly surprised to see I'd sold over a thousand dollars in comic books and records over the weekend. I confirmed the payments had processed and began preparing the items for shipment while Gigi chewed on her stuffed cat under my desk.

The bell over the front door rang, letting me know I had a customer. My hair wasn't standing up all over my body, so I knew Lyric hadn't stopped by with Daisy. Of course, there was no telling how late he'd sleep after staying up more than half the night baking goodies.

"Hey, Daniel and Mark. How are you guys enjoying your summer break so far?"

"It's going great," Mark said enthusiastically. "I finally earned enough money doing chores around the house to pay for the Superman comic book you're holding back for me." Chaz and Kyle's adopted teenage son was adorable, and so was his boyfriend. "Dad is going to freak when I give it to him for his birthday."

"You're buying it for Chaz?" I asked. I knew Chaz, Kyle, and Mark all bonded over their shared love of comic books and superhero movies. I thought Mark's excitement was about owning the book himself but knowing he wanted to buy it for his dad made it more special. "You're in luck, my man," I said excitedly. "I'm having a big sale this week."

"You are?" Mark asked.

"I don't see a sign," Daniel commented.

"I was getting around to it," I assured him. "Twenty-five percent off."

"Wow, I bet I could find something for Daddy too. Do you have any new *X-Men* stuff?"

"I just found a vintage Wolverine figure from 1993 at an estate auction," I told him. "How about I give you the Superman comic book and the Wolverine figure for the original price I was going to charge you?" The Wolverine figure was probably worth triple what I was going to make off Mark, but some things were more important than money. I couldn't put a price on the excitement in Mark's eyes from knowing he was about to surprise both his dads with something they'd love.

"Wow! My dads are going to be so excited. Thank you, Memphis." Mark threw his arms around my waist and hugged me tightly.

"My pleasure."

The bell over the door rang again while I was ringing Mark's purchases up at the register. My body instantly told me who came through the door. I was equal parts happy he was there and concerned I would never look at my store the same after he left his mark on it.

"Whoa!" Daniel said. "Your dog is huge, mister. Does he bite?"

"*She* doesn't bite," Lyric said. "Her name is Daisy, and she's extremely friendly. You're welcome to pet her if you like."

Daniel waited for me to hand Mark's purchases to him then they greeted the dog together.

"You're a beautiful girl," Mark said softly, sounding a lot like Kyle who doted and fussed over his patients at his animal hospital.

Lyric looked up from watching the boys with Daisy and caught me staring at him. *I want you. I want you so bad it makes my teeth ache.* How the hell was I supposed to forget that?

"Thanks again, Memphis," Mark said suddenly, pulling my attention back to him.

"No problem. I hope your dads enjoy their presents."

"Oh, they will."

Lyric approached the counter after the boys left. "I had this

48

strange dream I left a note on the counter for you. It said too much without really saying much at all."

"I don't recall seeing a note." I resisted the urge to pat my pocket to make sure I hadn't dreamed it too. "That's what you get for eating too many sweets in the middle of the night."

"Yeah, I bet that's it."

"I didn't expect to see you up and around so early. The library doesn't open for another hour, and I'm not sure what time the historical society opens."

"Hmmm," Lyric said, running his finger over the edge of the glass display case as he walked closer to me. "How about you give me a private tour."

"Um, well, this is pretty much it," I said.

"No office? No room to store inventory?"

"I have an office, but it's very small. There's barely room for a desk and a chair. We'd be very cramped."

"I love tight, dark spaces, Memphis. Show it to me."

CHAPTER SIX

Lyric

J UST A FEW HOURS BEFORE MY VISIT TO HIS STORE, I HAD WARNED him away from me in a hastily written note. I wish I could blame alcohol or drugs for the incident, but I wrote those words stone-cold sober. I thought I was honest, but upon reflection, I was cruel. What kind of asshole expresses how much he wants someone then turns around and tells them to stay away in the same breath? My stupid letter was a variation of the same dick moves used by heroes in television, movies, and books to warn someone away. I want you, but I can't have you. I love you, but I'm not good for you. In each of those instances, the warning only acts as an accelerant on a fire, and the couple usually falls head over heels in love.

Memphis wasn't an actor on a television show or a fictional character in a novel; he was real, and so were his feelings. I also didn't want or need Memphis to heal or fix me with his love. I wasn't broken. I was…jaded and cynical. I wasn't trying to be the chump who secretly lured prey into his web by appealing to their attraction to the unattainable man. I was trying to be honest with Memphis in a way that didn't make him think he was the problem. Then a curious thing happened. My plan backfired on me. According to the note he left in response, he readily accepted my offer of friendship without regret that there would be no sexy shenanigans between us. I should've been relieved, but I was irritated.

Had I imagined the lusty way he looked at my body? Had he not licked his lips while staring at my nipple piercing like he couldn't wait to take the metal hoop between his teeth and give it a good tug? I stood alone in his kitchen eating a slice of cake and trying not to choke on my remorse for leaving that stupid note. I knew Memphis was the kind of guy who accepted my words at face value and would back the fuck off rather than pursue me and try to change my mind. That should've made me happy, but instead, I wished I had never written the stupid note in the first place.

That regret grew tenfold when I walked into his store and saw him surrounded by the records, comics, and memorabilia he loved so much. His enthusiasm and excitement while discussing the teen boy's purchases was palpable and fed my lust. I wanted to see him that joyful over my kiss, my hands on his body, or my cock. Instead of apologizing for the letter, I pretended I had dreamed the whole thing, and Memphis went right along with it.

What did it mean though? Was he trying to make me feel better about myself, or did he want to pretend that I didn't warn him away? Could he accept my terms of no-strings sex? I needed to know, but instead of asking him outright, I asked him for a private tour. I could tell by his wide-eyed expression he knew what I meant. Memphis licked his bottom lip as if he could already taste the kisses I planned to steal.

"My office is...um...this way," Memphis stuttered out. I followed so close behind him I could feel his body heat.

Just a kiss. Just a kiss. Just a kiss.

But then I was enclosed in that tiny office with him and I couldn't stop my mind from wondering about the noises Memphis would make if I filled a different tight space. The desk at least looked sturdy enough to support his weight. If not, I could always push him up against the wall.

"Yeah, so this is it. Not very impressive," Memphis said, looking around the space like maybe he was trying to see it through my eyes.

"I'm not a very sophisticated decorator unless you count posters of villains as art."

"Art is in the eye of the beholder," I said, stalking closer to him until I had his ass pressed against the desk.

"I thought that was beauty," he whispered as my lips inched closer and closer to his.

"That too." I placed my hands on either side of his neck and stroked my thumbs over his racing pulse. "Tell me to go away and I will."

"No," Memphis whispered against my lips.

"You really should," I warned. The rough timbre of my voice made Memphis tremble, but I could tell it wasn't from fear.

I was stronger than this, or at least I thought I was, but maybe I'd just never met anyone who reached me on such an elemental level. It was fucking scary, but not tasting Memphis was far scarier. I kept my eyes open and locked on his as I made my final descent. The bell over the door jangled as I was about to press my lips against his.

Memphis whimpered when I pulled back from the kiss. "I've had more walk-in customers this morning than I had all last week."

"Yoo-hoo? Hello, Memphis."

"It's Bonnie Stillwater. She works for Maegan," he whispered, tugging the hem of his T-shirt to make sure it hid his excitement. "She's probably here to see you."

"Superfan?"

"No, well, maybe. I don't know what Bonnie likes to watch on television, but I do know her husband is Homer Stillwater, the curator at the historical society. Maegan probably informed her you were in town and would want to talk to Homer."

"Oh, that's a good thing then." I was relieved it wasn't someone who wanted me to pose for pictures or sign something.

"Memphis, are you here? The door was unlocked." Bonnie's voice grew louder as she approached my office.

"I'm here, Bonnie. I'm just going over something with Lyric.

We'll be right out."

"Ohhhh," Bonnie said. "Do you need me to come back?"

"No!" Memphis said quickly.

My body screamed, "Yes."

"Tell you what," Bonnie said. "Why don't you send Lyric over to see me when you...finish."

Memphis moaned but softly enough only I heard it. Damn, I wanted to make him moan long, hard, and loud. "He'll be right over, Bonnie." He didn't say anything else until we heard the bell jingling when she opened and shut the door behind her. "She's going to tell Maegan, who will tell Milo, we were in here making out or worse."

"Worse? Fucking is so much better than making out."

Needy little whimpers escaped Memphis once more, and he sat down hard against the desk. "Lyric, don't tease me like that. I don't know the reason for the sudden change between writing the note this morning and now, but you've got me reeling."

I inhaled a shaky breath and wondered what he must think of me and my mixed signals. I must look like a total flake to him. *Stay away, Memphis. Kiss me, Memphis.* My mood changes were so sudden I'm surprised I didn't give us both whiplash. When we were apart, I could use reason and logic to convince myself I didn't really need or want Memphis, but it all disappeared the moment I looked into his big, brown eyes. All I could focus on when I was near him was how much I craved him. Bonnie's timing, although annoying, was impeccable, because we wouldn't have stopped at kissing. I didn't want to do anything that Memphis would regret later.

"I'm sorry, Memphis," I said gruffly. "My behavior is...was..." I couldn't think of an adjective.

"Human," he supplied for me. "You're human, Lyric. Maybe you forget because you deal with so much paranormal phenomenon all the time. You also seem like a guy who carries a great weight upon his shoulders, and occasionally, a guy needs to cut loose and live a little. Maybe your brain is trying to deny what your body demands."

"Cut loose and live a little, huh?" Memphis's words tempted and dared me more than he could ever know. "I'll give it some thought."

"Don't overthink it," Memphis cautioned. "Maybe just…react."

I wanted to fucking react all over his sexy, messy self. I settled for straightening his glasses again. "Are you sure it's okay if Daisy stays while I do the library and historical society thing? I shouldn't be too long." We both looked over to where she and Gigi lay together in a ball.

"Positive," Memphis replied. "Let me know if you need my assistance later." His eyes widened when he realized how that sounded. "With investigating," he rushed to clarify.

Laughter rumbled from my chest, sounding like a rusty skill I hadn't used in a long time. "I'll let you know if I need your help later."

I left without saying another word because the longer I stayed in that little office with Memphis, the harder it would be to leave. My heart, body, and mind went to war over Memphis while I tracked down Bonnie Stillwater at Curious Things, Maegan's antique store. The minute I walked into the shop, I was overwhelmed by whispers, smells, and sensations, making my spine tingle. People didn't realize just how much energy objects held long after their owners had passed away, and some spirits who couldn't pass into the afterlife clung to the objects that tied them to this world. It took me years to train myself to turn down the volume on the noise these objects made to preserve my sanity.

The woman I suspected to be Bonnie was talking to a customer at a register. Maegan smiled and walked over to greet me. "That didn't take long."

"That's because we weren't doing anything salacious." *Yet.*

"Don't forget, Lyric. I own this building, and I know damn well how small that office is. I tried convincing Memphis to make his office larger, but he wanted to have as much retail space as possible. I don't think he was anticipating guests."

"I was only dropping Daisy off to Memphis so I could go to the library." Why did I feel like I had to explain myself to Maegan? She didn't seem upset.

Maegan leaned a little closer and lowered her voice. "I won't tell Meddling Milo about this incident after Memphis convinced him this morning to ease up on his matchmaking attempts."

I swallowed the bait—hook, line, and sinker. "Is that so?"

"Yep." I waited for Maegan to say more, but she didn't. Did she want me to be more assertive and show more interest? I might've caved but Bonnie saved me.

"It's so nice to meet you, Lyric," she said sweetly, not all offended by the non-existent banging that was going on in Memphis's office. "You're even taller in person than you appear in your show." Then her eyes widened. "I'm sorry. Did that make you feel uncomfortable?"

"Nah," I said, wanting to put her at ease. The term fan is a condensed version of the word fanatic. I've met many fans, like Bonnie, who enjoy the show, the cast, and crew without making us feel weird. Then you meet the fanatics or see rabid online posts from people like Myla and Elvie, and it makes you want to hide in your house and never come out. "It's nice to meet you too, Bonnie."

"Homer is at his doctor appointment, but he should be at the historical society around noon if you'd like to meet with him."

"That would be great," I told her. "I'll start by looking at old articles on microfiche so I can make a list of questions for Homer."

"I bet you spend a lot of hours doing mundane things like looking through microfiche, don't you?" Bonnie asked.

"I do, but I enjoy it," I replied. "It's fun to see what type of information made it to print through the different eras. It tells a lot about the mindsets of the people living in that community."

"Good or bad, the Blissville Daily News hasn't changed much since it was founded in 1835," Maegan said. "The vast majority of information will be about things going on locally and in the state. The national and world stories off the AP wire are pretty limited."

"And getting smaller," Bonnie added. "Other than the gossip

section, the paper tries to maintain a positive outlook but do so in a way that isn't manipulative or misleading. Our paper never endorses political candidates either. Opposing candidates are given the opportunity to speak directly to the constituents in op-ed pieces, but the paper will not endorse one over the other."

"Interesting," I said. "Gossip section though?"

"It's not called that," Maegan said, giving her employee a wry grin. "It's an advice column that gets carried away."

"Like 'Dear Abby'?" I asked.

"Yes, but our weekly column is called Amelia Knows Best," Bonnie said. "People write in *anonymously* to ask questions about how to handle sticky situations."

"The most fun is trying to figure out who is asking for the advice," Maegan admitted. "Sometimes the identity of the writer is pretty damn obvious. There have been times where people used the column to get a little revenge on someone else."

"I assume the person answering the questions has changed over the years," I said.

"Yes, but the editor won't reveal which staff member is answering the questions as Amelia," Maegan answered.

"I suspect it's someone freelance," Bonnie added. "The tone sounds far more sophisticated than it used to even a year ago, but the staffing hasn't changed."

"So, recent changing of the guards so to speak."

"It seems that way," Maegan agreed.

"That's one mystery I'll let you solve," I told them. "Who founded the paper in 1835? That would've cost a lot of money. Was it Bliss?"

"Actually, no. It was Anthony's good friend, Wallace Bennington III," Bonnie stated. "He was a steel and iron tycoon from New York also."

"Really?" I asked. "You had two wealthy tycoons setting up shop and building a town here? Together." My spidey sense was going off.

"Once upon a time, this sleepy town was a progressive place to live," Bonnie told me. "You'll learn more about it from reading the articles and talking to Homer. He has several artifacts in the little museum that belonged to Wallace and Anthony."

"Sounds great. I'll check in with you later, Maegan, to make arrangements to start investigating at Bliss House."

"Better yet, why don't you, your assistant, and four-legged friends come over for dinner tonight?"

"Please don't feel like you need to feed me," I told her. "I'm a low maintenance kind of guy."

"We'll order from the diner or have pizza delivered," she said. "It's no trouble at all."

I did need to start my investigation, I had asked Memphis to assist me, and we would all need to eat. "Let me buy, and we have a deal."

"Lyric, that doesn't seem fair at all."

"Life isn't fair, Maegan. I buy or..." *What?* The deal wouldn't be off because both the ghost mystery and Memphis had me by the balls. I wasn't budging from town until I explored every part of Bliss House and Memphis's body.

"Fine," she ceded. "Don't think you're going to make a habit out of it."

"This might be something I wrap up in a night or two," I told her.

"Oh," she said softly, sounding disappointed.

"You never know with these things though. Not all spirits cooperate. I think it's possible Anthony loves that house as much as you do."

"He's welcome to stay if it's what he truly wants," Maegan said. "I guess we'll figure it out as we go."

"What time do you want us to come over?"

"How does six sound to you?"

"Perfect. See you tonight *with* dinner."

I said goodbye to the ladies and resisted the urge to stop back by Vinyl and Villains. I could've used the excuse that I needed to tell

Memphis about the plans I made for us, but I knew I'd end up with him in the little office. I could no longer deny I wanted to spend as much time buried inside Memphis's ass as possible, but we needed to set some ground rules first. I didn't want our first time to be in some dark, cramped space; I wanted to lay him on a bed and take my time.

At the library, I got the surprise of my life when I saw who was working behind the desk. I'd been to hundreds of libraries in hundreds of small towns, but I had never once come across a hunk of a man who looked more suited to the gridiron than the library. This was no sixty-five-year-old woman with eyeglasses either perched low on her nose or hanging from a chain around her neck. This librarian wasn't wearing cardigans and a skirt down to his ankles. Well, I couldn't see his ankles, but he was wearing faded, well-fitting jeans. He wore an I Know I'm Sexy smirk instead of the sour expression I was accustomed to.

"Can I help you?" There was no mistaking the double entendre when he raked my body from head to toe. As sexy as he was, there was only one guy I wanted to get naked with at the moment. *Memphis*. If I were lucky, I was a few hours away from tangling my fingers in his messy curls while I rocked my dick in and out of his body.

I offered the man a pleasant but impersonal smile. "My name is Lyric Willows. I'm here investigating the history of the Bliss House. I'd like to look at archived copies of The Blissville Daily News that you might have on microfiche from say 1848 until 1852." Normally, I'd tell them it was for a television show which usually guaranteed cooperation from most people.

Not this bruiser, who crossed his massive arms over his broad chest. "Does Maegan know you're here?"

"She's the one who asked me to come. Why don't you give her a call to check out my story? I just came from her store."

The big man picked up the phone and dialed her number while I stood there listening to the brute's side of the conversation as he sized me up through narrowed eyes. The conversation took longer than I expected, but I just calmly waited.

"You check out," he said. "Sorry about that. Maegan and Milo are good friends, and I don't want anyone to mess with them. The name is Tucker Garrison." He extended a meaty hand toward me which I accepted. Luckily, he didn't crush my hand and render it useless. "I'm filling in for my grandmother while she attends her monthly ladies' brunch. It's been a while since I pulled the microfiche and loaded it into the reader."

"I have a lot of experience using the reader. I just need the film. How about we start with January through June of 1848? Once I'm done making notes, I'll ask for the next six months."

"Works for me. The reader is in the back room with the computers." Tucker pointed to an area over my shoulder. "Go ahead and make yourself comfortable while I pull the slides."

After I got my notebook and pens out of my backpack, I sent a quick text over to Memphis. *Investigation at Bliss House starts tonight. We're taking dinner over for Maegan and Elijah.*

Better add Milo and Andy to the mix. They won't want to miss this, Memphis replied.

Can I put you in charge of finding out what everyone wants to eat from the diner?

Memphis sent a laughing emoji before he answered me. *I know that by heart. Besides, a person only needs to throw a dart at the menu and order whatever it lands on. Can't go wrong with Edson and Emma's food.*

I was about to tell Memphis we needed to have an important conversation later, but Tucker arrived with my first round of microfiche slides. I put my phone inside my backpack so I wouldn't be distracted. The quicker I got this done, the sooner I could meet with Homer, and maybe I'd have time to collect that kiss I'd wanted earlier from Memphis before we headed to Bliss House.

CHAPTER SEVEN

Memphis

I DON'T KNOW WHY THE HELL I WAS SO NERVOUS. I'D HAD RUN-INS with Anthony Bliss or whomever haunted Maegan's house before and lived to tell about it. Of course, Lyric wasn't there on those occasions. What if I made an ass of myself? What if I dropped his expensive ghost-detecting equipment? I would bet Milo's left nut Lyric hadn't purchased his EMF detector from Amazon.

"Don't be nervous, Memphis," Lyric calmly said from the passenger seat beside me.

"Me? What makes you think I'm nervous?"

"You just blew through that stop sign back there."

"Fuck!" I slowed down and gathered myself before I hurt someone. "Sorry about that."

"Don't apologize to me," Lyric said. "I'm not the one who dove out of the way to avoid getting run over."

"Stop being so dramatic."

"Check your mirror," Lyric instructed.

I glanced into the rearview mirror and saw Mrs. Hawkins holding onto the stop sign for support. "Fuck!"

"Is that one of your favorite words?"

"It's an all-purpose word," I told him as I stopped my car and put it in reverse.

"What are you doing?"

"Apologizing." I eased back to the intersection, made sure it was clear, then continued backing up to the other side to where Mrs. Hawkins now stood with her hands on her hips looking angrier than a wet hornet.

"And just what do you have to say for yourself, young man?" she demanded when Lyric rolled down his window.

"I am so sorry, Mrs. Hawkins. I should've paid closer attention and not let myself get distracted while operating a vehicle. It won't happen again," I assured her.

"See that it doesn't, Memphis Sullivan." Mrs. Hawkins said firmly. Then she looked at my passenger for the first time. "Who are you?"

"My name is Lyric Willows, ma'am."

"Lyric Willows. Were your parents hippies?"

"Mrs. Hawkins," I chastised. "That's not very friendly. Lyric is a visitor, and we want to make a good impression."

"I'm too old to mince words, Memphis. I could die during my next breath."

"I sure hope not," I told her.

Mrs. Hawkins leveled me with a nut-shriveling glare. "I didn't say I wanted to die, just that it's a possibility. Especially with you zooming through a four-way stop in your love bug." Then she turned her attention back to Lyric. "Well, how'd you get a name like that?"

"My mother was a free spirit, to say the least, ma'am," Lyric said softly. "My father was a little starchier, but he couldn't tell her no."

Was. I felt a genuine sadness that Lyric referred to both of his parents in the past tense. Was it why he was so stoic and somber?

"Most of my friends call me Ric for short," Lyric told her. I doubted I'd be one of them no matter how up close and personal I became with his body. I loved his name, especially how the whimsical sound contradicted his somber personality.

"I like Lyric fine," Mrs. Hawkins said. "It's just a bit unusual."

"I prefer unique but unusual is okay too," Lyric teased her, earning a slight blush. "It was nice meeting you, Mrs. Hawkins. I'm certainly glad Memphis didn't run over you."

"I couldn't agree more. I hope you enjoy your stay in Blissville, Lyric."

"I'm certain I will, ma'am."

My brain kicked around all the many ways I could make his stay in town enjoyable. Lust grabbed me by the balls when Lyric looked over at me and smiled wickedly. He knew what I was thinking.

"Memphis, you make sure to show him a really good time."

"You can count on it, Mrs. H." I tore my eyes away from my walking wet dream and focused back on the elderly lady. "I truly am sorry I nearly ran you over."

"You're forgiven."

Neither Lyric nor I spoke again until we were a block away from Maegan's house. "Memphis, I want to stop fighting this attraction to you."

"I want you to stop fighting it too," I admitted. "What will it take for that to happen?"

"A conversation."

"You mean like making me swear I won't fall in love with you or something?"

Lyric snorted. "Yeah, but it sounds pretty damn arrogant hearing you say it out loud."

"I hate to shoot myself in the foot here, but it's very arrogant. I know you're not sticking around Blissville, and I'm not looking for commitment, marriage, and babies." I pulled into Maegan's driveway and parked behind Andy's truck. I half turned in my seat and faced Lyric after I turned off the engine. "You and I can fall into bed with each other without falling in love. I might fall in insta-love with your dick, but your heart is safe from me, and mine is safe from you."

"You sound certain," Lyric said dryly.

"And you sound disappointed." I tipped my head to the side. "Have we discussed it enough or will there be more talking before we fuck?"

Lyric looked out the windshield and blew out a long, shaky breath while I held mine waiting for him to respond. When he looked at me, his eyes had darkened with emotion. "Yeah, we're on the same page."

The held breath hissed out of me, earning a twisted smile in return. "Good to know. We better get inside before Milo starts planning our wedding." We both opened our doors and got out. Lyric let the pups out of the back seat while I retrieved the food from the trunk located in the front of my VW Beetle with the engine being in the rear. Lyric joined me to grab his bag of equipment.

"He's that invested in your happiness, huh?"

I shut the trunk and smiled up at Lyric. "Why do I get the feeling there's a hidden question in there somewhere."

Lyric shrugged. "I don't want things to get weird or complicated when they don't need to be."

"Lyric, you spend your days whispering to ghosts. How much weirder or complicated can it get?"

"A love triangle is pretty damn weird and complicated," he replied.

"Lyric, you've seen Andy and Milo together a few times. Have you ever seen two men more in tune with one another?"

"That's not in doubt."

"What or, should I ask, whom do you doubt?" I raised my hand when he started to answer me. "Have you ever met someone who you instantly connected to in unexplainable ways? I mean people who must've been your friends in another life because they knew you too fucking well. They could complete your thoughts and sentences as easily as breathing?" Lyric swallowed hard but didn't answer me. "That's how it was with Maegan and Milo. I felt like we'd shared a womb or something. They were the parts of me I didn't know were missing until everything clicked into place. There has never been anything sexual between Milo and me."

Lyric nodded then whistled for Daisy to follow him, signaling that the conversation was over, or at least tabled for the moment.

"Hey, guys," Maegan said when we stepped onto the porch. "Did you have a productive day, Lyric?"

"You could say that again," he said wryly.

"I did too, Mae," I said excitedly like a kid who was desperate for approval. "Are you going to ask about my day?"

"I was getting around to it," she teased.

"I have a great lead on an estate about ninety minutes north of here," I said casually. "A guy I met at a recent convention—"

"What guy?" Milo, Maegan, and Lyric all asked at once.

"Oh, wow," I said, shaking my head. "He's married…to a nice lady who also likes comics—" I began before one of them cut me off again.

"Like that's ever stopped a guy from trying," Andy said.

"Looking for a third," Milo added.

"Guys!" Mae admonished. "Cut it out."

Lyric just stared at me as he patiently waited for me to finish my story. "I met Sal and Elizabeth at a convention and told them about my business. I explained how you and I often search estates together though looking for different things. Elizabeth jotted down your website address and Sal saved my business card. Sal's cousin, Sonny, is looking to liquidate some assets he inherited from his folks. The way Sal tells it, Sonny's mom was a bit of a hoarder who still had those vintage blue glasses. He called them Blue Lindas or something."

"Blue Libbey," Maegan corrected.

"Yeah, that sounds right. Sal also said Sonny's dad was a big comic book fan with an impressive vinyl record collection."

"That's an amazing lead for us. What's next?" Maegan asked.

"We eat dinner," Milo suggested. "I'm wasting away to nothing, and I need my energy for Slugger."

"Milo, must you always think about your stomach and your dick?" his sister asked him.

"No, I often think about Andy's stomach and dick too."

"Honey, I'm home," Elijah said as he entered the house. "I smell meatloaf, mashed potatoes, and green beans."

"You smell the green beans?" Lyric asked in disbelief.

"I do when they come from Edson and Emma's. They add bacon to theirs." Elijah rubbed his hands together gleefully. "Let's do story time while we eat."

"What was the book event you held for Valentine's Day?" I asked Maegan.

"Blind date with a book."

"Let's do that with the takeout containers. I pass them out blindly and we eat whatever we get."

"Give me the meatloaf and no one gets hurt," Elijah playfully growled. At least I thought he was kidding. "Wait, don't even bother opening them." He took a deep whiff of the air and picked up a container off the table. "This one." Elijah opened the box container and his loud whoop signaled he'd chosen wisely. "The rest of you guys can do the blind date with a dinner thing."

"Sounds good to me," Maegan said. "What about you guys?" Andy, Milo, and Lyric nodded in agreement.

I passed out the containers while Elijah made drum roll noises. Milo made the oh and ah noises like the crowd on a game show while we each revealed our dinner. Lyric ended up with the country fried steak, mashed potatoes, and buttered corn. Maegan chose the pulled pork, macaroni and cheese, and coleslaw. Milo picked the shepherd's pie with a side salad. Lady fortune must've been on my side because Lyric was ready to stop fighting his attraction to me, *and* I picked my favorite dinner.

"Is that chicken and dumpling stew?" Lyric asked, sounding wistful.

"Um, yeah. Would you like to trade?" I asked trying not to reveal how much I didn't want to turn loose of my dumplings.

"That's okay," he replied, shaking his head. "Doubtful they're as good as the ones my grammy made. Most northern folks don't make dumplings the same way they do in the South, although it looks pretty close."

"It's Emma's grandmother's recipe," Maegan said. "She's from Alabama which is pretty Southern."

Lyric looked even more intrigued, so I speared a dumpling and blew on it to make sure he didn't burn his mouth. I looked up from my fork and locked eyes on steely gray ones that said eating the dumpling was the furthest thing from his mind. I moved the fork to offer it to him anyway. Lyric kept his eyes locked on mine when he opened his mouth and wrapped it around my fork. I heard the slight scraping of teeth against metal as he pulled back. I knew the instant the flavors hit his tongue because he closed his eyes and softly moaned as he chewed.

"Fuck, that's good," Lyric said after he swallowed then licked his lips in case my dick wasn't hard enough already.

"Is that some kind of foreplay?" Milo whispered.

"I almost feel like a pervert for watching," Elijah said.

"Maybe we should all go into the kitchen," Andy suggested, snapping me out of my fog of lust.

"Nobody move," I said firmly. "Lyric has news he wants to share with you while we eat, and then we'll begin our investigation."

"Um, yeah," Lyric said, returning his attention to his country fried steak. "This smells delicious, but I doubt it holds a candle to the chicken and dumplings."

"My offer to trade stands. I love the country fried steak."

"No way. I agreed to the terms, and I'm a stickler for honoring my agreements." I knew he was also talking about our agreement to fuck without strings. I needed to show him I could and would stick to the agreement also, so I tucked into my dumplings without a shred of regret.

"Damn, this is good too. How do you guys stay so fit with food like this in such proximity?" Lyric asked.

"We work out a lot," Elijah said.

"As much cardio as our hearts can handle," Maegan said, licking her fork.

Lyric chuckled. "Let's chat about what I learned today," he said, steering us into safer waters. "Today's trip to the library and historical society generated more questions for me than answers, but I have an idea which direction I think we need to go."

"I'm so excited to hear all about it," Maegan said eagerly.

"We've frequently talked about Anthony but discovering that a second tycoon was living in the middle of nowhere really stuck out to me. What were the odds? What was the history between the two men, if there was one."

"They definitely had history," Maegan said. "They were friends in New York City before either of them moved to Blissville. Anthony moved here with his family, and Wallace followed afterward."

"I think the men were more than friends, Maegan. I think it's possible Anthony did indeed run away in 1850."

"Are you basing this on something you found or gut instinct?" she asked.

"A little of both. I looked through two years of newspaper clippings which included many photos of the two men. I think it would be easy for people to miss the fondness in their expressions if they weren't looking for it."

"Huh," Andy said.

"I compared photos of Anthony with Melanie and Anthony with Wallace, and there was a noticeable difference." Lyric tilted his head to the side. "Also, Wallace Bennington III fell of the face of the earth not too long before Anthony disappeared."

"He moved west, right?" Milo asked. "So many people had wanted an opportunity to find their fortunes during the California Gold Rush, but the rich just got richer, and the poor got poorer."

"That's true," Lyric agreed. "The thing is, I spent hours online searching for information about Wallace Bennington III, and there was not one mention of him living in California. A man like him wouldn't move west without buying a hotel or something."

"True," Maegan said softly. "He announced his departure and the townsfolk accepted it at face value. What about his family? Weren't they looking for him?"

"He was an only child and a confirmed bachelor. Once his parents passed away, there was no one to look for him. I did some digging, and he sold the newspaper for a song, most likely just to unload it. He sold his steel and iron works company for a shit ton of money though. It was enough to start over with a new identity and the man he loved."

"Wow," I said softly. "That sounds romantic."

Milo winked at me from across the table. "Then Anthony faked his death and followed Wallace west a year later?"

"It was more like eight months, but yes. That's what I believe. Anthony relied on people believing he perished as part of the curse," I said. "I think the men changed their appearances as best they could and started over."

"Back then, it could've been as simple as shaving their faces and changing their style of clothes."

"If Anthony left here of his own free will, then who is haunting this house?" Elijah asked.

"That's what we're going to find out."

CHAPTER EIGHT

Lyric

"**A**NY IDEAS WHERE I SHOULD START?" I ASKED MAEGAN.

"The attic," they all responded.

Aiming a crooked smile at Memphis, I said, "Sounds like we have a date with an attic."

All I could think about was being alone with Memphis long enough to claim the kiss I'd planned to give him in his office. The rest could wait until we were alone at his house, but no living or dead person was going to keep me from kissing Memphis up in that attic. Regardless of his blasé comments earlier, we needed to have a conversation before I got him naked. Lust made you bolder, but it also made you the ultimate rationalizer. I didn't want Memphis to compromise anything to be with me, because I wouldn't change my mind. No matter how good sex would be between us, I wouldn't wake up the morning after wanting to live a happily ever after with him.

"I'm ready," Memphis said as he rose to his feet.

"We'll hang back here," Maegan said.

"Yeah, we don't want to get in the way," Milo added.

"Unless you want someone to hold the video camera on you…I mean, for you," Andy offered. I looked over in time to see Milo jab him a good one with his elbow, making all the air in Andy's lungs whoosh out of him. "Never mind," he squeaked.

I exchanged a smile with Memphis. "We'll be back in a bit," I told them.

"Don't rush on our account," Elijah said.

"You guys have serious issues," Memphis said then left me standing there by myself. It felt like I was standing in front of the firing squad, which wasn't too far off the mark if Memphis wasn't being honest with me and ended up hurt by my inability to give him more than sex.

"Um…yeah," I said then hurried after him, only stopping long enough to grab my bag of equipment before heading up the grand staircase. I caught up with Memphis just as he reached the top. I set my bag down and he spun around and faced me. I backed him up until I had him pinned between me and the wall then lowered my head until my lips hovered above his. "I don't think I can wait."

"So don't," Memphis challenged.

I fucking knew it was a mistake to give in to temptation, but I'd never wanted anyone as much as I wanted him. I couldn't live the rest of my life without knowing if his lips were as soft as they looked. I would never kiss another man without wondering if Memphis tasted better. Kissing him might ruin me for everyone else, but it was a risk I was willing to take. Correction: had to take.

I cupped his jaw with my hands and softly pressed my lips to his. Fuck! They were even softer than they looked. A few presses of my lips against his weren't enough to tide me over, but I wanted complete privacy before I kissed him like I meant it.

"Come with me," I said, taking a step back. I grabbed my bag off the floor, grabbed Memphis's hand, and led him down the hall to the attic door.

"You might want to find something to prop the door open so we don't get locked in," Memphis told me.

"Afraid of the things I will do to you up there?" I jokingly asked.

"Not in the least," he responded, but I already knew that because his brown eyes had darkened with lust. "I do want to be able to leave the attic whenever we're done *investigating* though."

"The door sticks?" I asked, opening the door.

"No, it locks from the inside." Memphis stepped around me then demonstrated how the inside handle didn't turn. I didn't notice it before because the door was left open when I checked out the attic during my initial visit.

"How did you discover that?" I asked with a raised brow.

"The ghost locked Milo and Andy up there together." Memphis chuckled then explained a little about their relationship before I met them. "I think Anthony smelled the sexual tension between Andy and Milo and decided to lock them in the attic so they could work things out. I heard Milo yelling and banging on the door before it got really quiet. When I opened the door suddenly, they spilled onto the floor with glazed eyes and flushed faces."

"Then what?"

"Well, Milo didn't offer up any information, and I didn't ask him to kiss and tell."

"Not that part," I said, stepping into him so he could feel the erection straining behind my jeans. "I can guess what happened once they were alone again. I meant before they left to scratch the itch."

"They argued some more then Andy went back upstairs to check for leaks while I talked to Milo. We both got a whiff of pipe tobacco and ran out of here."

"I thought you were calm under pressure," I asked with a quirked brow and tilted head.

"I normally am, but I reacted to Milo's panic." Memphis cocked his head slightly to the left. "Come to think of it; I bet Milo was trying to outrun his feelings for Andy."

"I doubt anyone outruns something like that," I said. "And by that, I mean lust."

"You don't believe in love, do you?" Memphis asked sadly.

"I believe that it happens for other people."

"Just not for you?"

"I've learned the hard way love is an illusion; it's nothing more than smoke in the mirror." He looked so sad, and that was the last thing I wanted him to feel. "Great pleasure awaits you upstairs... If you dare."

"Oh, I dare." Memphis stepped back and flipped the switch on the interior wall of the staircase. "This light is courtesy of the modernization touches Maegan added to the house. It's a big improvement over what was here before."

I was disappointed the attic was so well lit because I'd hoped to kiss Memphis in a dark corner. It wasn't that I felt the need to hide, but I thought it would add to the ambiance of a stolen kiss up in the attic.

I admired his ass as we ascended the steps just like I did at his house when he showed me to my room. Okay, I did more than admire the second time around; I imagined how his perfectly rounded ass would feel in my hands or pressed against my pelvis as I slid my dick inside him the first time. I just knew it would grip me tighter than anything I'd ever felt and challenge my stamina because as much as Memphis stimulated me physically, something about his personality made him irresistible to me. I was a moth to his flame.

When we reached the top of the steps, Memphis looked around the room and started to laugh. "Victoria," he said, answering my unasked question about what he found so funny. "The mannequin." Memphis pointed to one of those headless antique mannequins made from metal.

"Oh wow, that thing is probably worth a fortune," I told Memphis. "What's so funny about her?" He told me Victoria startled Milo when he and Andy made their infamous voyage into the attic. They'd only had flashlights, and Victoria was wearing a white dress at the time. I could see how someone would see that in their peripheral vision and think it was a ghost. "Maegan gave her a name so she'd be less scary to him. I think he nearly shit his pants. No one lets him live it down e—"

His words died when I pressed my lips firmly to his. I'd heard enough about Milo and Victoria already and needed to taste him. Memphis parted his mouth in surprise at my attack, and I used it to my advantage and slid my tongue into his mouth. In response, Memphis formed an O with his lips and sucked my tongue like he would a cock. Things were going to get out of control fast if I wasn't careful. Memphis looked like such a mild-mannered guy with his messy hair, guileless eyes, and black-rimmed glasses, but he was anything but when he slid his hands into my hair and became the aggressor in the kiss. I tasted a hint of desperation on him, and it only made me hornier. Instead of pulling back and slowing things down, I cupped his ass and pulled him tighter against me while tangling my tongue with his.

A crash sounded at the opposite end of the attic, making us jump apart in surprise. I looked in the direction of the noise and noticed the box that was on top of a stack had been knocked to the floor. Then I detected a hint of pipe tobacco at the same time a tingling awareness snaked down my spine. *Showtime!*

I placed another quick kiss on Memphis's parted lips and retrieved my bag. As a medium, I often was able to communicate with ghosts. Sometimes they would show me things in visions, and other times they would speak to me. The voices didn't always come through loud and clear. Some didn't communicate with me through the psychic channel; they used the human world to talk. That often came out distorted, and I used an EVP device named after the electronic voice phenomenon it picked up. It detected things the human ear never could and made the voices easier to understand.

"Let's do an EVP session," I told Memphis, who nodded in agreement. "Anthony Bliss, are you here with us?" I waited for a moment to see if I detected a voice spiritually or in person. I also searched the room for any physical signs he was present with us in the attic. I picked up the EMF reader that detected a fluctuation in electromagnetic fields signaling paranormal phenomenon might be present.

"Will you hold this for me?"

"Sure," Memphis said in awe.

"I've calibrated this device to sense spikes higher than what you'd typically find in homes from sources such as power lines and electrical outlets. Attics tend to spike higher in older homes like this one because it's where the main electrical line comes in since electricity was added many years after construction. New homes have underground lines that feed an exterior meter base, where this one is fed from an electrical line down the outside wall of the house to the meter base on the ground level. It's a huge source of energy and skews the readings."

"Right. You like to investigate any readings over two point one."

I'd forgotten he watched the show. I wasn't sure how I felt about Memphis knowing a lot more about me than I did him; it seemed like an unfair advantage. I suddenly felt awkward in ways I'd never experienced investigating before, which was silly. It wasn't like I was performing for his pleasure. I'd save that for when we were in bed. "Are you comfortable walking around the room with the reader?" I asked Memphis. I needed space from him to think clearly about the investigation.

"Are *you* comfortable with me walking around the room with the reader? You don't sound very sure."

"I am." I wasn't. I needed space from him, but I didn't want it at the same time. *Focus, Lyric.* "Why don't you start in that corner next to Victoria."

"Damn, my kiss must've sucked if you're sending me to the corner," Memphis said with a little pout. "The farthest corner away from the activity where you'll be investigating. I don't think it's a coincidence."

"Oh, you sucked all right, but I know you felt how much I liked it. I think you also know things wouldn't have stopped with tongue-sucking had the ghost not interrupted us." *Fuck me; I wanted to taste him.* "You caught me. Maybe I'll have my dick under control

74

by the time you work your way over to me."

Memphis snorted. "You'll be hanging out with Victoria by then."
Guilty.

"Be glad I don't trust myself around you and think of how it will play out when we get back to your place."

"Fair enough," Memphis said then eagerly headed in the opposite direction from me. I stood there staring at his firm ass until he called me out on it. "I can feel your eyes on my ass. I prefer your hands, so let's get going."

Knowing I was busted, I turned and headed over to where the boxes were knocked to the ground. "Are you trying to tell me something? Is there something special about these boxes, or were you trying to get my attention?"

"Readings are all pretty normal so far," Memphis said softly, but I swear I felt a paranormal presence. "Oh! There it goes. Reading four point six and now five point three."

I briskly crossed the attic to reach Memphis. "Are you the ghost of Anthony Bliss? What happened when you disappeared? What's special about this attic to you? Were you the one they locked inside?" After my last question, the lights flickered, and the digital display showed a spike of nearly ten points. I was on to something, but I didn't want to anger the ghost and make Maegan's life miserable. "We want to help you, Anthony. We want to tell the world what really happened to you in 1850. Can you help us?" The lights flickered faster and went out completely, leaving the fading daylight coming through the attic window as our only light source.

"There!" Memphis pointed toward the boxes. "I saw a shadow move. It's too bad you don't have your video camera out. I think we're going to need the help of one other person." Most people would've assumed the excitement was causing Memphis to see things, but I could *feel* the ghost's presence.

Memphis was right, but I resented another person interrupting our time together. The solution would be to set up several cameras for another session. The lights came back on full force, and I could feel that our ghost was gone.

"We're alone again," I told him.

"Did the ghost speak directly to you?" Memphis asked.

"No, but not all ghosts realize it's an option. If this is Anthony Bliss, he's probably been trying to reach out to humans since he died. They either weren't aware or were too afraid. He has no idea some humans walking the earth can chat with him. That is my ultimate goal, but I'll take what I can get."

"Do you think he ran away to be with Wallace?" Memphis asked me.

"I do. It wouldn't have been hard to reinvent themselves in a place like San Francisco with the kind of wealth they had. I just need to prove it."

"Wow, this mystery is turning out to be more exciting than I ever dreamed possible," Memphis said in awe.

"Let's head downstairs and chat with Maegan about what we've witnessed so far. Then we'll collect our dogs and head on back to your place, so I can transfer the data from the EVP session into my software program that scrubs all the background noise and clears up any paranormal sounds."

"Sounds awesome."

We packed up the equipment and headed for the stairs. When we got to the bottom, we saw the door was shut. Memphis looked over his shoulder at me with a raised brow.

"I didn't shut the door," I told him.

"You didn't prop it open either," he countered. He was right; I didn't. Memphis started knocking loudly and yelling until he felt my hand snake around and pressed against his stomach as I stepped up against his body. "Oh," he said, firmly pressing his ass against my erection. "Maybe this isn't so bad." Memphis started to turn toward me when the door opened suddenly.

Milo stood in the open doorway with a smirk on his face. "Didn't you learn anything after the last time?" He shook his head and added, "Never mind. It's none of my business."

Memphis chuckled. "Since when?"

"Since this morning." Milo winked then asked, "Did anything *paranormal* happen up there?"

"Yes!" Memphis replied excitedly. "We want to tell everyone together."

I followed Memphis and Milo down the staircase and into the dining room where everyone else patiently waited.

"The gang's all here," Milo said. "What happened up there?"

I opened my mouth to answer, but Memphis spoke up first. I smiled as he told them every little detail except for the way he sucked my tongue like a pro or the kiss that followed. When he finished, everyone turned to look at me.

"I'm going to upload the session into my computer to see if our ghostly friend had anything to say. I'd like to come back and set up some video equipment in the attic tomorrow morning. Maybe try another session tomorrow evening? Is that okay with you guys?" I asked Maegan and Elijah.

They both agreed, and I promised I'd come over early enough I wouldn't interfere with their work schedules. Memphis and I both refused the offer of coffee and dessert so we could hit the road. I hoped they thought we turned them down over our enthusiasm to play back the recorder and weren't aware just how badly I wanted to get Memphis naked and beneath me.

For the first time in my career, I was going to put my physical needs before an investigation.

CHAPTER NINE

Memphis

"DON'T RUN OVER ANY LITTLE OLD LADIES," LYRIC SAID ONCE I'd pulled out of Maegan's lane and headed across town. "I don't think I can wait long enough for the cops to investigate the accident. I need to be inside you, Memphis." His desperation nearly made me come in my pants. "I'd hate to shock the citizens of Blissville by bending you over the hood of your car." Lyric pointed out the windshield like he was pointing out the exact spot where the fucking would occur.

"First, the hood is back there," I reminded him, pointing behind me with my thumb. "The trunk is in the front."

"Either one would do. What's the second thing."

"Um… I can't remember. All I can think about is you bending me over the hood or trunk and yanking my pants down."

"Drive faster, Memphis."

I should've been able to drive the short distance from Maegan's house to mine without incident, but then again, I shouldn't have listened to Lyric.

"Fuck!" I exclaimed when the red and blue lights flashed in my rearview mirror.

"I'm sorry, Memphis," Lyric said. "I'll pay for your ticket."

"Oh, you're going to pay all right. As soon as we get back." I rolled down my window and looked up to see Joey Simanski shining his light inside my car like he didn't fucking know who I was.

"Sir, I need to see your license, registration, and proof of insurance," Joey said firmly, with virtually no warmth in his voice.

"Joey, come on. Why are you acting like you don't know my name?"

"I'm trying to act professional and not show you deferential treatment because I know how tightly your ass grips my dick. License, registration, and proof of insurance. Please." *Great!* Making an enemy of one of the cops in town wasn't my brightest decision. Hell hath no fury like a woman scorned really needed a reboot to include gay men.

I blew out a frustrated sigh and leaned forward so I could pull my wallet out of my back pocket while Lyric rummaged around in the dashboard until he came up with the registration and proof of insurance. "Here you go, Officer Simanski."

"Where were you headed so fast?" Joey asked me. "I clocked you doing ten over the posted limit."

"I'm half of a block away from my house, Joey. I think it's pretty obvious."

Lyric responded to my angry tone by placing his hand on my thigh. Maybe he wanted to offer comfort, but it only riled me up more. Joey didn't miss the gesture either.

"That explains it," he said dryly. "I remember how you get when you're horny. I need to run you through the system to make sure there aren't any warrants out for your arrest. If not, I'll write you a ticket and let you get on with your night. It shouldn't take too long, but our system has been acting funny all night." Meaning he planned to drag this out until he got tired of dicking me around because I no longer wanted his dick around.

"Wow," Lyric said when we were alone again. "What possessed you to fuck him?"

"He had a bad attitude and owns a real pair of handcuffs," I replied flippantly. "That was an irresistible combination."

"Appears to me you've resisted it just fine, and Officer Asshole doesn't like it."

"It turned out he was more hearts and flowers than I realized. I thought we had a good thing going until he wanted to take me home to meet the family." I shrugged. "That's when it all started going downhill. I learned a valuable lesson."

"Don't fuck people living in your own town?" Lyric asked.

"No, but that's a good one too," I told him. "Don't judge a book by its cover."

Lyric leaned toward me, and I met him halfway. "If he's going to keep us here for a ridiculously long time, I think we should make the best of it."

"The best of it could mean that I come in my pants."

"Let's give him something to get pissed about, Memphis."

I knew Joey's bright headlights illuminated the interior of my car, and he could see our heads inches away through the space between our seats. It might've been stupid to irritate the cop even more, but I couldn't resist the dark promise I saw in Lyric's eyes. I also saw he'd leave the decision up to me, which I liked a lot. There wasn't much for me to decide, especially after Lyric's pink tongue darted out to moisten his lips just in case I wanted to be bad with him.

I wanted to be bad; I wanted to be really fucking bad. Lyric's eyes dared me, and his lips tempted me, so I took the challenge. A low growl escaped my lips seconds before I pressed them against Lyric's. This wasn't a soft, getting-to-know-you kiss; it was a grab-you-by-the-balls kiss with teeth and tongues that made us forget a world existed beyond our connection. That is until a very annoyed cop cleared his throat outside my window. Even then, I wasn't willing to pull my lips away from Lyric's. I felt his mouth curve into a smile against mine before he pulled back, breaking our kiss. Lyric's eyes and wicked smile promised "soon." Did I look as dazed as I felt? Lyric reached up and straightened my glasses then blew out a long sigh before he faced forward to look back out the windshield with that crooked smile still planted on his face.

"I hate to break this up, but I need to get back on patrol," Joey said snidely. Yeah, right, he was prepared to sit there for as long as he wanted, and I wasn't about to let it slide.

"Wow," I said dramatically. "From what you said, I expected to be here for a long time. I'm so happy your computers are suddenly working efficiently. Can I have my ID, registration, and proof of insurance back now, Officer Simanski?"

Joey handed those items back to me plus a speeding ticket. "The fine and deadline to pay are on the ticket. The county judge shows up every other Tuesday if you want to challenge the ticket."

"Nah, I was speeding, so I'll pay the price."

"You're lucky I didn't tack on extra charges for lewd behavior." So much for Joey just giving me a ticket and moving on.

"Lewd behavior, Joey? We were only kissing." He sure didn't have a problem fucking me buck-ass naked in the back seat of his cruiser behind the high school late one night the previous summer. "That's a charge I'd fight."

Joey opened his mouth to say more when dispatch radioed him. "Slow it down, Memphis," he said bitterly before walking away. His words seemed to hold more weight than just telling me not to drive so fast.

I had no intention of slowing down, but I did make it back to my house without further incident. We let the dogs run around the back yard and do their business while Lyric pushed me up against the side of the house and made out with me. I hadn't turned on the light by the back door and the heavy cloud cover shielded us from prying eyes. I wanted to rip my clothes off and feel his hands on my skin, his naked body pressing me down and taking what he wanted—what we both wanted.

"If I had a condom and lube on me, I'd take you right here and damn the consequences," Lyric said roughly against my lips. "I won't be gentle—"

"I don't want gentle, Lyric. Let's get the dogs and go inside."

Lyric let out a sharp whistle, and the four of us headed inside. I'd barely shut the door before we were on each other. I lost my shirt in the kitchen, and he lost his in the living room as we made our way toward the steps. I went for Lyric's button and zipper on his jeans before we made it to the stairs. I tore my mouth away from his so I could look at the massive erection straining against his underwear.

"You make Big Bob look like Average Bob," I whispered huskily. Fuck, I couldn't wait to feel the fullness of his penetration.

In answer to my boldness, Lyric released my jeans and slid his hand beneath the elastic of my underwear to tease the crack of my ass with one long, wicked finger. I let out a needy whimper when the calloused pad of his finger brushed across my pucker. I quickly attacked his mouth to avoid making a fool of myself by begging him to fuck me right there on the stairway.

In my fantasies, I was suave and confident, touching him in ways that turned him to putty in my hands. In reality, I wasn't sure where to put my hands. I wanted to touch him everywhere at the same time. Growing up, my parents took me to a restaurant every Sunday that served up delicious food cafeteria style. You'd get your tray and slide it down the line picking out what you wanted for an entrée and side dishes. I always got overwhelmed when we reached the end of the line where I got to choose a dessert. There were always so many, and I worried I would make the wrong decision. I mean, what if I chose the chocolate parfait over the cheesecake and it sucked? As a kid, there was no reasoning I'd get a fresh pick the following week. All I knew was that moment.

Lyric was the biggest smorgasbord of deliciousness I would ever get my hands on, and I couldn't choose where I wanted to start. I wanted to trace my fingers over the ridges of Lyric's abdominal muscles and every tattoo with my tongue, but I was paralyzed by…lust. I wasn't guaranteed anything beyond that moment, and I knew I was blowing it with every passing second. Instead of taking full advantage of the situation, I stood there stiff as a dick, trying not to cream my underwear when he pushed just the tip of his finger inside my ass.

"Touch me, damn it," Lyric growled when he ripped his mouth away from mine.

He sounded as desperate as I felt which I took as a good sign. It bolstered my courage, making me brave enough to tug the hoop ring through his nipple with my lips.

"Fuck, yeah," he roared like a porn star, fisting my hair and holding my head against his chest like he thought I might bolt. *As if.* "You're going to be a little spitfire in bed, aren't you?"

I couldn't verbally reply unless I let the hoop slip from my mouth, which neither of us wanted. Instead, I fisted Lyric's cock through his black underwear and… I tore my mouth free of his nipple ring and pushed against his hand in my hair so I could look at what I'd just discovered.

"Holy Mother of Pearl, you have an apadravya piercing," I said, but it almost sounded like an accusation. My knees knocked and threatened to give out. All my focus went to peeling back the elastic band of his underwear to expose the piercing just beneath the glans. I brushed my thumb over the leaking tip, spreading his pre-cum over the head of his dick while admiring the round balls on either side of the barbell. I was already anticipating them pegging my prostate. "You're going to wreck me in the best possible way."

"That's the plan," Lyric said roughly.

Heaven awaited me in my bedroom, but instead of leading Lyric up the steps, I dropped to my knees on the stairs so I was face to cock with the beast.

"Don't you dare, Memphis. I've been thinking about my cock inside you all day long."

He might as well have whipped off a red cape and waved it at me like a bull. I pressed my hand against his abs until he was flush against the wall. "Just a little taste." I flicked my tongue out and licked a circle around the head, gathering his salty essence. One little taste wasn't enough, so I tugged his jeans and underwear down farther to expose more of his erection.

"Memphis, let's go upstairs," Lyric said half-heartedly. Then his fingers tangled in my hair as he pulled my face closer to his eager cock. I sucked the head into my mouth so exuberantly that I nearly chipped a tooth, but it didn't discourage me. "Or maybe you can just put me out of my misery right here."

I responded by taking his cock in as far as I could without gagging. It was my first time blowing a guy with a piercing, and I wasn't used to working around one, but I was more than willing to practice until I got it right.

"Fuck!" Lyric yelled loud enough to bring the Matrons running over. Maybe I was better at it than I thought. "I want to fuck your face, but it can wait. I want inside that sweet ass." I continued working his cock in and out of my mouth like I hadn't heard him until I felt his legs tremble.

I pulled off quickly, rose to my feet, and ran up the stairs. By some miracle, I didn't trip over my own two feet and break my dick on the way up. Lyric caught me at the top of the stairs and pushed me up against the wall. His eyes promised wicked retribution before he swooped down and claimed my lips in a possessive kiss. My heart raced erratically, and I thought it might explode in my chest before I knew what it was like to lie beneath him in a bed.

I pulled away from his kiss and began walking backward in what I hoped was the direction of my bedroom. Lyric had me so turned around I could be walking toward the staircase and certain doom and wouldn't even know it. I paused to toe out of my shoes and shove my jeans and briefs down my legs. Once I kicked them off, I stood in front of him completely naked while he looked at me through hungry eyes. I turned around and saw I had indeed been heading toward my room.

Lyric let out a playful growl when he got his first good look at my ass. I felt his pursuit even if I didn't hear it. For as big as he was, Lyric moved as silently as smoke. "Please tell me you have condoms and lube in here because walking a few feet down the hallway seems like an insurmountable feat right now."

I pulled open the bedside drawer and held up the condoms and lube for him to inspect. I tossed them on top of my comforter then positioned myself on my hands and knees in the center of the bed, parting my legs enough to entice Lyric. I wasn't sure what it was about him that made me act so fucking bold, but I reached for the bottle of lube, flipped open the lid, and drizzled the cool liquid down my crack.

Lyric clenched his jaw tight while he removed the rest of his clothes and strolled over to the bed. "I can see why that cop can't get enough of you, Sullivan." He placed his hands on the back of my knees and slowly slid them up until they rested just beneath the curve of my ass. "You have the face of an angel and a body made for sin. There's a boldness about you that tempts a man to want things he has no business asking for."

Little did Lyric know, he was the only man who brought this side out of me.

CHAPTER TEN

Lyric

I AM SO FUCKED. I AM SO FUCKED. MY ATTRACTION TO THE SWEET, and sometimes awkward, Memphis was already intense, but his boldness sent my lust soaring to stratospheric heights. It was like he sensed how badly I wanted him and fed off it. Or, maybe he was just a natural siren. I knew before I rolled the condom down the length of my cock one time in his bed wouldn't be enough.

Memphis dipped one finger inside his ass, stretching and fucking himself for a few heartbeats before adding a second digit. I'd watched countless hours of porn and had even gone to a few sex clubs over the years, but somehow, Memphis preparing himself for my dick was the most erotic thing I'd ever seen. A guy like him deserved sweet kisses and a gentle lover, but that wouldn't be me. At least not the first time.

Or the second, third, fourth, and so on…

"Bring that beast over here and fuck me," Memphis said, pumping his fingers into his ass as far as they would go from that angle. Did he know how desperate and sexy he sounded?

I coated my cock with lube then added one of my fingers to his. "Two just aren't enough." Of course, I could sink my digit in deeper than his two could reach. I bent my finger and tagged his prostate, making him moan loud and needy. "You want me to fill your greedy ass?" Fuck, something about Memphis brought out my inner porn star.

"Fuck, yeah." It was good to know I had reduced him to running on autopilot also.

I placed one knee on the bed, and said, "I won't be gentle, Memphis. Are you sure?"

"Oh my God. I'm about to come. It's so fucking hot that we're fingering my ass together, but I want to come on your cock."

I climbed the rest of the way onto the bed and positioned myself behind Memphis before I removed my finger from his ass. Memphis removed his too and whined, making me think the emptiness made him ache. I was about to press the broad head of my cock to his hole and push in, but I had a sudden urge to look into his eyes when I slid balls-deep inside him the first time. *Another first for me.*

"What are you doing?" Memphis asked in a stricken voice when I got back off the bed. My reply was to grab his ankles, pull him flat onto his stomach, then roll him over. "Oh!" he exclaimed when I spread his legs and pushed them back until his knees nearly touched his chest.

"Hold your legs right there and don't move."

Memphis swiftly did what he was told, freeing up my hands to do very wicked things to him, such as stroking his dick with my right hand while feeding my cock into his ass with the left.

"Fuck! You're so big!"

"We both know you can take it like a champ though, don't we?" Still, that didn't mean I was going to ram my cock inside him like a fucking brute. Stating I wouldn't be gentle wasn't the same as being cruel. "Nice and easy, Sullivan."

"I… Oh fuck, it burns." I started to withdraw, but Memphis shook his head desperately, knocking his glasses crooked again. "Give me more."

"Breathe and push out," I encouraged as his pucker strangled the head of my cock. "That's it, baby." *Baby?* Memphis squirmed, but I couldn't tell if he was trying to get my dick deeper inside him or dislodge me.

"Stop being a dick and give me your dick."

I had my answer, so I pushed forward to sink my cock another couple of inches inside his tight clench. It took every ounce of strength I had to halt right there and let him adjust to my size.

"Oh! Oh my God!" Memphis's eyes rolled back in his head, and I knew my piercing was pressing deliciously against his prostate. He tried rocking his hips up and down to fuck himself on my cock when it was only halfway inside him, but his position left him at my mercy. "Ric," he said pleadingly. "More, please."

I pulled back and punched forward in shallow thrusts, tagging his gland over and over while he panted and moaned beneath me.

"I'm close, so fucking close."

I didn't need him to tell me because I saw the way his body tensed, his balls retracted tighter against his body, and his cock jerked. I waited until the first splatter of cum hit his chest before I penetrated him fully.

"Uhn," Memphis grunted as I fucked him through his orgasm.

After he came, I gripped his hips and pulled his ass so it hung over the bed a few inches. "Put your legs on my shoulders," I instructed.

Memphis looked drunk and boneless, so I propped his calves on my shoulders, held him by his thighs, and gave him the fucking he'd begged me for.

"Yes! More!" His yells of pleasure and the sounds of our skin slapping together echoed throughout the room.

I became the rutting beast I'd warned him about as I pistoned in and out of his ass, chasing the orgasm I feared might wreck me. Lust and anticipation built inside me, promising heights of pleasure I'd never known. My orgasm crashed into me like a tsunami, and I held Memphis's legs tight against my chest while I buried myself as deep inside him as I could and flooded the condom. The pleasure went on and on until it became painful, and still, I couldn't stop rutting.

Black dots swam across my vision, and I wobbled on my feet a second as dizziness washed over me. "Sullivan, I think I fucked myself blind."

"Everyone knows you only go blind from masturbation," Memphis said sleepily.

When my vision cleared, I looked down to see him smiling happily at me. I felt my heart pinch painfully in my chest. I realized I was in deeper trouble than I first thought when I caught myself wishing I could see that same dopey grin smiling at me first thing in the morning. That kind of life wasn't in the cards for me, and I was a fucking bastard for using Memphis to get off. I could tell he saw the change in my demeanor when his body stiffened against mine, and I realized his legs were still thrown over my shoulders and my dick was still buried in the ass I held onto with a death grip. Memphis was basically impaled on my cock with no place to go unless I released him.

I wanted to release him and step back so I could erect my shield again, but I didn't. I slowly lowered his legs then leaned over him until he stared at me with big, brown eyes that pleaded with me to kiss him. I didn't do after-sex cuddling, nor did I kiss a lover while their body returned to normal function, but that's exactly what I wanted to do with Memphis. I'd already crossed too many lines, so instead of kissing him, I offered a wry smile while straightening his glasses before I gently removed my cock from his ass.

I turned my back and headed to the bathroom to clean up before I could change my mind. *Shower, comfy clothes, and get to work solving the mystery that brought you to Blissville.* I admonished myself under the hot spray until I thought enough time had passed that seeing Memphis wouldn't be as awkward. Yeah, right. When has the aftermath of a fuck and run been anything other than awkward? I didn't totally disappear, but I mentally checked out right in front of him then ran to hide in the shower while I gathered myself.

I heard the bathroom door creak open. "I don't mean to intrude," Memphis said hesitantly. All traces of boldness were gone, furthering my guilt. "Mind if I clean up a second?"

Man, I was a fucking dickhead. I left him lying there covered in his cum without offering to help him up or let him use the shower first. "It's your house," I said, hoping I sounded contrite and not sarcastic. "Oh wow, that didn't come out the way I meant it."

Memphis chuckled. "It's okay, Lyric." When he came, he'd shortened my name to Ric. My friends and family had used that nickname before, but never anyone I had sex with because I never allowed them to get familiar with me. It felt too intimate which was why Memphis probably went back to using my full name. That's if he was even aware he'd shortened my name. I'd liked it when he said Ric more than I should have.

I heard the water running for less than a minute followed by movement on the other side of the curtain. I wanted to peek around and see if Memphis was still naked but checking out his ass would lead us right back to his bedroom. Who was I kidding? I'd use any and all surfaces firm enough to support us. It got so quiet I thought maybe he'd left until I heard him peeing. Another new experience for me since I never stuck around long enough to shower on site or listen to my hookup take a piss while I cleaned cum off my cock.

A grin spread across my face until Memphis flushed the toilet. Like with most houses, water pressure was diverted from other sources to carry waste through the plumbing, but that was the least of my problems. What followed could've gone two ways—ice cold or scalding hot water. I held my breath to brace myself but lost my shit when I was blasted with water so cold it felt like small chunks of ice pelted my body instead of water droplets.

"Fuck me!" I roared then nearly slipped in the tub when I hastily reached for the faucet to shut off my ice bath. I yanked back the curtain and saw Memphis doubled over laughing behind the hand he'd pressed to his mouth. "Sullivan, did you do that on purpose?"

Memphis stood straighter, and it was then I realized he still was completely naked. I stepped over the edge of the bathtub and advanced on him. Memphis stiffened and lowered his hand. "I'm so sorry. Did you get burned?"

I couldn't answer him with the lump of longing lodged in my throat.

Memphis gasped when I pressed him against the vanity with my naked, wet body. "You're freezing. I promise I didn't do it on purpose."

"I'm not sure I believe you," I said, staring at his delicious lips.

"What can I do to convince you?"

I should've asked him to hand me a towel or step aside so I could get dressed. I did neither of those things. I cupped his neck and slowly lowered my lips. "Warm me up."

Memphis closed the gap and attacked my mouth with renewed hunger like we hadn't just fucked. I forgot all about the cold ending to my shower and that I needed to avoid him for both of our sakes. I got lost in his kiss, his touch and allowed him to warm me to my soul.

"I'm so glad you're a nervous baker," Memphis said an hour later while he licked the batter off one of the beaters. It was so hard for me to concentrate on my software program when that deft tongue tempted and teased me. How was that even possible? I was certain I'd ruptured a nut when I'd fisted both our cocks in his tiny bathroom and jerked us both off.

"Who said anything about nervous?" I asked after I finally tore my eyes off his tongue. Okay, I only looked up because his tongue stopped licking. Once I made eye contact with him again, that tongue darted out and took a long, leisurely lick. Fuck! There was the boldness that drove me wild.

"It was implied when you told me that baking and watching that baking show helps relax you," Memphis replied. "Do I make you nervous?"

"Why are you so bold?"

"Honestly?" he asked.

"Of course."

"I'm not usually this bold, but you bring out something in me." He dropped the semi-clean beater in the sink and pulled the other one out of the bowl and brought it up to his mouth. "I'm not sure what to make of it."

I wasn't sure what to make of it either. On the one hand, I liked that I made Memphis bolder, but on the other, I didn't like that I affected him. It made things more…complicated. I didn't do relationships because my life was enough of a cluster-fuck without adding romance to the mix. "You don't make me nervous, Sullivan." *The way I react to you makes me nervous.* "I bake to relax, and I bake when I need to keep my hands busy to distract my brain or drown out the chatter."

"Chatter? Ghostly chatter?" He dropped the beater in the sink without licking it. "Are you hearing some right now?" He ran his fingers through his curls, making them stand up all over. He peered at me with widened eyes while licking his lips nervously.

"I was pointing out some reasons why I bake. I haven't picked up any 'ghostly chatter' in your home."

"Have you picked up chatter here in Blissville?"

"Of course," I said calmly. "Restless souls are walking the earth everywhere. In some places, like hospitals and nursing homes, the noise is overwhelming. We took a field trip to a Civil War battlefield when I was in junior high, and the volume of paranormal activity left me with crippling migraines for days afterward."

"You just pick up the chatter when you're walking around?"

We were venturing into unchartered territory. I didn't discuss my personal life or details about my abilities with anyone. The only person who understood me was my maternal grandmother because she also had the gift. Grammy taught me everything she knew, including how to block out the noise to preserve my sanity. Emory, as a psychic, understood me to some extent, but he didn't see, hear, or communicate with the dead. I'd refused one interview request after the other with networks, magazines, and various organizations because protecting my privacy had always been my top priority when I agreed to do the show. I didn't feel pressure to prove my abilities were legit, and I didn't care if it pissed anyone off. Of course, many thought my aloofness added to my appeal and accused me of being an asshole to boost ratings.

Sitting in Memphis's kitchen waiting for the cakes to bake while fighting with my fickle laptop was the first time I wanted to open up and talk to someone other than Grammy or Emory. Memphis wasn't looking for a scoop for an article, he wasn't trying to catch me out and prove I was a charlatan, and he hadn't elevated me to some paranormal investigator God-like status. He was just curious.

"I do, but I've learned to block it or at least turn it down so I can function. It was overwhelming at first, but I had an excellent teacher." As much as I liked Memphis, I wasn't willing to talk about my grandmother.

"I'm sorry, Lyric. I didn't mean to pry. I find it fascinating, but I don't want to make you feel uncomfortable, so why don't we talk about Bliss House. How are you coming along with the software?"

I wondered if Memphis could hear my sigh of relief across the room and see me visibly relax. I was happy to avoid an unpleasant conversation where I would basically remind Memphis I wanted to fuck him as often as possible without connecting on the most basic personal level. I didn't mind discovering his favorite foods, television shows, or even comic book villains, but that was as deep as I wanted things to get.

"It's getting there," I replied. "The software isn't the issue; it's my outdated laptop. These things are only good for a few years before they're nearly useless, and I've had this one for seven years."

"That is a long time for a laptop."

"I keep updating software as best I can, but it's simply not fast enough to do what I'd like." I glanced up and found Memphis watching me with his head tilted slightly to the side. "What?"

"Nothing," he replied, shaking his head, but a sweet smile spread across his face. "You're superstitious, aren't you?"

"No," I said quickly, but even I heard the defensiveness in my voice. "I'm just lazy."

"Uh huh."

"Lazy and cheap," I amended. "Why buy a new computer when I have a perfectly good one?"

"Is the software compatible with Mac?"

"Yeah, why?" I asked, narrowing my eyes.

"I have an awesome MacBook, and I'm willing to let you borrow it so we might be able to hear Anthony talking to us faster. Or maybe you'd rather wait for your computer to update. How much longer does it say?"

"It's only at seventeen percent," I mumbled.

"Wow, it was at fourteen nearly half an hour ago when you decided to bake a cake." He crossed the kitchen and leaned down until we were eye to eye. "Come on, Lyric; live a little. Play with my shiny toys."

"I've seen your toys," I quipped. "You're a braver man than I am, Sullivan."

His face turned an adorable shade of pink. Memphis rose to his full height and placed his hands on his hips. "You're going to tease me about that forever, aren't you?"

I could've reminded Memphis we didn't have forever, but it felt unnecessarily cruel. Instead, I went with, "Fuck yeah."

CHAPTER ELEVEN

Memphis

LYRIC FINALLY RELENTED AND AGREED TO BORROW MY LAPTOP, so I went upstairs to retrieve it from my room and made sure there were no traces of that stupid *Willows Whisperers* site for him to find. He'd mentioned he needed to log in to his account and download the software to my laptop, so cleaning out my browser history just seemed like an excellent idea.

"Here you go," I said, breezing into the kitchen after I completed my mission.

"What took you so long? Were you hiding your porn?" Lyric asked. "Who knows, maybe we're in to the same stuff."

"You caught me." I sat the laptop in front of him. "Here you go."

"She *is* a thing of beauty," Lyric said, petting her.

"*He*," I corrected.

"What's this beast's name?"

"It's not important," I replied. "What matters is that you can download the software in seconds and upload your data so we can hear if Anthony communicated with you." I typed in my password to unlock Daken. Lyric didn't need to know I named my laptop after my favorite Marvel villain. "I'm kind of surprised you didn't want to listen to the recording before…"

"Before we fucked?" Lyric finished for me. "I had my priorities straight." He aimed a crooked smile at me and added, "You made it too hard for me to concentrate." Did that mean he'd fucked me out of his system now? *God, I hoped not.* I felt like we were just getting started.

"Are you hungry? I can make some popcorn." I needed to do something to stay busy while he got everything set up. I don't know why I was suddenly nervous. Hell, maybe I should've baked something. I'd experienced so many fucking emotions with him that night it left me feeling turned upside down and inside out. I felt bad for making things awkward between us by asking personal questions.

"Who's nervous now?" Lyric teased while he typed a web address into the browser.

"I'm just excited," I told him. "I've seen you in action on your show, but I get to experience it live in my kitchen. That's pretty fucking cool."

Lyric looked up at me with a raised brow. Did it make him uncomfortable that I watched his show? Then a smile spread slowly across his face. "It's pretty exciting for me too."

"It never gets old?" I asked, figuring that question was safe territory.

"Parts of traveling get old like lumpy hotel beds and weird foods, but I truly love what I do."

"What's your favorite city?" I asked.

"In the United States?" Lyric clarified.

I'd forgotten he'd traveled overseas to film specials. "The US and abroad."

"New Orleans is my favorite US city, and Scotland is my all-time favorite destination." There was an awe or wistfulness in his voice that made me a little jealous of the cities.

"I've never been."

"To which?" Lyric asked.

"Either. Blissville is the farthest I've traveled away from home."

"Really?" He sounded shocked.

"I'm stuck in a rut, to say the least. I love living in Blissville, but I would like to do more traveling someday."

"Where would you like to go?" Lyric asked me while plugging his USB adapter into my MacBook.

"Ireland, Scotland, London, France, and Italy top my international bucket list. In the US, I'd love to visit California, Washington, and Oregon on the West Coast, plus Hawaii and Alaska."

"Those are all beautiful places." Lyric looked up at me and grinned. "Are you ready to listen to the EVP session?"

"Hell yes. Bring on the ghosts!" I dragged a chair closer to Lyric, so I could look at my laptop. "The software erases the background noise and makes it easier to hear what the ghost is saying, right?"

"Yes, but it does more than that. See the chart at the bottom?" I nodded. "It looks like an EKG that registers a heartbeat, right?" I nodded again. "This detects pitches in noise, so the higher peaks indicate someone, or something, is speaking, where lower peaks could be something as innocuous as the hum of an air-conditioning unit."

"Why are there two graphs?" I asked.

"The program knows my voice, so it separates my questions from the responses. What I need to do now is play it back and mark where your voice is on the recording, so I can isolate your voice as well. I can tell I'm talking here," Lyric gestured to the top graph and then to the bottom graph where it registered the responses, "and some voices react immediately after. Is it your voice, Anthony's, or both?"

"That's so cool. Next time, I'll remember not to talk while you're doing your thing." I felt heat spreading up my neck when I realized how presumptuous I sounded. "If you need my help again, that is."

"Relax, Memphis," Lyric calmly said, bumping his shoulder into mine. "You did great for your first time. There's no way to keep an investigation completely quiet. On the show, large portions get cut out before it's aired."

"Yeah?"

"Yeah, like Jerry farting all the time. Hell, the microphones the crew use are so sensitive they can pick up the sounds of Alicia making out with Mack when they're a few floors above us." Wow! Either those mics were phenomenal or those two were especially boisterous when they made out.

I breathed a sigh of relief because I always wondered if Mack and Lyric had a thing going. Their friendship and on-screen chemistry were impressive. I mean, I didn't think Lyric was fucking me while in a relationship with Mack, but that didn't mean his heart wasn't already taken just because his body was available. Okay, maybe relationship wasn't the right word since Lyric claimed not to want one, and just because Mack was in to Alicia didn't mean he wasn't also attracted to Lyric. Or, Lyric could be in love with a straight guy. Fuck, even my inner dialogue was rambling. This man short-circuited my brain. I forced my thoughts to move on before I accidentally let one of my rogue thoughts slip.

"So, haunted houses make them horny?" I asked.

Lyric chuckled. "The paranormal energy might add to Mack and Alicia's already explosive energy." My jealousy detector didn't pick up any indication this bothered Lyric in the least.

"Is that why Mack usually isn't around when you have the EMF reader out?" I teased. "I don't think I've ever seen Alicia on the show." Of course, I knew who she was from comments made on the fan page and rolling credits at the end of the show, but I very well couldn't show Lyric what a freaking fanboy I truly was.

"She's our assistant and has never been on camera." Lyric snorted. "She's only been caught on the microphone."

"Do haunted houses make you horny? Is that what happened at Bliss House?"

Lyric stopped playing around with his program and looked at me. "I wish I could blame the thrill of ghost hunting for this insane attraction I feel for you, but I can't, and I won't lie about it either. I wanted our time in your bed to be a one-and-done thing, but it wasn't. I already missed your ass before I pulled my dick out. I tried to convince myself in the shower it was enough, but I knew better. In fact, I'm looking at you right now and thinking the sooner I listen to this evidence, the sooner I can learn every inch of your dick with my mouth. Do you like receiving blow jobs as much as you like giving them, Memphis?" I swallowed hard and nodded. "Then let's get to work because I'm having a tough time focusing on anything except my throbbing dick with you sitting so close to me. There are no spirits in this house to blame my arousal on."

"Okay," I whispered shakily. I boldly reached over and felt Lyric's erection through his shorts, making him shiver. *God, the things this man did to me and the way he made me feel.* Then I took his left hand off the table and placed it on my dick so he could feel we were in it together. "Let's get to work."

"Fuck me, you're a firecracker," Lyric growled. I expected him to remove his hand right away and click play, but instead, he stroked my dick a few times while I gripped the sides of my chair and gritted my teeth. "We won't make it back to your bedroom this time. I hope the Matrons won't barge in here and catch me on my knees in the kitchen with your cock in my mouth and my dick in my hand." Lyric gave me one last hard stroke then removed his hand, making me whimper at the loss. "Let's do this."

"So we can do each other," I added.

When Lyric hit play, his entire demeanor changed. Our erections were forgotten as he focused on isolating voices that didn't belong to the ghost. I always hated hearing my voice on a recording, but I could listen to his deep voice for all of eternity. Lyric even let me isolate sections and flag them for scrubbing after a quick demonstration, which was fucking cool.

"Now, I scrub the recording and give it another listen. We will no longer hear the flagged sections on the recording, and those spikes on the bottom graph will disappear. I'll keep doing this until all I have is my voice and the ghost's."

"What happens if you scrub too deep? Like maybe you removed something you didn't intend?" I asked.

"A backup file is kept between each round. See that?" Lyric pointed to a data box at the right of the screen. "Each version will be stored here. I can rename them with notes to indicate exactly what I remove each round. Like this," he said then clicked on the only version available. He right-clicked on it and named it the Bliss House initial EVP session then indicated that he and I were the only people present. "The next round, I'll note your voice was scrubbed from the recording. I'll continue doing it with each round."

"That's so freaking cool."

"Right?" he asked excitedly. "I have a friend from high school who is an incredible software designer."

"I like how he also made it user-friendly," I added.

"She," Lyric corrected, "and I think that's her best advantage as a designer." A wry smile spread across his face. "Her passion is video games though. She sent me a beta version of her newest creation. If you're a really good guy and come down my throat, I will show you. As long as you can keep it a secret."

"Coming down your throat or the game?" I asked. "What if I wanted to paint your face instead?"

Lyric closed his eyes and breathed deeply through his nose while I adjusted myself under the table. An image of me splattering his sexy face with my spunk then smearing it around with the tip of my dick popped into my head.

"I wanted your confidentiality about the game," Lyric replied. "Pretty sure the people in the next county will be able to tell by your joyous shouts just how skilled I am at blowing you."

"Hit the fucking button, man," I demanded. Lyric's dark chuckle rumbled from him as he hit the button to begin scrubbing the recording.

The process was more tedious than it ever looked on television, but I was completely enthralled and lost track of time. The cakes had finished baking and were cooling on a rack long before we finished making the recording as pristine as we could get it.

"Other than Alicia and Mack, have you ever recorded something you weren't supposed to hear?"

"Who said Mack and Alicia don't want us to hear them?" Lyric asked with a wry grin. "Honestly, yeah, we've picked up a few things. Mostly silly fights, but we did record a husband sneaking off to phone his girlfriend for dinner plans while his wife was in a different part of the house."

"What a dick."

Lyric laughed. "We thought so at first, but then realized he was talking to his wife. They were either role-playing or just horsing around. You should've seen the horrified looks on their faces when they found out. We weren't going to rat out the husband, but there were other things on the recording we needed help with, like an odd, whiny sound that turned out to be their air-conditioning unit. He wasn't cheating, but they didn't intend for us to overhear them playing around."

"Sounds to me like you need to warn some bitches," I teased.

"We normally ask them to leave the premises, or at least let them know not to speak during an EVP session."

Lyric finally stopped when he felt that nothing remained except his and Anthony's voices. There were spikes on the graph after Lyric's questions, so we truly expected to hear something. Some spikes were higher than others, but Lyric cautioned me not to get my hopes up too high.

"Are you trying to tell me something," Lyric asked.

"Yes," an eerie voice said.

The hair on the back of my neck stood up. I automatically reached over and braced myself by gripping Lyric's thigh. *Holy shit!*

"Is there something special about these boxes, or were you trying to get my attention?"

"Yes," the ghost replied.

Yes, they were special, or yes, the ghost wanted to get his attention? Lyric needed to start asking open-ended questions, so the ghost had to divulge more. Could the ghost divulge more? I dug my fingers in his thighs in anticipation of the next question.

"Are you the ghost of Anthony Bliss?" Lyric asked.

"Yes."

Lyric and I performed identical fist pumps in the air.

"What happened when you disappeared?"

I kid you not; I held my fucking breath.

"Asylum."

Lyric and I silently mouthed the word as we stared into each other's eyes. My heart fell to my stomach. They'd sent him to an asylum?

"What's special about this attic to you? Were you the one they locked inside?"

"Yes."

"We want to help you, Anthony. We want to tell the world what really happened to you in 1850. Can you help us?"

"Asylum. Where's Wallace?"

Once the recording finished, we sat in the kitchen in stunned silence.

"Something about the way he said asylum made me physically ill, especially when he added his possible lover's name in the mix," I told Lyric. "Did Melanie Bliss discover the affair and have him committed? Did Wallace really leave town or was he dead?"

"I don't know if women were given enough authority to do something like that back in the eighteen hundreds. Men routinely had their wives committed because they were just as much a man's property as his prize chicken."

"That's so fucking wrong," I said through gritted teeth. "All of it."

"I think I need to look deeper into Melanie Bliss's background. Not much was written about her, but it's most likely she came from a prominent family herself. Is there a lawyer or judge in her family tree who'd have her husband committed for humiliating her? I think it's likely."

"Or a local esquire she charmed into doing her bidding," I added.

"Homosexuality would've been extremely taboo in that period, especially for someone as well-known as Bliss. He probably established this town thinking he could hide his secret."

I snorted. "Small-town life is the worst place to try and hide a secret."

"I have a feeling Anthony learned that the hard way," Lyric said softly. I could tell he was as moved as I was.

"This will break Maegan's heart," I told him.

"I agree. That's why I think we should find more facts before we tell her too much. I need to try and stay objective while I investigate the paranormal activity in her house."

"Lyric," I said softly. "I can't believe I'm going to say this, because my desire for sex dwindled when I heard the A word, but I think it's even more important you suck my cock in this kitchen."

Lyric slid his hand around to cup the back of my head, cradling it gently. "Because we can?"

"Yes," I whispered. But then I started to cry before Lyric could lean forward and kiss me. "I'm sorry." I tried to get up from my chair so I could leave the room before I made a bigger fool of myself.

"Oh no, you're not getting away that easily," Lyric said, hauling me onto his lap. He held me safely in his strong arms and let me weep over a suspected injustice that occurred one hundred and sixty-eight years prior. "You need to knock it off, Memphis," he whispered huskily in my ear.

I pulled back and looked into his eyes. "What? Crying?"

"Stop being so fucking attractive."

"My eyes surely are red and swollen, my nose is runny, and—" My words died when he pressed his lips against mine for a long but chaste kiss.

"I've forgotten how beautiful humanity can be, but you've reminded me." He gave me one last quick kiss before he closed my MacBook and rose to his feet. "Do you know what you need right now?"

"Um, an amazing blow job that makes me frighten people in the next county?"

"A giant slice of my grammy's triple fudge cake and a tall glass of milk. I need to whip up the icing."

Honestly, it did sound better than sex right then. "Can I lick the beaters again?"

"I will let you lick anything you like."

I placed my elbow on the table then rested my chin on the palm of my hand while watching Lyric whip up a large batch of chocolate icing. He moved with confidence and skill as he built the layers of cake and icing, telling me he'd made it many times in his life. When he finished, he cut us both a huge piece and poured a large glass of milk.

"Where's yours?" I asked, gesturing to the glass.

"You were prepared to shoot your load down my throat or all over my face, so I figured sharing a glass of milk was no big deal."

"Well, when you put it like that," I said before taking a big bite of the best cake I'd ever had in my life. "Ohmyfuckinggod."

"What's that, Firecracker?" Lyric asked with a smile. "I couldn't hear what you said with your mouth full of the best cake you've ever had."

I nodded my head in agreement because I was ruined for life. "Oh. My. Fucking. God!"

"You're welcome," he smugly said before digging in.

I thought I was too exhausted and emotionally drained to do much of anything else, but I learned how wrong I was when Lyric reached over and cupped my crotch after we devoured the cake. "About that blow job…"

CHAPTER TWELVE

Lyric

I WOKE THE NEXT MORNING WITH A RAGING HARD-ON AFTER THE blow job I'd given Memphis in his kitchen replayed on an endless loop in my dreams. He had tasted as delicious as I predicted, but he still found a way to surprise me when he took the lead. One second, he was leaning against the kitchen counter for support while I worked his cock in and out of my mouth, and the next, he stood up straight and took over by fucking my face. Memphis stared at me through eyes darkened with lust and dominance as he gauged what I could take. I could take anything he wanted to give me, and I did. I'd never forget the way he fisted my hair or the grunts he made when he snapped his hips forward taking his pleasure.

His first two spurts hit the back of my throat before he pulled out and finished shooting on my face. I shot my load on the kitchen floor as he smeared his cum all over my lips with the tip of his flushed cock.

"Best of both worlds," Memphis said in a voice roughened by his shouts of pleasure.

It was later than either of us intended to stay up, so we cleaned up quickly and headed up the stairs. Kissing Memphis goodnight at his door and walking away felt wrong. After I finally drifted into a fitful sleep, my dreams consisted of fucking Memphis or holding him close while he cried his eyes out over Anthony Bliss's fate. We had no solid evidence anyone had committed Anthony to an asylum, but just the thought was enough to crush Memphis. I'd never seen a more beautiful soul than his nor had I encountered anyone else who challenged the way I saw my future. That alone should've been enough to make me pack my bags and leave, but I couldn't. Check that; I didn't want to leave yet. I had a mystery to solve, and a man to make memories with that would last me for a lonely lifetime. The internal battle left me feeling more exhausted than when I pulled an all-nighter while investigating.

I wanted to turn off the alarm I'd set on my phone and go back to sleep, but I'd promised Maegan I'd be at her house early enough to set up video cameras in her attic before she went to work. My throbbing dick's demand for release would need to wait until I was alone in the shower. As much as I wanted to crawl into bed with Memphis, I knew I needed to rein myself in a bit. I stumbled into the hallway doing the zombie shuffle while trying to rub the sleep from my eyes and somehow managed to stop at the bathroom when all I wanted to do was keep on shuffling until I reached the warm, welcoming body in the next room down the hall.

Without paying attention, I opened the bathroom door and was blinded by the bright light. The sounds of Memphis brushing his teeth penetrated my foggy brain, and I squinted to see him. I almost regretted not backing out of the door immediately because a sleep-rumpled Memphis was the sexiest thing I'd ever seen in my life. I allowed my eyes to roam down his leanly muscled body until I reached the *X-Men* boxers hanging low on his hips. Memphis's dick hardened before my eyes, his comic book heroes forming a tent around the thick column of flesh. All bets were off.

"I can't be late to Maegan's," I said as I reached for Memphis.

He pulled his toothbrush out of his mouth and smiled wryly. "I guess you better fuck me fast then." Memphis dropped his toothbrush in the holder and rinsed his mouth while I turned on the shower to get the water heating. Then I brushed my teeth while he retrieved condoms and lube from his bedroom. By the time he returned buck naked, I was minty fresh, my boring boxers were on the floor, and steam started to build in the small space.

My mind spun with the many ways I could take Memphis in the shower until I found the one that nearly fried my brain. I hungrily kissed him beneath the hot spray while touching him everywhere I could reach. Lust clawed at my guts making me desperate to feel his ass squeezing my dick. I broke our kiss so I could lube my fingers and work him open before I jizzed all over him just from kissing and heavy petting.

Memphis reached behind him, seeking out my dick. "Huh-uh," I said, slapping his hand away. "Too soon." His dark chuckle caused goose bumps to pop up all over my skin even though the steam in the shower made it feel like a sauna.

"Did you lie in bed and think about fucking me all night long too?"

"In every dream and every waking minute," I admitted. What was the point in denying it? I removed my fingers from his tight clench and reached for the condom. "I want you to use my dick to get yourself off." My voice sounded so gravelly I hardly recognized it. "My dog broke your favorite shower toy, so I will offer myself up as the next best thing."

Memphis moaned. "Oh my God. I would never prefer Big Bob over you."

Once the condom was on, I pressed my back against the cold tile wall and pulled Memphis's hips until he was lined up against my cock. I dropped my hands to my sides and said, "You take over from here."

Memphis bent over at the waist, raised up on his tiptoes, and reached between his legs to grasp my cock. He let out a soft growl when he eased himself onto the rigid length. I wanted to grab his hips and fuck him hard and long but not more than I wanted to watch him use me.

"Fuck me, Memphis. Just like you would Big Bob."

"Lyric," he moaned, rocking his hips back and forth. Sometimes Memphis pulled himself nearly all the way off before sinking back until I was balls-deep inside him. Other times, he fucked himself on just the broad head of my dick. I loved watching his ass swallow my cock and had to grit my teeth and distract myself with algebraic formulas to keep from coming too soon. I swore to myself I wouldn't touch him with my hands, but I said nothing about keeping my dirty mouth to myself.

"Is that how you fuck yourself?" I asked. "Would you rather have the toy instead of my throbbing dick inside you? Did he stretch you as wide? Do you want me to replace him or would you rather ride my cock as part of your morning ritual?" I wasn't fishing for compliments; I wanted to make him crazy with need so he would stop teasing me with slow thrusts and fuck me until we both came.

"I can't get enough of you, Ric. I don't want to come yet. Feels too fucking good." He was too coherent to be lost in lust. I couldn't allow that.

"You're a sexy fucker, Sullivan. Use me."

"I'm so close," Memphis said in a near whimper. *Thank God!* "Touch me, Ric."

"Touch yourself, Firecracker. Come for me then I'll fuck you with everything I have."

Memphis raised his torso up a little higher and reached for his cock with his left hand while bracing himself by holding onto the curtain rod with his right. He slammed his ass against my pelvis while fucking his fist as his moans climbed higher in pitch until he cried out my name and came around my cock.

"Oh, Ric," Memphis sighed as his knees buckled. He grabbed the curtain suddenly just as I grabbed onto him to keep him from falling.

My hips started thrusting as if they had a mind of their own, and soon, I was powering into him while he spurred me on with, "Yes! Yes! Fuck me harder, Ric!"

Memphis yanked the curtain rod so hard he pulled it off the wall and it, along with the curtain, crashed to the floor. I was too far gone to worry about the water splashing onto the floor. I held his hips in a bruising grip and fucked Memphis like I might not get another chance. As I started to come, I pulled Memphis upright against my chest, sinking my teeth in the tender flesh of his neck where it curved into his shoulder and flooding the condom I wore.

Memphis reached up and tangled his fist in my hair as I licked the marks I'd left behind in his skin. "Did I hurt you?" I asked.

"It hurt so good." Fuck, he was dangerous. I wanted to keep pushing and learning what we were capable of. "We're making a terrible mess though."

I gently guided Memphis off my cock and reached for the curtain rod so I could hang it back up. Memphis carefully removed the condom from my dick and began washing my body with the bar of soap.

"We have to be good," I told him when he lingered on my cock and balls long enough to make my dick twitch. "Can't keep the lady of the house waiting."

"I know," Memphis sighed. "Promise me we'll pick up where we left off."

I could easily promise him damned near anything when he looked at me with those soulful brown eyes. "Deal."

"Good morning, fellas," Maegan said, opening the front door wide when we stepped onto the front porch. The dogs rushed ahead of us and went in search of Lulu while we casually stepped inside. Maegan's eyes flicked back and forth between us, and her megawatt smile nearly blinded me. Yeah, Memphis and I weren't fooling anyone. "I didn't expect to see you here this morning, Memphis." I hadn't originally planned to bring him.

"Last minute change of plans," Memphis said, echoing my private thoughts. "You don't mind, do you? I thought the two of us could set up the equipment faster then Lyric can use my setup at Vinyl and Villains to do some research based on what we uncovered last night."

"I'm dying to know what it is," Maegan said excitedly.

"Your ghost is Anthony Bliss," I told her. "He was the one locked up in the attic."

"Oh no," Maegan said, covering her mouth. She slowly lowered her hand as tears filled her eyes. Dammit. I should've waited until I had solid answers before I said anything at all. "Do you know why? Did it have to do with Wallace or his disappearance?"

I released a long, shaky sigh before I opened my mouth to reply. By then, Memphis stepped up and reached for her hands.

"Mae, we don't know exactly what happened to either Wallace or Anthony. I'm pretty sure Lyric's suspicion the men were in a relationship was correct, but we need more evidence to make some connections. Anthony only communicated with single-word answers or fragments that didn't make a coherent statement. We're going to get to the bottom of this. It doesn't do you any good to get upset when we don't have any answers yet." I thought of the way Memphis cried against my chest and knew he was trying to delay causing Maegan the same kind of sorrow.

"Okay," she said softly. "That makes a lot of sense, and I will be patient. I have to head to Books and Brew now, but Elijah is around for another ninety minutes if you guys need anything. He just went upstairs to get dressed."

"Thanks, Mae," Memphis said then leaned forward to kiss her cheek. "We'll see you in a bit. You know I can't resist a mid-morning snack and cup of java."

"You're going to waste your taste buds on our muffins and scones when you can eat his creations?" Maegan asked, pointing at me. "Lyric, I will hire you to make all the pastries and baked goods for

Books and Brew if you ever get tired of traveling around the world solving ghostly mysteries. Your kind of talent is hard to find."

I felt myself blushing a little. My baking hobby was something not many people knew about me, including Jerry, Mack, and Drew. I'd brought in some of my creations, but they always thought I'd stopped at a bakery on my way to work, and I let them think it. Memphis was the only person who knew about my obsession with *The Great British Baking Show*.

"Thanks, Mae," I replied. "I'll keep that in mind. I honestly have no idea where my future stands with the network. I do have other things I've kept on the back burner I plan to explore if I decide to part ways with the network. I might pursue them even if the show resumes." It made more sense to keep doors open rather than close them.

"I assure you our bakery doors will always be open to you."

"Should I be jealous?" Elijah said as he came down the stairs. "All I've heard Maegan talk about since she sampled your baked goods is how skilled you are in the kitchen."

"*Kitchen* is the key word there, Elijah."

"I know, Freckles. I love giving you a hard time." *I just bet he did.* "I'm going to walk my lady out, and I'll be right back, fellas."

We headed upstairs to get started when Elijah and Maegan went outside. Memphis and I worked well together as we set up five different cameras in the large attic space.

"Are you going to record all day?" Memphis asked.

"I'm not going to record until we do our next EVP session tonight." I looked at Memphis after we finished setting up the last camera. "Are you sure you don't mind me hanging out at the store? I can research at home and stay out of your hair."

"No way," he said adamantly. "I'm too invested to wait until tonight to find out what you learn."

"If I learn anything," I reminded him. "I stumble into a lot of dead ends." The air around me seemed to crackle and pop and awareness washed over me, signaling we weren't alone in the attic.

"Lyric?" Memphis asked. "Are you okay?"

"He's here," I whispered. "He feels really sad today." I closed my eyes and silently reached out to him. *Talk to me, Anthony. Let me help you.* The sensations grew stronger as if he was trying to break through the barriers to speak to me. Anthony disappeared as quickly as he had arrived. "He's gone now. He's trying to reach out to me."

"Can you use one of his favorite objects to try to connect with him? Perhaps his favorite pipe?"

"I'll try that tonight," I assured him. "I think he just needs a bit of guidance."

We headed downstairs where we found Elijah drinking coffee and scowling at something on his phone. He snapped his head up to look at us when he realized we entered the room. "All finished?" he asked, but I noticed his smile appeared brittle. I hadn't picked up on any animosity from him when he joked about Maegan gushing about my baked goods, so I didn't think I was the source of his displeasure.

"We're all set. Are you sure you don't mind us coming back tonight to record another EVP session?"

"I'm positive," Elijah replied. That time his smile was genuine and free of hesitation. "I was just kidding earlier."

"I know," I assured him. "My traipsing through the attic is still intrusive. I would understand if you preferred to wait."

"Can I ask you something about the investigation?" Elijah said in a sobering tone. "Maegan seemed upset about something you said even though she tried to distract me with kisses."

"Man, I'm sorry. I should've just kept my mouth shut until I had some concrete answers."

"I'm not busting your balls, Lyric. I want to know what you suspect happened. It's the detective in me. I want to be the one to break it to Maegan when the time is right."

"You want to know what I suspect or would you rather wait to hear when I have concrete answers? I don't want to put you in a position where you're keeping secrets from Maegan. I know you want to protect her, but I get the feeling she's not a shrinking violet, and I bet she has one hell of a temper."

A crooked smile appeared on Elijah's face. "You can say that again." Then he released a sigh and said, "You're right. You can tell us at the same time. I'll be there if she needs me, but I won't treat her like she's helpless and can't handle bad news."

"Good call, Elijah," Memphis said.

"We'll see you tonight around seven, if that works for you," I told him.

"Seven is fine with me unless you want to come over a bit earlier and grab a bite to eat."

"We don't want to impose," I told Elijah.

"It's not an imposition if we've invited you. Besides, you brought dinner last night. How about we grill out some burgers and hot dogs?" Elijah asked.

"Sure," I agreed. "See you tonight."

"Where to?" I asked Memphis as we rounded up the dogs and headed out to his Beetle. "The Bat Cave?"

"Eww, no," Memphis replied with a scowl. "Never the Bat Cave."

"Not a fan of Batman?"

"Nope," Memphis replied. "We'll call our headquarters the X-Mansion." I remembered his *X-Men* underwear and the posters I saw in his office. Memphis was a big fan.

"To the X-Mansion we go, Firecracker."

CHAPTER THIRTEEN

Memphis

"SO, DO YOU DISLIKE ALL SUPERHEROES OR JUST SOME OF them? It's obvious from the name of your store that you favor villains. Or did you pick that name because it's catchy?" Lyric asked after I unlocked the back door and let us inside Vinyl and Villains.

"I love villains, and the name is catchy."

"Why do you love villains so much?" Lyric wanted to know. "Is it the bad boy thing?"

"Partly," I admitted, "but I think it has more to do with villains making the story more interesting. I mean, superheroes tend to be a tad bit predictable and boring. Sometimes their morals won't allow them to make tough decisions."

"Are you referring to their refusal to kill the bad guy?"

"How many people die while they wrestle with their conscious? If someone is trying to destroy the world, then you take them out before they can do it. There's no prison to hold evil like that. You gotta send them straight to hell."

"You sound like my grammy's fire and brimstone preacher, Firecracker."

I grimaced because that's the last type of person I wanted to resemble. "I suspect the preacher and I would have vastly different opinions on what behaviors would constitute death for punishment."

My mind went straight to Anthony Bliss, and I couldn't help wondering what kind of hell awaited him when someone forcefully removed him from his home.

"I can see that I upset you, Memphis. I'm sorry."

"I was thinking about Anthony's situation again," I admitted. "You're not responsible for the fate that befell him." I nodded my head toward my small office. "Let's get you set up then I'm going to open for business."

"Who's he?" Lyric asked, pointing to the large poster of my favorite villain behind my desk.

I could feel myself heating up with embarrassment. "Um, that's Daken."

"I take it he's from *X-Men*? I recognize those steel blades protruding from his hands. Is he Wolverine's evil brother or something?"

"Son," I replied.

"Huh. How'd the good guy end up with a villain for a son?"

"Wolverine's pregnant wife was killed by the Winter Soldier. He didn't know his child survived. Daken is a trained assassin."

"His tattoos and mohawk are hot," Lyric said, studying the poster.

"He's bisexual too." I waggled my brows.

"Man, I hope he retracts those blades if his partners like fisting."

I cringed. "Ouch."

"Right? So, this is your fantasy guy, huh?"

"I think he's sexy as fuck, but he's nowhere close to my fantasy guy."

Lyric turned away from the poster and looked at me with a knowing smirk. Had he heard something in my voice to give me away? I knew I better be careful before he bolted. "Yeah?" he asked, taking two steps to bridge the gap between us. "Who is your fantasy man?"

"I...um..." Lyric slowly lowered his head until his lips were close enough I could touch them with the tip of my tongue if I were bold enough. Was I bold enough? When it came to him, I was.

Someone knocked loudly on the front door, jerking me out of my sex-fogged trance. I glanced at my watch and noticed it was five minutes before opening time. Whoever it was knocked again.

"It sounds like you have your first customer of the day," Lyric said, taking a step back.

"So it seems," I agreed. "I've never had such an eager customer before. I better go let them in." I stopped in the doorway and said, "Password for my computer is Daken2. I'll be back as soon as I finish up."

I had my fair share of enthusiastic customers at Vinyl and Villains, but none had ever knocked on the door before I opened. I expected to see eager teenagers Daniel and Mark on the other side of the glass, but it was an eager man instead. I barely managed to stifle a groan when I saw who waited for me. Joey Simanski looked at me with a forlorn, puppy dog expression. Why couldn't he leave well enough alone?

"Hey, Joey," I said when I opened the door. "Did I park illegally or something?"

"I deserve that, I guess."

"That and much more," I told him. "What do you want, Joey?" He seemed startled by my directness, but I just wanted him gone so I could return to Lyric. Discovering what happened to Anthony Bliss was much more important to me than listening to Joey offer up a lame apology.

"Fair enough," he said softly. "I just wanted to apologize for my rude behavior last night. I was jealous."

"I appreciate the apology. Thank you." I moved to close the door, but his hand shot out to prevent it.

"Why are you in such a hurry? I know it's a few minutes before opening time, but you usually have the door unlocked and ready to go at least ten minutes early. You're not acting like yourself, Memphis." I knew damn good and well what the jerk was implying.

"Joey, I'm well past the age where I need someone warning me away from a bad boy." I smiled wryly at him then delivered the death blow. "Besides, don't you know that only makes us want them more." I released the door, and it slowly closed in his stunned face. It was time to open for business, so I didn't lock it before I turned and headed toward the counter to put the till in the old-fashioned cash register. I had hoped Joey would take a hint and leave, but I knew he had more to say when the door immediately opened again.

I slowly turned to face him and was shocked by the anger on his face. "You're an asshole, Memphis. I can't believe I apologized for the way I acted when you're the one who should be sorry."

"Sorry for what?" I asked him. "That I didn't fall in love with you, Joey? I told you I wasn't looking for love or a relationship. You told me you understood and were on the same page as me. Were those lies so I'd have sex with you?"

Joey scowled at me from beneath the deep V in his brow. "Listen, Memphis..."

"I think it was a simple question, but maybe you need to hear it again. Did you lie about being on the same page so I'd have sex with you?"

"It was incredible sex, wasn't it?" At the time I thought it was, but I knew better after the previous night with Lyric. I wasn't a big enough jerk to crush Joey's ego though.

"Joey," I slowly said while trying to find a kinder way to let him down.

"Babe, I could use your... Oh, I didn't realize you had a customer." Lyric stopped suddenly in the store and looked between Joey and me. I knew damn well he'd overheard the conversation and was doing his best to rescue me from an awkward situation. "I could use your help when you're done. It's nice to see you again, Officer."

"Uh, you too, sir." Joey looked back at me. "I can see that you're busy, so I'll head out."

"Okay," I said. "Take care, Joey." He left without saying another word, but the awkwardness remained in the air.

"Maybe I should change your nickname from Firecracker to Heartbreaker," Lyric teased.

"I don't think either of those names apply to me," I said wryly.

"You underestimate yourself, Memphis." There was something new in his gray eyes, an emotion I'd never seen in them. I didn't know what to make of it, so I changed the subject to something with less potential to fuck up the happy vibe we'd found together.

"Did you find something interesting?"

"Yeah, I read up on your lover boy, Daken. He is evil as hell. I'm shocked by your devotion to him," Lyric said in mock disapproval.

"He's just misunderstood," I said in a playful, pleading tone for him to understand. "The right guy can show him the way to righteousness." Lyric snorted. "I thought you were going to use my computer to do some more research on Anthony Bliss."

"I was just assessing the situation," Lyric told me. *Assess the situation? As in competition?* Nah, that was ridiculous. If anything, he was just curious. "I've started compiling a list of asylums in the area too, but I heard Officer Heartthrob giving you a hard time and wanted to intervene."

"I appreciate it."

"I kept my search to a one-hundred-and-fifty-mile radius. I think that makes the most sense."

"There was Wellview Asylum in Cincinnati and another one called Montgomery County Asylum in Dayton, Ohio. I think there was one up north and another in Kentucky," I said.

"How in the world did you know that? Did you google them last night?"

"I watched a documentary about haunted asylums not that long ago, and those four were mentioned. The Cincinnati and Dayton asylums stuck out in my memory since they were so close. Do you think they would've stashed him away at a location so close to home?" Then another thought occurred to me. "Say Melanie did have a judge in her family tree who committed Anthony to an asylum, would there have been jurisdiction restrictions? If the judge was in New York, would he be able to have an Ohio resident committed to an asylum here, or would he have been taken back to New York?"

Lyric smiled broadly. "Those are excellent questions, Firecracker. Let's see what we can dig up on Melanie Bliss."

My office was cramped as hell with two humans and two dogs, but we managed. Of course, I practically had to sit on Lyric's lap, but neither of us complained about the proximity to one another.

"Here," Lyric said after searching for a few minutes. "Melanie's maiden name was Harlow. Let's see if we can find a state supreme judge by that name. I've only started a remedial search into the judicial proceedings during that era, but I think an involuntary commitment requires an order from the state supreme court. Probate judges can issue temporary hospitalization in some situations, but not a permanent commitment."

"The judge also could be a good family friend. Maybe they called in a favor to a judge who lived closer. Transporting Anthony back to New York seems too risky. He'd have several opportunities to escape or tell someone," I told Lyric.

"Unless they kept him sedated."

"Jesus, there are too many unknowns," I said in frustration.

"You're so adorable, Firecracker." Lyric hooked his elbow around my neck and pulled me closer. "We'll figure it out by crossing one thing off the list at a time. The first step is looking for a supreme court judge with Harlow as the last name. If that doesn't turn up anything promising, then we'll move on to her mother's maiden name."

"What's that?" I asked.

"Smith," Lyric said with a smirk, making me groan. Of course, it had to be one of the most common names in America.

"Let's not forget, we might be able to get a lot of answers from Anthony's ghost or the trunks he knocked over. Remember, he said 'yes' to my question about the trunks, but I wasn't sure if he was agreeing he was trying to get my attention or that they were special."

"I thought Maegan looked through all of them, but I could be wrong. It's possible she didn't realize the items she found inside were significant to his disappearance."

"There has to be a public record of the court docket from when he went to trial," Lyric said.

"That's if they used his legal name."

"Memphis."

"Hmmm?"

"Will you stop putting up roadblocks before we've even begun?"

"Oh, I'm so sorry," I said. "I was thinking out loud. I didn't mean to discourage you."

"Good to know."

"If I were, I'd say the records probably went up in flames during a fire or something."

"Firecracker, I'm going to put you over my knee and..."

"Yes!" I cried out.

"Let me out of here so I can go chat with Maegan before I follow through on my threat."

"And here I was hoping it was a promise," I teased. Lyric's eyes turned a smoky, dark hue.

"Do you want to feel my palm smacking against your pert ass, Memphis?"

"Go talk to Maegan," I said, swiftly rising to my feet and stepping aside so he could exit.

Lyric stood up, but he didn't seem to be in a hurry to leave my cramped office. He cupped his hand around my neck and held me in place for a languid, soul-consuming kiss. When he finally broke our kiss, he asked, "What kind of mid-morning snack would you like? From Books and Brew," he quickly clarified.

"Um, how about a blueberry lemon scone and a medium salted caramel coffee. Milo knows how I like it." I chuckled when Lyric raised his brows. "He knows how I like my *coffee*."

"I'll be back in a little bit, okay?"

"Sure. I'll check my email to see if Sonny has responded. I saw the way Maegan's eyes lit up when I mentioned the Blue Libbey glasses."

"I'd like to tag along with you and Maegan," Lyric said, surprising the hell out of me.

"Really?"

"Absolutely. You've seen me in action, so I think it's only fair that I get to see you do your thing also."

"It's fine with me. You're already used to crawling around in dark, dirty places."

"That I am."

Lyric dropped a quick kiss on my lips and left me to do my thing in his absence. The bell over the door let me know I had my first real customer of the day, or so I hoped. I smiled when I saw it was Jake. "What's up, Nurse Jakie?"

He cringed because he wasn't a fan of the show *Nurse Jackie,* and calling him Jakie reminded him of his great aunt who used to pinch his cheeks. "I *was* prepared to drop some cash in here, but now I'm not so sure. Maybe I should check out that vintage vinyl record store that opened in Cincinnati this weekend. I bet they won't abuse me."

"My apologies," I said with as much contrition as I could muster. "What vintage vinyl record store?"

"I think it's called Spin Tables and Superheroes."

"Are you winding me up or did a vinyl record store open this weekend?"

"I'm only joking about the name," Jake replied. "It's called Vintage Vinyls. From what I've heard, it doesn't have nearly the selection you have, and I bet the owner isn't as cute." Here's the thing about Jake, he's fucking beautiful. He exudes goodness through his pores. Most guys would give their left nut for a chance to be with him, but I've never returned his interest.

"I don't know about that," I replied, hoping he would move on.

"I stopped by to see if you were able to find The Smith's 'The

Queen is Dead' album. I've found replicas but not an original."

"I think I do have a lead for you. I found some on eBay in the UK, but I have a reliable source in the States who thinks he can get his hands on one for you. I think he'll charge you a hundred bucks which includes shipping."

"What will be the final price then?" Jake asked.

"What do you mean?"

"Memphis, you can't spend your time tracking down records and comics for people and not get compensated."

"Jake, it took me ten minutes to send an email to my friend. I can't charge you for that. If I'd spent hours or days, then it would be a different story. He's supposed to call me soon and let me know if the record he found is in good enough condition. I'll let you know what I find out."

"Thanks, Memphis, but I still don't feel right not compensating you. Would you at least let me take you out to dinner?"

"I, uh…"

"Babe, here's your breakfast. I know how cranky you get when your blood sugar gets low." The man had impeccable timing, and that was twice he called me babe in one morning. I was starting to like it too damn much. "Oh, hey," Lyric said. "I didn't know you had a customer. I'll take our breakfast into your office and wait for you there."

"Thanks, babe," I told him. I turned back to Jake who stared after Lyric with widened eyes. "What did you ask me? That man robs me of the ability to think straight."

"Um, it was nothing. Just let me know about the album, okay?"

"Sure, Jake. Have a great day."

"Uh, yeah. You too."

After Jake left, I returned to my office where Lyric sat behind my desk with his legs propped up, although I couldn't figure out how he found the room to pull it off. "You're mighty popular here in Blissville, Firecracker."

"Not really," I replied casually. "Just with those two."

122

"Have you *dated* them both?"

I snickered at the way he said dated. We both knew what he meant. "I only 'dated' Joey. Jake is too good and wholesome for me."

"I can see that," Lyric said, nodding his head. "I don't even want to know what you got up to with Officer Hard-On."

"Why not?" I prodded.

"While I'm here, I only want to think about you getting naked with me. Everyone else ceases to exist for you." I almost snorted. Couldn't he see no one else stood a chance with me?

"I'll give it my best shot." Hey, a guy had to make himself a bit of a challenge. "Why don't you hand me that scone, and we can get back to searching the internet for more information."

"Come a little closer, and I'll give you what you want." *Was he still talking about the scone?*

Lyric lowered his legs to the ground when I walked behind my desk. Instead of returning to the chair I had recently vacated, I straddled his lap and looked into his stormy eyes. "Give me what I want."

CHAPTER FOURTEEN

Lyric

"**G**IVE ME WHAT I WANT."

Those words bounced around my brain all day—sometimes they were strung together to form a sentence, and sometimes they were fragments, but still potent nevertheless.

"Give me."

"I want."

"Give."

"Want."

"Give me what I want."

I could've given us what we both wanted, but I needed to show some fucking restraint around him or I'd end up sounding like those guys who showed up at the store trying to get him into bed. Sure, one offered an apology and the other offered dinner, but I knew what both of them wanted, and they couldn't fucking have him. Memphis was mine. *Whoa!*

That was the possessive thought that had me reaching for his blueberry scone instead of his zipper. Yeah, I fed it to him one bite at a time like a lovesick sap while he straddled my lap, but our dicks stayed in our pants. When he finished eating, Memphis remained where he was and fed me the muffin I'd chosen for myself in the exact same way. Our dicks were hard, and I couldn't seem to keep my mouth off him, so I knew it was only a matter of time before I bent him over the desk and fucked him. As much as I wanted that, I needed space to think and get myself under control even more.

I left Daisy with Memphis and Gigi after a long kiss then went back to the Blissville Public Library to see what else I could find. Memphis's office was barely big enough for one person, let alone two grown men and two dogs. I also didn't think I could handle a third gentleman caller showing up to woo Memphis away from me. *Woo him away? Gentleman caller?* I sounded like those Harlequin romance novels my grammy used to read. I sure liked the thrusting part though. Yeah, I liked thrusting into Memphis's demanding body way more than I should.

Stop thinking about sex and solve the damn case, Willows.

"Can I help you?" a blue-haired lady behind the counter asked. I don't mean the silvery-blue treatment some older ladies use; I'm talking neon blue that shouted at you across the room. She looked to be the age I would expect Tucker's grandmother to be, but it was hard to say.

"Yes, ma'am. Are you Tucker's grandmother?"

"Yes, I am." She smiled broadly. "Are you dating my Tucker?"

"No, we just met when I stopped in to look at old newspaper articles on microfiche yesterday. I'm only in town for a brief time while I investigate the Bliss House mystery."

"So, you're the handsome stranger staying with Memphis Sullivan on Maple Lane." When I raised a brow, she explained. "The Matrons were at bingo last night."

"Ahhh," I replied. They knew exactly who I was but chose to keep my identity to themselves. There's always a risk of someone recognizing me, but it was so much easier when it didn't happen. I decided to reward The Matrons with some baked goodies if I could keep my dick out of Memphis's ass or mouth long enough. "Mind if I head over to the computers and do some more research?"

"Go right ahead," she said with an easy smile. "Let me know if you need me to pull microfiche for you."

"Thank you, ma'am."

The first thing I did was check that hideous website to make sure Elvie and Myla hadn't tracked me down. I couldn't look this shit up on Memphis's computer. I didn't want him to think I was a self-absorbed asshole who got off on having a fan club. The first thing I noticed was Myla posted an announcement stating Steven Riser was added as an admin to the site and would take a more active role. I'd seen that pompous windbag's posts many times. He never came right out and said I was doing things wrong because he'd incur Elvie's wrath; he blamed it on production for skewing the way the investigations were portrayed. "Ghost Hunting for Dummies," he called it. He appealed to the network to take off its restraints and turn me loose to show what I was really capable of.

"Someone has been watching too many episodes of *Supernatural*," I whispered. I scrolled down through the feed to see what Myla Trey was up to. She was the most annoying and dangerous out of the group with her creepy-as-fuck stalking tendencies. It didn't take me long to find her latest post.

"I have it on good authority our fearless leader is either in Southern Ohio or Northern Kentucky investigating an unsolved mystery dating back to 1850."

Damn you, Myla. Who the fuck feeds you this information? As I was cursing internally, a rebuttal from NerdBoy88 popped up.

"Once again, your information is faulty as hell, Myla. My sources tell me he's in Kingston, New York, investigating rumors of a haunted lighthouse." The post accompanied a picture of me standing in front of a lighthouse. The thing was, I'd never investigated or visited the lighthouse behind me in the photo, and the image of me was at least a year old since I was missing a few tattoos on my left arm. That meant this guy, whoever he was, photoshopped an old picture of me in front of a lighthouse I'd never visited. Not only that, he did it in a way that made it look real. I held my breath to see if Myla noticed the missing tats because I was sure she probably had them all memorized. Hell, I was surprised she hadn't guessed the size of my dick from the bulge in my jeans.

"Road trip!" came Myla's response a few minutes later. "Any Willows Whisperers in the area who want to go on a hunt for our favorite ghost hunter?" I didn't hunt ghosts; I investigated paranormal hauntings and tried to give the restless souls some freaking peace.

I forced myself to get off the site and get to work on the Anthony Bliss situation. I pulled out a notebook and began making notes of names in Melanie Bliss's prominent family tree. Her grandfather, Earl Harlow, was indeed a judge who lived in Boston, Massachusetts, but he wasn't attached to a supreme court there. Her father, Edgar Harlow, followed his father's footsteps into law school but never became a judge. Tracing her mother's lineage got a bit trickier since it looked like her maternal grandparents were immigrants from Europe. Edgar Harlow's marriage appeared to be a love match rather than a business arrangement he made with a prominent family for their blue-blooded daughter in exchange for money or privilege.

The only way I discovered any of that information was from archived newspaper articles about Anthony Bliss because women in that era didn't get mentioned in the newspaper unless the narrative was framed around their husbands. Larger libraries in the US made articles and important archives available online rather than tedious sorting through microfiche. I searched through both the New York State Library and Massachusetts State Library for hours looking for as many tiny details as I could find. There were so many articles about Anthony Bliss my eyes started to blur but very few about his wife. Most of them contained news about Melanie's charitable deeds and how well it reflected upon her husband's reputation. The New-England Courant, where Benjamin Franklin gained his apprenticeship as a printer, was the paper with the most information about Melanie Harlow Bliss, but these articles were framed to make her father look well instead of her husband. It was there I learned that both the Harlow daughters attended Mount Holyoke College in South

Hadley, Massachusetts.

I remembered from a previous article that Anthony Bliss attended Williams College in Williamstown, Massachusetts. I suspected they were introduced through mutual friends they'd made at the colleges but couldn't confirm how they were introduced. I didn't think how they met was nearly as important as their parting, so I made notes and moved on. The last search I wanted to perform was on Wallace Bennington III. I was making assumptions that Wallace was Anthony's lover, and Anthony was committed to the asylum for being a homosexual. I had no proof of it, and how could I be certain Anthony wasn't telling me Wallace had him committed to the asylum?

I learned Wallace also attended Williams College, where he would've met Anthony Bliss. I did a search combining both their names and came up with some photos of them in their early days at Williams College. It appeared someone had scoured photographs looking for the men once they became known as two men who helped build the industrial age in America.

One caption beneath a photo read: *Anthony Bliss and Wallace Bennington III playing cards in the common room.* The men sat on opposite sides of a small table smiling at one another. To the untrained eye, a person would say the sly tilt to their mouths meant they both thought they had the winning hand. I knew better because Memphis and I had shared those same smiles earlier that morning. Those grins said, "I know what you taste like, I know the feel of your skin pressed up against mine, and I know the sounds you make when joy bursts inside you at my touch."

"Is everything okay, sir?"

I was a man who walked through haunted houses for a living, yet a woman in her seventies scared the daylights out of me in the well-lit library. I jerked in my seat and turned around. "Excuse me?"

"I didn't mean to startle you. I happened to look over and you seemed pale."

"Like I'd seen a ghost?" I asked, earning a smile.

"Or found something that upset you."

Finding additional photos that furthered my belief that Wallace and Anthony were lovers before they disappeared wasn't what upset me. It was acknowledging Memphis looked at me like Wallace and Anthony looked at one another, and I was pretty sure I looked at Memphis the same way. I wasn't a guy who wanted love, commitment, and picket fences. Memphis said he didn't need those things either. I'd even heard him tell Officer Simpleton that falling in love with him was never on the table. I couldn't deny that I felt a need for Memphis I'd never experienced with anyone else, and I wasn't just talking about physical things.

I wanted to see him laughing over something funny I said. I wanted to see his delight over learning something new about paranormal investigating. I wanted to make him hum deep in his throat because the cake I made for him was the best he'd ever had. I wanted to hold him against me while I slept, and that is something I never craved with another person. He made me want so many fucking things. I needed to get the fuck out of Blissville before it was too late. No matter what Memphis said, he was falling as hard for me as I was him. It was completely crazy because I hadn't known him long enough to crave him this desperately. Then again, hadn't I already admitted it felt like I already *knew* him?

"Something just caught me by surprise is all," I replied. "Thank you for your concern." The librarian smiled softly and let me return to my research.

I hadn't made any progress on the asylum angle, so I decided to figure out Wallace's role, if any, in Anthony's disappearance. He sold his newspaper then fell off the face of the earth when he moved to San Francisco. I did a combination search of his name and the city, but nothing came up. I searched steel magnates living in San Fran at the time, but none of the men were Wallace. He could've changed his appearance but not that much. Did he start a new business venture with his new life on the West Coast during the Gold Rush? Hotels? Brothels? What would a man like Wallace choose? The hotel seemed more in line with his old life, so I did another search for wealthy hotel owners and came across the name of an enigmatic owner who was seldomly photographed. In fact, there was only one picture of the elusive Denver Collins known to exist. My breath caught in my throat when I clicked on the photo to enlarge it. Denver Collins stood outside his luxury hotel he'd named Blissview. Even though he had his head angled down, I recognized his stance from pictures I'd seen of him with Anthony. That wasn't the only thing that stood out to me. The white horse with the unique heart-shaped gray spot on its flank was Anthony Bliss's horse, Starlight. The photo at least proved Anthony didn't suffer an accident while out riding his horse. It would've been easy enough for Wallace or Bliss to make transportation arrangements for Starlight prior to Anthony leaving.

There was no way in hell Anthony would've sent Starlight west with Wallace unless he planned to go too. I wanted to dig a little further, but I wanted to share the news with Memphis. I printed a copy of the picture and grinned like a fool that I had at least solved part of the mystery. I offered to pay for my printout, but the librarian refused.

I walked the few blocks back to Vinyl and Villains and saw Memphis was helping two older gentlemen look for vinyl records while two teenagers browsed the comics. Memphis smiled when he saw I had returned, and I wanted to cross the room and kiss him right then and there. Instead, I winked and pointed to the folded piece of paper in my hand. I had hoped he would finish with his customers quickly and meet me in his office, but I realized after waiting ten minutes, they weren't wrapping it up anytime soon.

I plopped down in his chair and moved the mouse to wake up his computer. It took me a second to understand I was looking at the member dashboard on the *Willows Whisperers* fan page. I stared in disbelief that Memphis would be part of such a destructive site, but then I saw the user name at the top of the screen. Memphis was NerdBoy88? He was the one purposely misleading Myla and the gang? I didn't know how to feel about it. I felt a little betrayed that he didn't at least tell me about his online activities, especially since he had nothing to hide. Of course, he had no way of knowing I was aware of the site since we never discussed it. There wasn't anything for him to feel ashamed about. Hell, he was my fucking hero! It wasn't like he was making up... Oh! The fan fiction story! If he told me about his efforts to thwart Elvie, Myla, and now that sweaty ball sack, Steven, then he would risk me checking out the site and stumbling onto his paranormal investigator porn.

I should've felt like my privacy was violated, but it wasn't. I should've felt sketchy about the entire situation, but I didn't. I should've told myself to get the hell out of there because Memphis was thinking about having sex with me long before we ever met, but instead I skimmed the rest of the content before clicking the command to put the computer to sleep so my Firecracker wouldn't know I learned his dirty little secret.

I fucked around on my phone so I would look busy when he sought me, but inside I was giddy over that last private message exchange I saw with Steven.

SlickSteve: NerdBoy88, where do you get your intel?

NerdBoy88: No can do, Stevie.

SlickSteve: Come on, my friend. I won't tell anyone.

NerdBoy88: Nah. You're going to have to get that pussy without my help.

SlickSteve: Excuse me? I don't know what you're talking about. I don't like your crude talk.

NerdBoy88: Dude, you have your head so far up Myla's ass you can't see the light. Get a clue, pal. Her G-spot ain't in that door, and I'm not going to be the one who helps you find it. Run along now, Stevie. I think your mommy is calling you from the top of the basement steps.

SlickSteve: You're a cocksucker!

NerdBoy88: Yes, I am and very proud of it too.

Don't fall in love with him, Lyric. Memphis deserves more than a vagabond lifestyle. He deserves to plant roots and build a life with people who aren't besieged by voices calling out to help them. He needs someone who will put him first, even if he's not aware that he does. He deserves the world, but all you can offer him is limited passion. If you weren't so fucking selfish and needy for him, you would've walked away from him before you knew what it was like to love him.

"Hey there," Memphis said sweetly when he entered the room. He stopped long enough to pet the girls before he planted himself on my lap just like he'd done that morning. "I'm famished. Are you in the mood for something to eat?"

Don't fall in love with him, Lyric. Don't fall in love with him, Lyric. Then Memphis leaned forward and pressed a sweet kiss to my lips, and I knew it was too late. I was a goner for Memphis Sullivan.

CHAPTER FIFTEEN

Memphis

I STARED INTO LYRIC'S TURBULENT EYES, WORRIED I WAS BEING TOO forward or too clingy, but the way he gripped my ass to hold me closer told me I was worrying about nothing. Still, he looked distant even when he held me near. It was the oddest sensation, like we were physically together but only I was firmly planted in the moment. Then he blinked and focused back on me.

"Where'd you go?" I asked, making sure I kept a light, teasing tone.

"Library."

"I meant right now. You look like you drifted away from me."

"Never that, Firecracker. I'm just trying to process all the things I learned today. It probably won't seem like a lot, but an investigation needs to start somewhere."

"Would you care to join me for lunch at the diner?"

"Are you closing early today?" Lyric asked, sounding concerned.

"I just close an hour for lunch each day. Well, I'm not open on Wednesdays and Sundays because I don't have much business on those days."

"You close up for lunch? Doesn't that make your customers angry?"

"Most people in this town take their lunches between eleven thirty and one, so I make sure I get lunch after the rush." I laughed because the four people I had in my store when Lyric returned was about as big as my rush ever got. "Besides, I've maintained consistent hours since I started, so the town is used to it."

"Do you want me to pick up a carryout order and bring it back here?"

A wry grin spread slowly across my face. "I'm thinking we could get into a lot of trouble if you do."

Lyric's mouth tipped up into a half smile. "I think you're probably right." He rose to his feet, taking me with him. I slid slowly down the front of his body, feeling the way he reacted to my proximity. "Ladies, we won't be gone long." Lyric refilled the water bowl I kept in my office then we made our way down the block to the diner.

As usual for that time of the day, there were only a few stragglers lingering at the diner. I let Lyric choose the booth and wasn't surprised when he chose one in the back so we could have some privacy. I couldn't wait to hear what put that smile on his face when he came through the door. It had to be something big. I nearly had a fucking heart attack when I saw him sitting behind my desk though because I was pretty sure I forgot to log off that damn fan site when the bell over the door rang alerting me I had a customer. I figured it would be a browser or possibly a quick sale and I would have the chance to hide my extra-curricular activity before Lyric returned. A second customer came in while I was still with the first, then a third and a fourth. Normally, I would've been stoked at the opportunity to make sales, but it felt like the universe was out to get me because he returned before I finished with my customers.

Of course, the second I saw his smiling face, I forgot all about my online activities while he was at the library until I walked into my office. It seemed like I panicked for no reason because he was busy looking at his phone and the screen on my computer was dark, indicating it was still sleeping. I was safe…for the moment. I still needed to devise a way to hide my ridiculous behavior from him when we got back. I loved spending time with him, but I almost hoped he would go back to the library for more research or follow another lead long enough for me to wipe my computer clean. I decided I had logged on to that site for the last time.

I looked up from my menu to catch him staring at me thoughtfully. My heart raced, and butterflies took flight in my stomach. I could no longer pretend lust was the only thing I felt for Lyric Willows. He made me want to chase the shadows I saw from his eyes and give him reasons to smile and laugh. I wanted to be someone he could confide in about the reasons he was so set against love and relationships. Mostly, I wanted to change his mind because I felt like we could have something special. I clenched my fists to keep from reaching for his hands across the table. We weren't on a date for fuck's sake. My heart plummeted when I realized how much trouble I was in.

Lyric raised a brow in question as if he could sense the change in my emotions. I'd never been good at hiding my feelings, so it was probably stamped across my face or broadcasted on my forehead like a jumbotron. Were the messages "falling hard for you" and "please don't hurt me" flashing in neon letters for him to see?

I could tell he wanted to ask me what was going through my mind, but instead, he asked, "What are you going to order? I don't think I want anything too heavy this late in the day. I didn't realize I was at the library for three hours."

"You must've found something amazing to distract you for so long."

"I did, and I'm curious if you'll see the same thing when you look at the picture I found from San Francisco." Lyric focused back on his menu, and I thought it was adorable the way his brow furrowed as he tried to decide what to eat.

"Do you have any food allergies or foods you absolutely hate to see on your plate?" I asked him.

"No and no," he replied, glancing up from his menu.

"Are you insulted when someone replaces beef with turkey in a burger?" I asked.

"Nope. I love a good turkey burger. Is that what you're going to order?"

"It's my favorite burger on the menu. The meat is seasoned deliciously and seared to perfection, and it's topped with a cranberry and citrus sauce so good it makes me want to write a poem."

"Wow," Lyric said, but I couldn't tell if he was impressed by the sandwich description or surprised by my enthusiastic response. "A poem, huh?" He leaned forward and lowered his voice. "Is writing a poem your first reaction to things that give you pleasure and make you feel good?" *Gulp.* "What about physical pleasure? Are you planning to write a poem about the way my blow job made you feel?"

I opened my mouth to respond, but I was distracted by someone clearing their throat. I could feel my face and neck turning red from the passion and embarrassment warring in my brain. I looked up at the person standing beside our table wearing a knowing smirk that signaled he'd overheard Lyric's question. I was accustomed to Daniella taking my order, but this guy could never be confused for her.

"Can I start you fellas off with a drink or do you need a minute? Lord knows I could use a cigarette right about now." He had a wicked gleam in his eye as he looked between us, and I knew his sudden urge had nothing to do with a nicotine craving.

"We'll have two turkey burger platters and Cokes," Lyric said dryly. He wasn't the least bit amused about the interruption, but neither was he embarrassed like I was.

"Are you new here?" I asked.

"I used to live here when I was a kid, but I missed it and moved back."

"Oh, you're Dustin. Emma told me you were in town, but she didn't say anything about you working here," I said.

"I go by DJ for short now. I just pick up a shift whenever Daniella needs a break from working and going to night classes at the community college."

"How nice," Lyric said dryly.

"They need to hire a second full-time server around here any-way. I don't know how Daniella has kept up with this over the years," DJ continued. He either didn't pick up on Lyric's displeasure or didn't care because he didn't acknowledge him. "I'll go place your orders and grab your drinks."

"Thanks, DJ," I said, offering a friendly smile.

Lyric let out an odd hum slash growl I'd never heard him make before. I glanced up and noticed he was watching DJ walk away. I followed his eyes and wondered if he was admiring his ass and may-be trying it on for size in his mind. I hated that thought more than I had a right to and jerked my head forward again. I was ill prepared for the emotion I saw in Lyric's dark-gray eyes. He looked angry but why? What had I said or done? He was the one I caught checking out the waiter.

"He seems just like your type," Lyric finally said, breaking the awkward silence between us. "He has that bad boy vibe and has plen-ty tattoos."

"You sure seem impressed with him," I snapped.

"Me?"

"Act like you weren't checking out his ass, Ric." Two things oc-curred to me. I'd tossed out the nickname I only used during sex, and we were having our first fight.

"Why are we fighting?" Lyric asked.

"We're not fighting," I replied. "Couples fight; we're having a spirited debate."

"Okay, why are we wasting time with a spirited debate about the waiter. You find him attractive, it's cool with me."

"What makes you think I find him attractive?" I asked. "You think I'm attracted to any guy who is tatted and gay?"

"You have a type, Memphis. You've said so yourself."

"Lyric, this is ridiculous." My mother used to say I was so calm she often felt like she needed to check my pulse to make sure I was alive. It wasn't that I didn't have a temper; it was just buried deep beneath the surface. It took a lot to get a rise out of me, and apparently Lyric had triggered that reaction. I was about to say more when two familiar, smiling faces walked into the diner and headed toward our table. "Incoming," I said to Lyric.

He looked over his shoulder, and I saw the tension fade from his body when he saw Emory and Jon were headed our way. "Hey, guys." Lyric scooted out of the booth and stood up to greet both men with a hug. "Have a seat and eat with us." He then walked over to my side of the booth so Emory and Jon could sit across from us.

I scooted over as far as I could get because I was still pissed at him. I nearly jumped out of my skin when Lyric squeezed my thigh beneath the table. Was he trying to apologize or maybe just ease the tension? Either way, it worked because I melted beneath his touch and was no longer pissed. I expected him to remove his hand once he felt me relax, but he left it there until DJ brought our drinks and took Jon and Emory's order.

As soon as the waiter left, Jon said, "Hey, he's your type, Memphis."

"Knock it off, Jon," I said.

"What? All work and no play makes... Ow! Fuck!" He turned and scowled at Emory. "What the hell did you pinch me for?"

"Memphis said to knock it off, Jon."

"I was just teasing him about his love of bad boys. I don't see what the big... *Oh.*" Jon faced us once more. "Sorry."

"You have nothing to apologize for, Jon. Everyone knows about my bad boy addiction."

"Excuse me," Lyric said before he shot out of the booth and headed toward the hallway that led to the bathrooms.

"I'm so sorry, Memphis. I didn't realize that the two of you—"

"We're not," I said, cutting Jon off. "It's fine."

"You don't look fine, Memphis," Em said softly. I wasn't fine. "I should've insisted Lyric stayed with us."

"Don't be silly," I argued. "You're reading way too much into this."

"I don't think I am. You've always said you couldn't see yourself falling in love and finding your sappily ever after, but I think that's because you hadn't met the right person." Emory's voice was soft, and he looked too worried I was setting myself up for the greatest heartache of them all. I had to look away before I did or said something stupid.

Needing to keep my hands busy, I began tying my empty straw wrapper in to knots. "Em, trust that I know what I'm doing, okay?" I didn't have a fucking clue what the hell I was doing, but at least I sounded certain.

"You know I love Lyric, right?"

"Hey," Jon said. "Your husband is sitting right here." I looked up and saw Jon holding up his left hand and pointing to his ring finger. His reaction made me laugh.

"I love him like you love Beau and Corbin," Emory countered.

"Okay, carry on then," Jon said magnanimously.

"Looks to me like someone needs a reminder of my devotion," Emory said.

"Anytime you want, baby."

"Oh lord," I said, fanning myself. "I'm choking on the pheromones over here."

Emory threw his head back and laughed at my discomfort. Seeing him happy made me forget all about my conflicted feelings for Lyric. I never thought I would see him smile and laugh again after his first husband died in a car accident. Emory pulled so deep inside himself there were times I feared we would lose him too. Then he met Jon, and it was like he stepped out into the sunlight after existing in a dark cave for many years. His expression turned more sober when Lyric returned to the table.

DJ returned long enough to drop off Emory and Jon's drinks and assure us that our food would be ready soon. He didn't attempt to make small talk, but maybe it had something to do with the scowl on Lyric's face. I wanted to reach over and comfort him like he'd done for me, but I couldn't convince myself to move. Whatever boldness he brought to the surface inside me had disappeared, leaving me confused and unsure for the first time since we met.

"What have you been up to, Lyric?" Jon asked. "Are you connecting any dots?"

"Some," Lyric replied, but all the enthusiasm he'd shown earlier was gone. I couldn't help but feel I was to blame. "I'm hesitant to say much before I have solid proof to back up my theory. Right now, it's a bunch of little clues I need to piece together to form a cohesive story."

"Like a jigsaw puzzle," Jon said.

"Exactly," Lyric said nodding his head. "You know what that's like, don't you, Em?"

"Sure do," Emory replied. "We get just enough info to hook us but not enough to solve the riddle."

"How's business for you, Memphis?" Jon asked. "Staying busy?"

"I am very busy between the shop and my online store. I also got a great lead for Maegan and myself to follow. I have a feeling we're going to find things that will make us both happy."

I could feel Lyric pulling away from me, both physically and emotionally. He sat with enough space between us that we weren't touching, not even our elbows, when DJ brought out plates and we began eating. I thought I was prepared for the moment Lyric decided that whatever we shared was over, but I had been lying to myself.

"Is there anything at all you can share about the investigation?" Emory asked when we were halfway through our meals. I was shoveling food in my mouth much faster than normal because I wanted to end this awkward lunch as soon as I could.

"I better not," Lyric said. "My theories will sound wild and outlandish."

"I like wild and outlandish," Jon said. "Makes for a much better story."

"Do you think you can help Anthony find peace?" Emory asked.

"I sure hope so, but there are never any certainties."

"What's next?" Jon questioned.

"I'm leaving for San Francisco tomorrow to follow up on a lead."

The sharp stabbing pain in my chest nearly stole my breath. "You are?" I asked, speaking for the first time since he returned to the table. I looked over at him, but he kept his eyes on the plate in front of him. Lyric's brief nod was the only acknowledgment my question received. That just wasn't good enough. "Is this a new development? Is that what you were so excited about telling me?" Lyric nodded again.

That folded piece of paper in his hand must've been an itinerary he printed up or something. Why would he have been so eager to show me that he was leaving? That wasn't the vibe I picked up from him earlier. His sudden mood change left me feeling a little dizzy and a whole lot overwhelmed. Something that felt like panic rose swiftly inside me, threatening to choke me. I needed to get the hell out of there before I made a fool of myself. Trying to find a legitimate-sounding excuse made my anxiety grow even stronger. Luckily, my ringing cell phone snapped me back to reality and provided the perfect excuse.

"Excuse me, but I've been waiting on this call."

Lyric rose swiftly so I could get out. I reached for my wallet to cover my food, but he gripped my wrist firmly. "I've got it."

I nodded without looking at him then answered my phone as I walked away. "Sonny, thanks for getting back to me so quickly." I felt Lyric's eyes on my back, but I didn't look at him. I needed time to get myself together, so he wouldn't know my assurance that I wouldn't fall for him was the biggest lie I ever told—to him and myself.

CHAPTER SIXTEEN

Lyric

I WATCHED MEMPHIS WALK AWAY UNTIL HE WAS OUT OF SIGHT. I wanted to call out his name or even follow him, but I sat back down at the table instead. I forced my eyes off the door and looked across the table at Emory and Jon. I was glad that neither man looked mad because it was obvious that I hurt Memphis with my surprise announcement. Then again, I think I would've preferred anger to the pity I saw in their eyes.

"Emory..."

"You don't owe me an explanation, Lyric. The last time I checked, both you and Memphis are adults and can make your own decisions." He broke eye contact briefly, and I wondered what thoughts ran through his mind. When he looked at me again, there was a crooked smile on his face. "I've never seen you run scared from anything though."

"I'm not scared, Em. I'm just not good enough for Memphis."

"Bullshit," Jon said abruptly. "That sounds like an easy out, and it's not your call to make."

"I agree with my husband," Emory said. "Lyric, I don't need psychic visions to know there are things in your past that haunt you. I admit I'm not an objective party here, but there's no one better at helping you eradicate those ghosts than Memphis."

"I think Lyric prefers to cling to his ghosts than banish them, babe," Jon said astutely.

"I thought you liked me, Jon."

"I do," he said quickly, aiming a disarming smile at me. "That's why I'm calling you out on your bullshit. Do you think you're the only scarred bastard who claimed not to want or be worthy of love? You're looking at two such mopes right here," Jon said, gesturing back and forth between himself and his husband. "We held fast to all the reasons why things shouldn't work rather than why they should. It took a brain tumor for this one," he pointed a thumb at Emory, "to come around."

"It wasn't just the tumor," Emory said dryly. "It just gave me the courage to do what I knew was right all along." Em leaned forward and kissed Jon softly on the lips before he faced me. "But hey, you keep on doing that living-lost-soul thing you've been rocking. It helps you get a lot of ass."

"Em…" Memphis was more than a piece of ass, and I'd known it from the start. If he were just a piece of ass, I wouldn't have been fighting the urge to go after him and apologize. Maybe even explain why I'm so set against love and relationships.

"I'm sorry, Lyric. I didn't mean to make you sound like a jerk. You're the furthest thing from it. I know you would've told Memphis the rules before you got involved with him."

"Rules?" Jon and I asked at the same time. It wasn't like I had a fucking list of things I expected from a lover.

"Let me clarify," Em said. "You have one rule: don't fall in love with you."

"Okay, you have me there." The problem in the situation with Memphis was I didn't follow my own fucking rule. I didn't think it mattered anymore after I shut Memphis out and dropped the bomb that I was leaving. Going to San Francisco to continue the investigation had always been in the back of my mind once I discovered Wallace's friendship with Anthony and suspected they were more than mere friends. Why would an extremely wealthy man like Wallace sell everything he owned to join the Gold Rush? I knew wealthy people liked to become wealthier, but he fell off the face of the earth and no one seemed to be asking why. But leaving the next morning wasn't even a blip on my radar until I became insanely jealous over that waiter, DJ. I hated looking at him and thinking that he would be happy to step in and warm Memphis's bed after I left Blissville for good. Hearing Jon echoing my thoughts turned my blood to ice.

It was ridiculously easy to make flight arrangements on my Delta app when I went to the restroom. Memphis never needed to know that my feelings for him had me running scared. What would be the point of telling him? Nothing had changed.

"Memphis is the kind of person you can confide in, Lyric, even if what you need to say isn't something he wants to hear. Just don't leave things the way they are right now. Make peace with him so you can leave with a good conscience."

I asked for two orders of banana pudding to go. Call it an apology or a peace offering, but I hoped it worked. Emory was right; I didn't feel good about leaving things like this. I found Memphis sitting at his desk. Daisy had laid her head across his lap, and he absently stroked her satiny ears while he looked at something on the computer screen. I set the desserts on his desk and scooted one toward him.

Memphis looked at the takeout container then back up at me. I wouldn't say his eyes were hostile, but they were certainly hesitant. I hated that even more than anger because he always seemed so bold around me. I could tell he was trying to figure out what my gesture meant.

"You didn't eat much because I acted like a dick. The least I could do was bring you some banana pudding."

"You give yourself too much credit, Lyric. My moods don't revolve around you."

I wished I could believe him, but I knew better. I was the reason he sat so stiffly in the booth beside me and pulled deeper into himself like a turtle hiding in its protective shell. I was the reason he left the diner in a hurry, not the phone call he received. Memphis made me want and crave and care. Those weren't things I'd ever felt for another man, and I was grappling with what to do. I didn't believe I was right for Memphis, but that didn't stop me from wanting to prove myself wrong. "Look, I fucked up. Okay?"

"You did," Memphis said, nodding his head. "You think banana pudding is going to make up for it?"

"Banana pudding and a heartfelt apology?" I asked.

"Let's start with the apology, and we'll see how it goes from there."

"I *am* sorry, Memphis." Those were words I rarely cared enough to mutter to anyone.

"What exactly are you sorry for?" It was obvious Memphis wasn't going to make this easy on me, and I deserved no less from him.

"I'm sorry I behaved like a dick. I'm sorry I run hot and cold with you. I hate that I pull you close sometimes only to push you away. I'm sorry if I made you regret anything that's happened between us because that's something I just can't live with."

Memphis's eyes widened like he was surprised by my honesty. That made two of us. "I have no regrets. I've lived more in the four days I've known you than in any other time in my life." He took a deep breath, like maybe he was trying to choose his next words. "Let's not ruin what little time we have left together."

"Fair enough. Would you like to know what I found out today?"

Memphis opened the container and plastic cutlery and started eating the pudding as I waited for him to answer me. I sat on the corner of his desk and dug into my dessert too. The only sounds in the tiny office were the hum from Memphis's computer and two dogs panting while hoping we would share our concoction.

"What's different about this banana pudding?" I finally asked. "I've never tasted anything quite like it." I licked the spoon clean while I studied my treat. "It's richer and more decadent, but I can't quite put my finger on it. I'm thinking condensed milk."

"That's one of the ingredients," Memphis said. "Cream cheese and cool whip are the other two."

"Cream cheese, huh?" I took another bite and savored the taste on my tongue. "It's the best damn pudding I've ever had."

"Okay, what did you find at the library? I'm dying to know what put that smile on your face when you walked into my store?"

"*You* were the reason for the smile on my face," I said before I thought it through.

"Then why the sudden mood change at lunch? Was it Jon's comment about DJ?" Memphis shook his head. "No, that can't be it."

"Yes."

"*Yes*? You were upset because Jon mentioned that DJ was my type?"

"Yes."

"Why?"

I set my pudding down on the desk. I couldn't swallow another bite anyway with my heart stuck in my esophagus. I cleared my throat a few times before I could answer him. "I was jealous."

"*Jealous*?"

Memphis sounded like I'd spoken in a foreign language. "You know, that reaction when someone wants something or someone you don't want to share. It's often accompanied by chest thumping, posturing, and pithy comments to hide the real emotions."

His mouth fell open, and he stared at me with unblinking eyes behind his cute glasses. I leaned forward and straightened them. Next thing I knew, Memphis shot out of his chair, launched himself into my arms, and attacked my mouth with his lips and tongue. I placed my left hand on the small of his back, holding him flush against me, while I fisted my right hand in his curls. This was the bold man who wormed his way into my heart when I least expected it. How could I think I could walk away from him and never look back? How the fuck could he mean so damn much to me after only a few days?

Memphis tore his mouth from mine, panting to catch his breath. "Were you planning on coming back?"

"Yes," I replied honestly. "I had planned to ask if Daisy could stay with you while I was in San Francisco. I will only be gone for a few days, but I'd rather not board her."

"I wouldn't let you board her, Ric. I can't stand the thought of her being alone in a cage when she can stay with Gigi and me." Memphis reached up and ran his thumb over my lips. "Is this too much for you? We don't have to… Mmmm," Memphis moaned into my mouth when I cut off his words with a fevered kiss. I wanted to strip him down and take him right there on his desk, but I felt like I had something to prove to him.

"As I was saying before you mauled me, I got jealous thinking that DJ would be keeping you company after I left town."

"Not going to happen," Memphis assured me.

"I couldn't go to San Francisco and leave things strained between us. I can't put the things I feel into words right now, but I don't want to pretend that you're just another hookup."

"Listen, Ric," Memphis said softly, "why don't we just take this day by day. No pressure. We enjoy each other's company and let's leave it at that."

"I like the way you think, Firecracker."

"Good, now show me what you found at the library. Oh," Memphis said suddenly as if he just thought of something. "Are we still on for Bliss House tonight?"

"I wouldn't miss it," I answered honestly. "I'm planning on doing an EVP session while we look through the trunks Anthony knocked over." I placed my palm on the back of Memphis's neck and stared into his eyes. "Then I want to spend the night tangled up with you."

Memphis briefly closed his eyes and hummed happily. "Tell me about the library, Ric."

"Let me show you instead." I pulled the folded piece of paper from my pocket and handed it to him. He looked at me for an explanation instead of opening it right away. "I decided to search for wealthy men living in San Francisco around the time that Wallace supposedly would've lived there. I figured a man of means such as himself wouldn't run brothels or do anything he felt was beneath his stature, even if he was living under an assumed identity."

"And what did you find?"

"Open the paper and see for yourself."

I could tell by Memphis's gasp that he knew exactly who he was looking at standing in front of the Blissview Hotel next to Anthony Bliss's horse. "Do you have a picture of Wallace on your phone?"

I pulled up the same photo that I thought of when I saw the picture. It was of the two men standing on the lawn at Bliss House during some social event. People were playing croquet in the background, but Anthony and Wallace appeared to be deep in conversation. Wallace and Denver's stance, with the left leg crossed over the right, were identical, as were the tilt of their heads, and the way both men put their hands in their front pockets.

"That's Wallace Bennington standing beside Starlight in front of the hotel he named after his lover," Memphis said. He looked up at me. "My God, Ric. He must've wondered what happened to Anthony every single day of his life. What do you hope to find out in San Francisco?"

"I want to learn more about the man he was and the life he lived. My gut tells me that I'll find answers there. Do you want to hear something exciting?"

"You don't call me Firecracker for nothing," Memphis teased.

"The original Blissview Hotel still exists, even though it's had several name changes over the years. Guess where I'm staying?"

"The Blissview Hotel?" he asked with a wistful sigh. "That's so cool. Please take a lot of pictures for me."

"It's called The Golden Gate Bridge Inn now, but you can count on me documenting the experience." I kissed his lips softly. "I have several things I need to take care of before I leave. Do you mind if I take the girls and head back to the house? I can pick you up after the store closes."

"Or I can walk home," Memphis said wryly. "The cool thing about Blissville is that nearly everything is within walking distance."

"I wish I hadn't made these plans so hastily as a jealous, knee-jerk reaction because it would be so much more exciting if you came with me. You're just as enthralled with this investigation as I am."

"When exactly did you make those knee-jerk plans?"

I grimaced because the truth made me sound mildly unstable at best or insane at worst. "When I went to the bathroom."

Memphis's eyes widened in surprise. "Whoa! You weren't in the bathroom that long."

"I have a Delta app to book flights, I already had the hotel website pulled up on my phone, and I used Apple Pay to book my room. The entire process took me about three minutes or less. I'm sure you were too busy talking to Jon and Emory to realize I was gone longer than normal."

"True," he agreed. "It wasn't like I was timing you."

"Do you want to hear the coolest part about the hotel?"

"It's reported to be haunted, right?"

"You got it."

"What's my prize?" Memphis asked, reaching between our bodies to cup my erection.

I had decided to lock his office door and bend him over the desk, but the bell over the front door jingled. "Saved by the bell, Firecracker."

Memphis whimpered softly and briefly closed his eyes. "I am normally thrilled when I have so many customers in one day, but damn it. I want to experience makeup sex after our little *spirited debate*."

"Oh, you're going to experience it all right, but I think it will be best if we wait until we're all alone."

"No attic shenanigans then?" Memphis inquired.

"Not unless you want it on film."

"Oh yeah," he said, but his eyes glazed over like he was imagining what we would look like fucking on camera.

"I need to get out of here while I can still walk," I told him while adjusting my junk.

"Maybe you should find time for a nap," Memphis called out when I reached the door. "Especially if this is the last night I'll see you for a while."

"I'll only be gone five days max," I told him, "but you have an excellent point." I didn't want to go three hours without touching, kissing, or getting naked with Memphis. I felt an intense urge to leave my mark on him—physically and emotionally.

I planned to love Memphis until the sun came up and tell him the things I never shared with anyone else. I would trust him to keep my heart and secrets because they suddenly seemed too heavy to keep to myself.

"Hey, Memphis," his customer called out. "Are you here?" I recognized that voice from the other day. It belonged to the kid who'd bought the gifts for his dads.

"Maybe he ran over to Books and Brew for an afternoon coffee," Daniel said. "I'd weigh three hundred pounds if I worked next to the bakery."

"I'd still love you," Mark told his boyfriend.

"Aww. I'll love you no matter what too."

Jesus, those teenage boys didn't have a problem communicating their feelings. I needed to step up my game. I dropped a quick kiss on Memphis's lips, whistled for the dogs to follow me, and walked out into the store. Mark and Daniel's eyes widened when they saw me coming.

"Hey, fellas. Memphis is finishing up a phone call." More like he was readjusting his clothes to hide his arousal. "He'll be right out."

"Thanks, mister," Mark said.

There was a lightness in my soul I hadn't felt since nineteen ninety-six when my world crashed and burned. I had no fucking clue what I was doing or how I was going to hold onto the feeling, but I was going to give it my all.

CHAPTER SEVENTEEN

Memphis

"I CAN'T TAKE THE SUSPENSE ANY LONGER," MAEGAN SAID WHEN we arrived at her house for the next attic session.

The word attic will now forever be synonymous to Lyric and me having sex in front of a camera amongst Anthony's trunks of belongings. Recording myself having sex with someone was never a fantasy of mine, but I couldn't help thinking about seeing the way he made me feel on film. I heard Lyric chuckle softly beside me, and I knew he was picturing *me* picturing *us*.

"Freckles, not even a day has passed yet," Elijah teased her. "Don't you want to wait until they have the whole story rather than bits and pieces?"

"What are you willing to tell me?" she asked.

"Mae, can we at least let the fellas in before you interrogate them, or are you planning on withholding their dinner until they talk?" Elijah asked.

"I guess you guys can come in," she said begrudgingly, "but no dessert until you talk."

"I'll tell you whatever you want to know," Lyric said. "This is your home, and I know how much Anthony and this house means to you."

"Do I want to know?" she asked me.

"If you're asking me if I'm a hundred percent sure what happened to Anthony, then the answer is no. I do have a copy of the EVP session if you want to hear what Anthony had to say. Unfortunately, it's broken bits that we're left to interpret until we find hard evidence to prove what happened."

"I think I want to know," Mae said, dropping down on the couch beside Elijah. "Right?" she asked her boyfriend.

"She wants to know," Elijah said. "She didn't sleep worth a damn last night which meant I didn't either. I can't keep law and order in this town on only a few hours of sleep each night."

"Is that right," Maegan asked. "I wasn't aware you felt so put out."

"Freckles, I'm never put out about putting out. I love helping you get tired any way I can. I was teasing you."

"Okay, we're veering off course here," Maegan said, a slight blush creeping up her neck. "Tell me, Lyric. I'm sure I want to know."

Lyric slowly and methodically explained everything he had learned, making sure to emphasize what was supposition versus facts he could verify with articles or documents he found online. Maegan gasped when she heard the recording and cried when she saw the photo of Wallace standing with Starlight in front of the Blissview Hotel.

"Oh my God," she said softly. "You really think Melanie Bliss had him committed because she found out about his plans to leave her? There's no way Anthony sent Starlight with Wallace if he wasn't planning to go too. I'm surprised that horse wasn't in the formal family photos."

"That's what I thought too," Lyric agreed.

"What about the asylum angle?" Mae asked.

"We've searched for anyone in the family trees, or even a friend of the family, who would've had the authority or connections to have him committed," I told her. "So far we're coming up with a big miss."

"What about someone bribing a person in charge at a facility? Let's be honest here, the doctors and administration at a lot of the asylums were not good people. For enough money, I could see them slipping a man in without a proper judiciary ruling."

"Damn," Lyric said, whistling between his teeth. "I didn't consider that."

"I'll look into that angle while you're in San Francisco," I said.

"San Francisco," Elijah and Maegan said at the same time.

"When do you leave?" Mae asked.

"My plane leaves at ten o'clock in the morning, so I need to be at the airport around eight thirty."

"I didn't ask if you wanted a ride to the airport. Tomorrow is Wednesday after all, so my store is closed. I can drop you off and you can save some money on long-term parking."

"I don't want to inconvenience you," Lyric told me.

"I wouldn't offer if I wasn't willing to do it," I answered.

"Okay," Lyric agreed easily.

"I hate that you'll miss French toast brunch tomorrow, but you have an open invitation when you return to Blissville."

"I appreciate that, Maegan." A muffled thump came from upstairs. "Sounds like someone is trying to get our attention."

"Not until after you eat," Elijah said. "I bet you could spend hours and hours up there."

"That's so nice of you, E," I said.

"Not really," he replied with a shrug. "Freckles won't let me eat until you do. Help a fella out, won't you?"

"I'm smoking a pork roast to make pulled pork," Maegan said, narrowing her eyes at Elijah. "We don't serve our guests hamburgers and hot dogs. I also have baked macaroni and cheese, coleslaw, and baked beans."

"That sounds amazing," Lyric said, "but hamburgers and hot dogs would've been fine too."

By the time we finished eating, I was so full I had to practically crawl up the two sets of steps to reach the attic. "We're back, Anthony," I said. "We're going to solve this mystery if it's the last thing we do."

"You're so fucking cute," Lyric growled in my ear. "I cannot wait to get you alone."

"Turn these cameras on and let's go," I said eagerly. "What do you need me to do?"

"Help me look through these trunks that have been knocked around a bit more while I try to communicate with Anthony."

"Anything special you'd like me to keep an eye out for?"

"Hidden journals or personal belongings that might hold some answers for us," Lyric told me. "I would love for you to find letters or telegraphs, but I won't hold my breath."

"Dear Sir. Stop. I found my husband in bed with another man. Stop. Will you help me commit him to the asylum? Stop," I said, imitating a telegraph.

"Doubt we find a smoking gun like that, but we could get lucky. Maybe Anthony's personal belongings were sent back to his home of record after he passed away."

"Hmmm, interesting theory." I was suddenly eager to sort through the five boxes to find clues. "Do your thing, Sexy."

I tried to split my attention between my search, listening to Lyric ask questions, and thinking of all the naughty naked things I wanted to do with him when we got back to my house. I was too distracted and nearly discounted a porcelain-looking jar as nothing special until I saw the Blissview Hotel logo on top of the lid. I picked it back up and studied it more closely. The ivory porcelain had turned a dingy, brownish yellow with age, but that didn't detract from its simple beauty with gold horses embossed all around the jar. I checked the lid again and it appeared that the handle might've been made of gold too. I opened the jar and was immediately assailed by the same tobacco smell I associated with Anthony's ghost. I expected to find tobacco inside, but all I saw was ash. Did he empty his pipe into the jar after smoking? Then it hit me. The ash was too coarse to be from a pipe, cigar, or any other form of tobacco.

I placed the lid carefully back on the jar and looked behind me to see what Lyric was doing. "Um, Lyric," I said shakily. "I think I found an important piece of the puzzle."

Lyric had been in midsentence but stopped and came over anyway. "What do you have there, Firecracker? That's a pipe tobacco humidor used in the 1800s."

"Check out the lid," I said.

"The Blissview Hotel," he read aloud. "I'll be damned. Those golden horses resemble Starlight, don't they?"

"They do, but that's not the most interesting part," I told him, opening the lid.

"Holy fuck," Lyric whispered. "I think you've found Anthony Bliss."

"Did they use cremation back then?" I asked him.

"I'm pretty sure they used cremation at least in the late 1800s. This is huge, Memphis." He set the humidor carefully on the ground beside us and began helping me sort through the crate I found it in. "He's not cooperating tonight. Maybe seeing us touch his humidor will get a reaction out of him." Lyric shook his head like he couldn't believe we found it.

"Do you think that means he made it out to San Francisco after all?"

"Either he went to San Fran and his remains were shipped back here after he passed, or Wallace's ashes ended up back here. Of the two scenarios, the first one seems more probable."

"I agree, but how would someone at Blissview know to send his remains back here? He wouldn't have used his real identity with a fresh start on the West Coast."

"Well, he either documented this address as his former address or Wallace made the arrangements after Anthony passed," Lyric said.

"The latter makes more sense. I don't think anyone asked questions if you had money back then. Besides, Anthony searching for Wallace does make it seem like he passed away first and wanted to know what happened to his lover."

"Damn, I hope I get a hold of a knowledgeable historian who can tell me about Denver Collins and if he had a male friend he spent a lot of time with while living in San Francisco."

"I won't lie, Lyric. I'm really fucking jealous of your trip right now."

"I wish you were going too," Lyric said then looked around the room. "I'm going to find Wallace for you, Anthony."

"Feel anything?" I whispered.

"He's here, but he's keeping his distance." Lyric closed his eyes like he was trying to connect with Anthony, but he reopened them after a minute. "Nothing. I'll review the footage on my flight."

We continued looking through the trunks, but it was mostly clothes, books, and pipe tobacco pouches. Nothing had Anthony's name on it, and the only item that had a connection to San Francisco was the pipe tobacco humidor slash urn which we took downstairs to show Maegan after we turned off all the equipment.

"Oh cool! A pipe tobacco humidor," she said when she saw it. "That's a large one too."

"It smells like the tobacco wafting through the air whenever Anthony is around," I told her.

"Really? I wonder if this is the item he's attached himself to."

"It would seem so," Lyric said. "Especially since we think it holds his remains."

"Whoa!" Elijah said, jumping to his feet and walking to Maegan's side. "His what now?"

Maegan slowly opened the lid like she expected something to pop out and get her. Elijah and Maegan peered into the humidor for a few seconds before she closed it. "Looks like cremated ashes to me," she agreed. "The question is: how'd they get here?"

"And when?" Elijah asked.

"I hope to find those answers for you and more while I'm in San Francisco," Lyric said. "I'll be in touch when I find something out. In the meantime, what would you like to do with Anthony's ashes?"

"I'll put them in a place of honor on the mantle above the fireplace, of course."

"Whoa, Freckles, can we talk about this?" Elijah asked, following behind her.

"We live with his ghost, babe. What's the harm in placing his ashes on the mantle?"

"We'll just show ourselves out," I called after them. If Maegan and Elijah heard me, they didn't acknowledge it. They just kept debating the humidor's proper place as Maegan set it on the mantle and took a step back. Maegan had her hands on her hips and her head cocked to the right as she studied the humidor.

Lyric and I chuckled as we followed our dogs out the door and down the porch steps. Daisy jumped in the back of Lyric's truck while Gigi sat inside with us. My mind switched from solving the ghost mystery to getting Lyric naked as soon as we were enclosed in the cab of his truck. Neither of us said anything during the short ride home, which only amped up the excitement that sparked between us. I tried to calm my racing heart while I watched the dogs play in the back yard and Lyric carried his equipment inside the house.

"Lyric?" I called out when I brought the dogs inside after they did their business for the night.

"Up here, Firecracker. Come alone."

I took the stairs two at a time and threw open my door. "Sexy, it's much more fun when we come together."

"I meant for you to leave the dogs outside the room." Lyric lay in the center of the bed lazily stroking his cock. "C'mere."

I toed off my shoes then stripped down faster than I ever had in my life. I didn't care that Lyric knew how desperate I was to feel him inside me again. As I approached the bed, he spread his legs wide, and he'd slipped two slick fingers inside his puckered hole, stretching himself.

"Oh," I said.

"Is this okay? I didn't even ask if you…"

"Hell yes, it's okay," I said, climbing between Lyric's legs on the bed. Lyric removed his fingers with a needy moan when I picked up the lube and oiled my fingers. His moan became a strangled groan for more when his ass tightly gripped my finger.

"More. Give me two."

"Who's the bossy bottom now?" I ignored his request because I figured it had been a long time since he'd bottomed. I wanted to make him feel good and drive him wild more than I wanted my own pleasure. I would wait until I was sure he was ready.

"I'm going to get even with you when you least expect it, Memphis. I will make you beg for my cock, and then I'm going to only give you an inch at a time until you cry."

Okay, he was lubed and ready. I slid a condom on and propped a pillow under his ass to raise his hips. I'd never tried it before, but the guys in my favorite porn scene sure liked it. Desperation and need clawed at my guts, urging me to claim and possess Lyric, but I slowly penetrated him while he gripped his pillow and continued to threaten me with a good time.

Lyric pulled his legs back and held his knees to his chest. He was surprisingly flexible for such a tall guy and sexier than any man had a right to be. Lyric's ass squeezed me so tightly I worried I would embarrass myself by coming before I was fully inside him.

"Fuck me already, damn it. There are so many things I want to do to you before I get on that plane in the morning. Don't hold back, Firecracker. Lose control and take me with you."

I punched my hips forward making us both roar with pleasure when I was buried as far as I could go. Then I fucked Lyric like he demanded until I felt the tingling in my spine that signaled the end was near. I reached between his spread legs and fisted his leaking cock. I never took my eyes off his while I jacked him off at the same pace I fucked his ass.

"Yes! More!" he cried out. I gave him more until I felt his body tense and his toes curl seconds before he splattered his chest and stomach with his release.

"Ric." I moaned his name as his ass milked the orgasm from me.

"C'mere," he said again.

I eased my dick out of him and fell onto his chest, not caring that I was lying in his spunk. All that mattered was Lyric holding me like he never wanted to let me go.

"You make me want to believe, Memphis," Lyric said then pressed a kiss against my damp temple.

CHAPTER EIGHTEEN

Lyric

MEMPHIS PLACED A KISS DIRECTLY ABOVE MY HEART THAT still raced for him before he lifted his head and looked into my eyes. "That's the sweetest thing anyone has ever said to me."

"Uhhh ohhh," I said dramatically. "Is that the death toll for our… um…relationship?"

Memphis playfully gasped and raised up even higher. "The R-word too? I think I need a minute." He acted like he was going to roll off me, but I wrapped my legs around his waist, securing him in my grasp. If he wanted a bad boy villain, I'd give him one, but on my terms.

I gave him my best villainous laugh then said, "I've got you now, Captain Firecracker, and I have so many wicked things I'm going to do to you."

Memphis pretended to struggle against me, but the only thing he accomplished was arousing us both. He gave up struggling in favor of kissing me breathless before he kissed down my neck and chest until he reached my pierced nipple. At first, he flicked his tongue over the hardened bud then he sucked it between his lips and tugged the hoop with his teeth.

"Fuck! I can't keep my dick down around you, Memphis. I wanted to talk to you about some things, but I can't think straight."

Memphis rose up on his knees and I watched him remove the condom from his dick then lean over the bed to discard it in the small trash can next to his bed. "Think gay then," Memphis said as he kissed a path down my stomach, not caring it was covered in my cum. "We can talk after I blow you." He looked up at me as he dipped his tongue in my navel. "You do want me to blow you, right?"

Only every day for the rest of my fucking life, but I scrunched up my face like I was giving it serious thought. "Meh," I said.

Memphis grinned as if I'd just thrown out a challenge. "That 'meh' is going to turn into 'Oh, Memphis' in about five seconds."

"Five seconds? You sure are... Oh!" I said when his tongue traced a circle around the head of my dick. Memphis playfully winked before he swallowed my cock. "Oh, Memphis."

My guy set a tempo that said he wasn't playing around either. His ass moved up and down as he rubbed one out against the sheets while giving me head. I loved that I had that kind of power over him, and it had me flooding his mouth too soon. Memphis groaned as he swallowed my release, but I could tell he hadn't come yet.

"Get up here and fuck my face."

Memphis moved up my body with superhero speed and began fucking my mouth with shallow strokes until I gripped his ass with one hand and teased his hole with the other. Then his rhythm faltered, and his thrusts became fast and choppy. Memphis braced one hand on the wall above his headboard and took turns pinching his nipples with his free hand. He was so fucking hot with his messy hair, crooked glasses, and wide-open mouth sucking air into his laboring lungs. He was everything I never knew I wanted but couldn't imagine my life without.

I moaned and savored his pre-cum on my tongue. The vibrations must've excited him even more because he hastily pulled his dick out of me and painted my neck, chest, and mouth with his cum. Then, as if he couldn't get any fucking hotter, he scooped his cum off my lips with his thumb and pushed it into my mouth. I sucked his spunk off his thumb then pulled him down for a long, languid kiss.

Memphis raised his hand and knocked twice on the headboard.

"Are you tapping out?" I teased.

"I have nothing left to give," Memphis replied dramatically. "Besides, didn't you say you wanted to talk to me?"

I did say that, and I meant it at the time, but I was second-guessing myself. I didn't doubt I could trust Memphis; I just didn't want to ruin a special night. Then again, how special could it be when I didn't let him see the real me?

"Shower first? I'm a bit sticky."

"Shower and ice cream," Memphis said. "I can sense that heavy things are weighing down your mind right now. Ice cream helps everything."

"Do you have rocky road?"

"Among others," Memphis said. "Come on."

I followed Memphis out of his room and chuckled at the baleful glares we received from our dogs for making them wait in the hallway while we fucked. I had fun staring at Memphis's ass while he turned on the shower and adjusted the water temperature. He reached back and parted his ass cheeks, showing off his pink hole. "Like what you see?"

"I love what I see."

Memphis seductively smiled as he approached me. "I'm desperate to make you miss me half as much as I'm going to miss you." I would've run for the hills buck-ass naked had anyone other than Memphis said those words to me. He made me want to hold on instead of run away.

I took his glasses off and set them on the countertop. "I'm going to miss you like crazy, Firecracker. I'll call you so much that you'll be sick of me."

"Hardly." He tipped his head to the side. "I don't know what to do with all these…feelings."

I chuckled because I was in the same boat. "Why don't we try not to worry about figuring it all out and just let things unfold naturally."

"Right? We've only known each other for like four days and half of those we spent naked. It all happened kind of fast."

"That's typical for people in my family," I said wryly. "Get in that shower and let me tell you a story." I liked to keep my hands busy while I worked through things, so why not soap up Memphis's gorgeous body while I explained to him why I was so leery about love? I squirted a generous amount of body wash in my hands and began soaping his chest by running my hands in a circular motion. "People in my family tend to fall in love fast and hard."

"How fast and hard?" Memphis asked.

"My maternal grandparents and my parents both believed they fell in love at first sight. My grandparents got engaged two days after they met, and my parents eloped the week after meeting at college."

"What about your paternal grandparents?" Memphis questioned.

I looked up from my task and caught him watching my face for reactions to his questions. He looked afraid he had upset me. "I like that you want to know about me, Memphis."

"You don't have to answer anything you don't want to, Lyric. I promise I won't be upset."

"I know, Firecracker. That only makes me want to tell you more." I gave him a quick kiss then returned my attention to washing his arms. "My paternal grandparents wouldn't know love if it bit them on the ass. Marriages were about business connections and protecting legacies and had nothing to do with love, affection, or even respect. I doubt Edward and Veronica Willows have ever said the word love to anyone in their lives."

"Wait," Memphis said suddenly, pulling my eyes up to his. "Are you telling me that Edward and Veronica Willows are your grandparents? Weeping Willows Estates? The Hilton family of the south?"

"Yep. My father was their only son."

"I'm so fucking sorry, Lyric. I don't think I've ever seen colder people in my life." If he knew who my grandparents were, then he knew the tragic story about their heir and his much younger wife. I knew it was only a matter of time before he made the connection. "Oh," he softly said when everything clicked into place. "I don't even know what to say."

"My father had always been a bit of a rogue which pissed the sperm donor and egg incubator off big-time. My dad's choice of academia over business or law rocked the boat but falling in love with one of his students sank it quicker than the Titanic. My mother was a young, free-spirited hippie and should've been completely wrong for my buttoned-up father."

"But they worked, huh?"

Oh, how they worked. "In a way that a symphony works, Memphis. Their differences brought out the best in each other. My dad's steady love kept my mom grounded while allowing her to soar. My mother's wild heart tempted my dad to take risks he would never have considered until she came along. They loved swift, hard, and complete. So much so, they often forgot the rest of the world existed."

"Including you?"

"Including me. Sometimes it was like watching an epic romance movie in person. Every time my father entered a room, his eyes would immediately seek out my mother. There were nights when he'd come home after a long day, and he'd sweep her into his arms and start dancing with her around the room for an hour or so. They'd talk about their days and how much they missed one another. Sometimes they'd dance out of the room, forgetting that I was sitting on the sofa."

"I'm so sorry, Ric," Memphis said softly.

"I wasn't completely neglected, and they did love me, Memphis. It's just the love they had for one another surpassed anything they felt for anyone else, including their only child. I loved when I had one-on-one time with them. Mom would take me to museums and theme parks and Dad would take me out on a boat or up in his small plane." I swallowed hard at the mention of his aircraft. "When my father's plane crashed off the coast of Savannah, my mother gave up living.

It didn't matter that her devastated son needed her, she only knew her world had ended. Not her parents, doctors, or even my desperate pleas could reach her. She just gave up."

I was sure he knew the rest of the story told in the papers, but no one really knew the whole story. "A week after my father died, I came downstairs and found my mother in the kitchen swaying to my father's favorite song while she made his favorite breakfast foods. Tears streamed down her face, but she smiled when she saw me. She told me it was Daddy's birthday and we needed to celebrate by eating his favorite foods. I ate everything on my plate even though I wasn't hungry. I wanted to make my mom happy, and maybe my dad too if he was watching over us like she said he was.

"After breakfast, my mom drove me to her parents' house for the day. She held me tightly against her chest and told me she loved me so much and she was so proud of me. Even though I was only ten years old, I knew something was wrong. I remember clinging to her and begging her not to go. She just rocked me from side to side while humming a lullaby, comforting my broken spirit and putting me at ease. I'll never forget the sad smile on her face the last time she looked at me."

"Hey," Memphis said. "I know what happened next. You don't have to say it out loud if it hurts too much."

"I need to explain why I've never wanted to fall in love," I told him. "My mom drove to Savannah and walked along the shore to the spot closest to the place my dad's plane went down. She walked into the ocean in broad daylight and never came back out. She was so far gone in her grief that she didn't think about her unborn child or me."

"Oh no," Memphis said, wrapping his arms around me and holding me tight. That was the part that was never in the news.

"She'd only discovered her pregnancy a few weeks before my father's death. They were so excited to have another child after years of trying, and I was excited I wouldn't be all alone anymore. I was so fucking mad at her, Memphis. She didn't love me enough to stay.

Looking back as an adult, I can see my mom had other underlying issues that made her grief feel insurmountable to her. It took me a long time to forgive her."

"I'm so sorry, Ric," Memphis said softly.

"To me, love was an all-consuming illusion that made people selfish. It was smoke and mirrors, or smoke in the mirror as some skeptics call my ability. You thought you saw something beautiful and rare, but it was an evil that would suck the soul right out of you."

"Ouch," Memphis said.

"A tad extreme," I agreed. "It wasn't just my parents' tragic love that soured me. I saw the absolute reverse when I visited the Willows after the funerals for my parents. They were virtual strangers to me, but I was the only tether to their son, so they decided they wanted to keep me. Luckily, that didn't happen."

"Your mom's parents won guardianship?" Memphis asked.

"Nope, they couldn't afford a lawyer who could take on the Willows, so I had to take matters into my own hands." I felt myself smile for the first time since we got in the shower. "I showed them what a nightmare a ten-year-old boy could be. I believe the words atrocious, unruly, and heathen were used to describe me. I got my way though and went to live with Jessa Rae and George."

"I'm sure having you there was a comfort to them," Memphis said then gasped suddenly. "The water is getting cold." He shut off the shower while I grabbed the towels off the rack. Once we dried off, we wrapped the towels around our waists and headed downstairs to get ice cream.

I continued to unburden my soul over rocky road and mint chocolate chip. "As a teenager and young adult at college, I watched one idiot after the next do the stupidest shit for love. Luckily, my grandparents had a beautiful relationship. It was the only thing that saved me from being one hundred percent fucked up."

"You're not fucked up at all," Memphis said. "Hell, my parents have an amazing relationship, and I still made shitty decisions when it came to guys. I was like the idiots from college you described."

"Was?" I asked hopefully.

"Well, there's this guy I met. He's the perfect blend of bad," Memphis tweaked my nipple piercing, "and good."

"Bad boy with a heart of gold?" I asked.

"Something like that." Memphis's easy smile slid off his face, and his expression grew serious. "Since we're having a heart-to-heart chat, I need to tell you I've done something I'm not proud of," he said slowly. "I should've told you before we had sex the first time. It's just that I wanted you so fucking bad I let lust cloud my judgment."

I thought I knew where he was going but didn't want to jump to any conclusions and embarrass him by saying the wrong thing. "Did you live stream us having sex for a web show or something?"

"God, no."

"It can't be that bad," I told him.

"That's your measuring stick?" Memphis asked. "Never mind. I don't want to digress too much, or I'll lose my nerve." He released a long, shaky breath before he said, "There's this ridiculous fan site on the internet called *Willows Whisperers*. I'm not sure if you're familiar with it."

"I'm aware," I said dryly, making him cringe. "Are you a member of my fan club?"

"Oh fuck, this is embarrassing," Memphis said, setting his pint of ice cream down on the coffee table. "I am, but I need you to know the website started out as a fun place to chat about episodes and stuff."

"And stuff," I repeated, trying hard not to laugh. "Fan fiction stuff?"

Memphis turned an adorable shade of pink. "Um, have you read any of that?"

"You mean the paranormal porn?" I asked, earning a groan. "Did you write a fan fiction story about me, Memphis?"

"Maybe." He squirmed so much on the couch I had to set my

pint of ice cream next to his and pull him onto my lap.

"Was it naughty? Will you let me read it?" I knew every fucking word, but I wanted Memphis to show me. "Better yet, read it to me."

"Oh, I don't think I could. It's too embarrassing. How about I tell you my username and you can entertain yourself while you're thousands of miles away."

"I want to entertain myself when you're inches away," I said, gripping his hips and pulling him to me. "At least tell me what the story is about."

I raptly listened as Memphis told me the story of the sexy paranormal investigator who fell in love with the clumsy but adorable owner of a haunted house. He tried to gloss over the sexy details, but I wouldn't let him.

"No skipping the horny details," I teased. "Better yet, why don't you show me what happened when the investigator got the cute homeowner naked for the first time."

Memphis was all too eager to remove our towels and ride me reverse-cowboy style until we both shouted our releases and fell asleep in a tangle of limbs on his couch. We barely woke up in time to leave for the airport and rushed out the door after making sure the dogs were set for a few hours.

There were still so many things I wanted to tell him, but I didn't want to start the conversation because we were running out of time, so we talked about trivial things like favorite breakfast cereals and our favorite Saturday morning cartoons we watched as kids. All too soon, we arrived at the departure drop-off at CVG International Airport.

"I'll call you when I get settled in," I told him.

Memphis pressed his lips to mine for a quick kiss. "You better." He was slow to release me after our goodbye hug and slowly walked backward to his Beetle.

"I really like you, Memphis."

The smile he gave me was the most beautiful thing I'd ever seen. "I really like you too, Ric."

I grabbed my bag and headed inside the airport before I changed my mind about going. I'd never hesitated to leave for an investigation before, but neither had I made such a bold declaration about my feelings. The sudden change after only a few days should've felt disturbing or scary, but it felt...great.

CHAPTER NINETEEN

Memphis

"**H**EY, YOU MADE IT," MILO SAID IN GREETING WHEN I WALKED into Maegan's house.

"Of course, I did. I don't miss French toast brunch. Feed me, Mama," I said dramatically.

"Mae said you took Lyric to the airport," Andy said.

"I dropped him off at eight thirty and brunch doesn't start until ten."

Five sets of curious eyes were locked on me. I could tell they were dying to ask questions but were trying to behave. I knew it wouldn't last long. I sure as hell wasn't going to volunteer any information.

"So, when can I come over and see Lyric naked?" Milo asked.

"What the fuck, Milo?" Andy snarled.

"I don't want to see his dick for my pleasure, Slugger. I need to balance out the universe. Memphis saw your dick, so I think it's only fair that we get to see what Lyric is sporting down below."

"Over my dead body," I growled. "I didn't ask to see Andy's dick. I was minding my own business and drinking coffee when he forced me to see it by strolling into the kitchen buck-ass naked. It's not my fault you neglected to tell your boyfriend you expected company."

"He has a point, Peach," Andy said. "Everyone is keeping their cocks covered up from now on."

"I guess," Milo grumbled. "So, how are things going between you lovebirds. Don't even bother trying to deny you're not riding him like a bull. It's written all over your face."

"I do not deny anything, Milo. I'm just not sharing the details with you guys over brunch."

"After brunch then?" he asked.

"Try never," I replied. "Just bask in the glory that you were right, okay?"

"Yeah, that works for me."

"What do you guys know about the mystery so far?" Andy asked. "What sent Lyric to San Francisco?"

My phone buzzed in my pocket, and I checked to see who the text was from. A sappy grin spread across my face when I saw Lyric's name on the screen.

Boarding the plane. I'll call you once I land in SF.

Safe travels, I replied. *I like you.*

I like you more, NerdBoy88.

Fuck! That meant he took what little I shared with him the night before and matched it to my paranormal porn.

Lyric's response was a series of emojis—ghost, squirt gun, house, eggplant, a jockey riding a horse, and water drops. Followed by, *I probably shouldn't have read that in the Sky Lounge though. Had to adjust my pants more than once. I want to reenact every second of that hot-as-fuck story. You left out a lot of the good parts last night.*

Aren't you mad?

Fuck no. I must say that the reality of you is so much hotter than fan fiction you. Gotta go. Talk soon, Firecracker.

I sent back three kissy-face emojis—something I'd never done before. Man, I had it bad.

"He has it bad," Milo whispered dreamily.

"I do," I admitted. What the hell was the point in lying? "One day at a time though."

After brunch, I decided to swing by Emory and Jon's house. I knew Emory would've worried about me after I left lunch the day

171

before, and I wanted to put his mind at ease. He greeted me with a big hug like always then stepped back to scrutinize me. "This is a far different expression on your face than the one you wore at the diner. Can I take it you and Lyric worked out whatever was bothering both of you?"

"Yeah, we're working on it. I just wanted to stop by and let you know I was okay. I had the feeling you were trying to warn me away from Lyric yesterday."

"Not at all," Emory said quickly. "I'm so sorry if I gave you the impression I don't like the two of you together. I think you're perfect for each other." A knowing smile spread across his face. "I'm no longer worried about it."

"Have you seen something?" I asked.

"I see lots of things, Memphis. I have excellent vision," Emory teased as he turned and walked toward his kitchen.

"Did you have a vision of Lyric and me as a couple?" I clarified.

"You know I'm not going to answer that." Emory poured a cup of coffee for each of us.

"Which means that you did. Will you at least tell me how long ago you had the vision?"

"No."

"Emory, that's not fair." I sounded like I did one Christmas when we were kids and he got the cooler *Planet of the Apes* figure. He wouldn't even trade me because he knew I wanted his. The jackass didn't even like *Planet of the Apes*.

"Yeah, well, you're still not getting my General Ursus, Memphis," Emory said, making me laugh. "Listen, remember how you once told me that you didn't want to know anything about a guy unless he was a serial killer?"

"Yeah, but back then I never really thought I'd meet a guy that I could..."

"Love?"

Gulp. "Like a lot."

"I will tell you Lyric isn't a serial killer."

"Hardy har har," I said.

"That's all you're getting out of me. Enjoy the fall, Memphis. You fucking deserve it."

"Thanks, Em."

"Pull up a coffee cup and tell me what you can about the Bliss House investigation."

"I'm not sure what I can say," I replied honestly.

He narrowed his eyes. "Are you being sincere or getting even with me?"

I snorted. "I'm sincere."

"Okay, then tell me about your week. It feels like we haven't sat down for a quiet chat in forever."

I regaled Emory with the stories about the Matrons letting Lyric inside when he showed up unexpectedly, nearly running over Mrs. Hawkins, getting pulled over by Joey, and asked out by Jake. "Add in one hot paranormal investigator, an intriguing ghost story, and too many nights of short sleep, and you get an exhausted Memphis Sullivan."

"Go home and take a nap, Memphis. We can catch up later. Why don't you come over for dinner tonight? Jon is making his famous lasagna."

"He does make amazing lasagna."

"Then it's settled. We'll eat around six."

"I'll be here."

I went home but was too restless to sleep. I needed something to do with my hands to ease my anxiety. I normally would love to draw, but I decided to do something else that would keep me connected to Lyric.

I logged onto *Willows Whisperers* and accessed the fan fiction part of the site. At first, I wasn't sure what I wanted to write, but I made sure to slap the NSFW and eighteen and older labels on it to cover my ass. I titled the piece: One Night in Bliss. While I wouldn't be challenging Chaz, Blissville's resident romance author, to a writing competition, I didn't think it was half bad. Now the question was, did I let Lyric discover it on his own or did I drop a hint and guide him to the story? At the last minute, I changed my mind about posting it on the site. I thought it would be more fun to send it directly to Lyric so only his eyes got to read my latest fantasy.

By the time I saved the completed story to my hard drive, my dick was hard enough to drive railroad spikes. I decided to ignore it and save it up for when Lyric got home because I was certain we'd have a night of marathon sex, especially if he were able to solve the Anthony Bliss and Wallace Bennington III mysteries which I had somehow stopped seeing as two separate incidents. In my heart, I knew they were connected. Anthony's spirit wouldn't rest unless we could tell him what happened to Wallace.

Instead of jacking off, I pulled out my sketchbook and opened it to a blank piece of paper. Within minutes, I was completely caught up in bringing a fantasy to life. This was so much different than anything I'd ever drawn before, but my God it felt right. Only my ringing cell phone snapped me out of my trance a few hours later.

"Hey, Firecracker," Lyric said when I answered the phone. "Still like me?"

"Who's this?"

Lyric chuckled. "You're a funny man."

"I have my moments. Did you have a nice flight?"

"It was eye-opening. I'm in the back of a Lyft heading to the hotel now."

I wanted to think it was a circumstance he witnessed during the flight, but I suspected he had spent a lot of time tracking my activity on *Willows Whisperers*. "And you're still talking to me. I'm impressed."

"I'm the one who's impressed. I mean, wow. You put a lot of effort into thwarting these assholes. I've admired that about you for some time. Well, not you, because I didn't know you were NerdBoy88 until recently, but I admired your attempt to distract Myla Trey from tracking me down."

"Oh my God! You've had a secret profile on the site all this time?"

"Not since inception, but for a few years now. It was cute at first, but then things got weird, and I figured it was best to keep an eye on things from the inside. I didn't want them invading my privacy and dissecting my personal tragedies." Surprisingly, none of them had ever mentioned Lyric's parents, so they either hadn't made the connection, or it showed they had a shred of decency inside them.

"Weird like people writing paranormal porn about you?"

"Okay, that was just hot even if I thought it was creepy the first time I read it."

"Wait, how long ago did you read that story?" I felt panic rising inside me.

"Um, that's not important," Lyric hedged.

"It is to me!" I exclaimed. "I don't want you to think I'm a crazy fan who will broadcast our intimate moments online. I'd never betray you like that."

"Breathe, Firecracker," Lyric said calmly. "I'll tell you everything."

"Okay," I managed to squeak out.

"First thing you need to know, I never got a freaky fan vibe from your fan fiction writing. I admit it was shocking at first, but then I thought it was fucking hot. I admit I wondered what NerdBoy88 was like on more than one occasion, especially when it became obvious you were an ally."

"I hate the way they talk about you," I said just barely above a whisper. "At first, I thought Elvie was nice because she always defended you, but then her methods became vicious. Myla and her cyber-stalking ways just pissed me off. I felt so guilty for being a member of the fan site but thought I would serve a good purpose if I threw roadblocks in their way whenever I could."

"I could tell your intentions were good, and that's why I didn't say anything sooner."

"What? How could you have said anything sooner? You didn't

find out until… Oh. You saw my computer screen when you stopped by my store after the library. Why didn't you say anything?"

"I didn't want to embarrass you, Memphis. I would never have brought it up."

"Why?"

"Because I trust you."

"I bet you don't say that often," I said in awe. Hearing that he trusted me meant more than knowing he liked me.

"You're right; I don't. And I never say things I don't mean."

"This conversation has taken a more serious tone than I expected," I teased. "Of course, you're in the back of a hired car, so I can't carry on the way I'd like to right now. I have a surprise for you."

"Yeah?"

"It's something special for your eyes only. I have your email address on your business card, but I didn't know who had access to it. I thought I'd ask you before I sent my latest installment of paranormal porn. This one might even have an illustration. I must warn you it made my dick so fucking hard, so you won't want to open it up until you're alone."

"Hello!" Lyric yelled excitedly. "Oh, not you, sir," Lyric said to his driver. "Firecracker, you made me startle my driver." Then he lowered his voice and whispered, "Illustration?"

"It's a pretty crude drawing at this phase, but I'm pretty pleased with it so far."

"I can't wait to see it. Hey, I just arrived at the hotel. I need to hang up and tip my driver. I'll shoot you a text with my email address as soon as I get checked in. I'll call you later to tell you what's going on with the investigation."

"Sounds awesome. Have fun."

"I will, and don't forget to send the latest episode of paranormal porn to me along with the illustration."

"I won't," I told him even though I was nervous. "I'm heading over to Jon and Emory's for dinner in a little bit. They won't mind if I bring Gigi and Daisy with me."

"Call me when you get back. Like you, Firecracker."

"Like you too, Ric."

I was still smiling like an idiot fifteen minutes after we hung up when his text came through with his private email address. I scanned the sketch to my MacBook then sent both the latest episode of paranormal porn, as Lyric called it, and the sketch I drew of the hottest part of the scene.

My phone rang a few seconds after I sent it. "You drew that?" Lyric asked. "You've been sitting on that kind of talent and no one knows? Jesus, I want to read the story that goes with this image so fucking bad, but I have an appointment with the concierge in five minutes. Her family has held the position since the hotel was first built. I bet they've handed down some amazing stories through the generations."

"Investigation first, pleasure later."

"What time will you be home from Emory and Jon's? Do you use Skype?"

"I'll be home by eight o'clock, and yes, I have a Skype account," I answered, knowing exactly what he wanted to do during our Skype session.

"Send me your Skype address, and I'll video call you after you get back. I should have plenty of time to do my research on the very important topic we'll need to discuss."

"Discuss? You mean jerk off on camera."

"Jesus, Firecracker. I need to go."

"Don't be meeting that woman with a hard-on, Ric. You'll give her the wrong impression."

"It will be rude if I'm late to my meeting."

"Some would say your monster cock trying to escape your jeans is rude too. Unzip your pants and let me hear you jerk off."

"And you look so innocent," he said hastily, but I heard the sound of him unbuckling his belt and unzipping his pants. "Do it with me. I can hear your arousal through the phone."

Neither of us lasted long as we listened to each other breathing heavily into the phone while we worked our cocks. There was nothing either of us needed to say as we chased a quick release. I knew we were both thinking about reenacting the image I sketched as soon as Lyric came home, and that quickly shoved me over the edge. We grunted our releases at nearly the same time.

"You have some shopping to do before I get back, Firecracker," Lyric said once he caught his breath. "I need to go wash up before I head out."

I had an image of his cock hanging out of his open black jeans. I almost whimpered but caught myself. "Talk to you soon."

I cleaned myself up after we disconnected and decided to head back to Emory and Jon's to hang out before dinner. I loved spending time with them and seeing Emory so deliriously happy. I grabbed a selection of the baked goodies Lyric had made since his arrival, whistled for the dogs to follow me, and headed out. I knew if I stuck around, I'd end up working on the rest of the sketches in the scene and forget to eat.

I wanted to make sure I had plenty of energy for my Skype session with Lyric later that night.

CHAPTER TWENTY

Lyric

"**M**ISS YANG?" I ASKED, KNOCKING ON THE FRAME OF HER open office door. The Asian American woman looked up and offered me a kind smile as she rose to her feet. "I'm so sorry for making you wait. I know your time is valuable."

"I should've been more considerate of your travel schedule and allowed you time to get settled first. Please call me Anh." She extended her hand across her desk, and I shook it.

"It's nice to meet you, Anh. Please call me Lyric. I'm used to traveling, so don't worry about it. Besides, you're doing me a favor, not the other way around."

"I wouldn't bet on it," she said. "You've heard our hotel is haunted, correct?"

"I have, yes. Are you hoping I can help the resident ghost, or ghosts, find peace?"

"That is my wish, yes," she replied. "I do believe we only have one ghost in residence though, and he mostly sticks to his private rooms?"

"His? Do you mean Denver Collins?" Who else would have private rooms on the premises?

"Yes, while most wealthy men in that era chose to live in Nob Hill, Mr. Collins chose to live on the top two floors of his hotel."

"That is unusual," I said. "Doesn't seem like Denver would've had much privacy."

"Oh, privacy was never an issue for him. He had secret entrances for himself and his live-in valet. There were strict rules about the times staff could access his rooms for cleaning and serving meals."

"Live-in valet?" I asked, my curiosity piquing. "Do you recall what this man's name was?"

"Tony Reid."

"You don't say?"

Anh Yang tilted her head to the side and studied me. "You know something, don't you?"

"I *think* I know something which isn't the same." I winked playfully. "Guests staying on the top two floors report seeing or hearing ghostly activity?"

"Guests aren't permitted on those floors. They've remained exactly as Mr. Collins left them when he passed away in 1901. It kind of feels like a shrine slash museum."

"All of his belongings are still up there?"

"Yes, sir. Only the staff goes up there to clean once a week. Would you like to tour his private residence?"

"Seriously? That would be amazing." I wanted so badly to ask if I could take some equipment to document any possible paranormal activity but didn't want to push my luck.

Anh reached into her desk drawer and pulled out a set of keys. "Let's go take a look."

I followed her without hesitation. I was close to solving this mystery; I could feel it in my bones. "I'm surprised you're not blindfolding me or something so that I don't see the secret entrance."

Anh's laughter was light and melodious. "That's not necessary, Lyric. I'll wipe your memory clean when we're finished."

I liked her spirited personality. "This hotel is spectacular, Anh. I was blown away by its opulence when I walked through the door. The attention to detail in the woodwork is breathtaking. Are these marble floors original?"

"All of it is original," Anh replied. "The hotel has been brought up to modern standards, but we've managed to maintain the integrity that met Denver's standards."

Anh led me through a series of service areas on the first floor, including the kitchen where a delicious aroma permeated the air. "I need to order whatever that is."

"That's our famous seafood trio platter," she told me. "The options depend on the season. Right now, the platter includes blackened salmon, crab cakes, and fried clams, along with corn on the cob, a tossed salad, and a dinner roll."

"I didn't realize how hungry I was until I smelled the delicious food." Up until then, I mostly focused on how horny Memphis had made me. I did feel a lot better after that quick jerk-off session with him, which allowed my other needs to make themselves known.

Anh pulled her cell phone from her suit jacket pocket. "Hello, Mr. Smithson. Can you please make sure that a seafood trio platter is sent up to Lyric Willows's room in an hour? The meal is on me, Mr. Smithson. Thank you."

"Thank you so much, Anh, but you didn't have to go to any trouble."

"It's my pleasure," she told me as we approached a non-descript-looking elevator. Instead of a button to call the elevator, Anh inserted a skeleton key into a lock and turned it. The typical silver elevator doors opened to reveal an interior as lush as the rest of the hotel. There were only two buttons to choose from, which were marked with a roman numeral one and two.

Once inside, I asked, "Is it true that someone in your family has held the position of concierge since the hotel was built?"

"It is true," she confirmed.

"Even though the ownership has changed many times over the years?" I asked.

"Only the management groups have changed, never the owner. Mr. Collins established a trust long before he passed away, and one of the things he made certain was that a Yang descendant would oversee the daily operation of the hotel. The other was that his private residence remained untouched except for the things he specifically donated to charity. Oddly enough, Mr. Collins didn't care if management changed the name of the hotel. The law firm acting as trustee has always seemed to have the hotel's best interest at heart when making decisions that impact the hotel and it's employees." She smiled broadly. "The day my father handed the reins over to me was one of the happiest in my life. We take pride in preserving the legacy Denver Collins left behind."

"I can see how passionate you are about your job," I told her. "It's also very evident in the demeanor of the staff that works for you. This is one of the most beautiful hotels I've ever seen."

"Thank you, Lyric."

"From everything I read about the Gold Rush, Asians weren't treated very well. I'm curious how the first Yang was placed in such an esteemed position."

Anh's happy grinned turned wry as she looks up at me. "Jun Yang saved Denver's life when their railroad car was robbed at gunpoint after he first arrived. Jun was on the stagecoach working as a servant and took a bullet meant for Denver. Luckily for my great-great-great-grandfather, the bullet missed anything vital, and it forged a relationship with the man who would change our lives forever."

"Fascinating," I said.

Anh stopped at ornate double doors with the same gold horses that were on the pipe tobacco humidor we found in Blissville. "There are several Gold Rush mining and prospecting experience packages nearby that tourists can buy, and one of them includes dressing in period costumes and getting held up while riding on a railroad car that runs between the mine and the nearby town."

"That's really cool," I told her.

"You ready to see Denver's residence?"

"I am." I closed my eyes briefly to center myself as Anh unlocked the door with the same key that granted us access to the elevator.

I was stunned when I walked into the living room. It was as regal as I would expect to have found in the wealthiest of homes in the late eighteen hundreds. I'm talking plush, velvet furniture that looked brand new, crystal light fixtures, and a floor-to-ceiling fireplace made of the same white and gold marble that was used throughout the hotel.

"It does look like a museum," I whispered.

"Why are you whispering?" she asked.

"I have no idea," I answered honestly. "What else is on this floor?"

"An informal dining room and a kitchen so the chef could come up here and make his food fresh for him and Mr. Reid. The dining room is through these doors."

When she told me it was an informal dining room, I expected an intimate setting and not a large mahogany table that seated at least ten people, but oddly, only had two place settings. One was at the head of the table, and the other was to the immediate right. The fine china used to set the table and the sterling silver tea set and eating utensils had to be worth a small fortune.

"When did construction on this hotel begin?"

"In 1843," Anh said.

"The Gold Rush didn't start until 1848," I said. More important-ly, Wallace didn't disappear until 1850. It was obvious the men had started planning their escape west together earlier than I realized. Wallace had started construction on the hotel before he knew there would be a Gold Rush to increase his wealth.

"I would say Denver Collins had a crystal ball or was a very lucky man. Would you like to go upstairs?"

"Absolutely," I told her. I expected Anh to lead me back to the elevator, but she took me through the kitchen instead. She opened the pantry then moved a back panel to reveal a hidden staircase. "Traveling in secret passages never gets old."

"I thought you might like it."

"Thank you so much for this tour, Anh." The stairway opened into a small sitting area that had a door on either side of the room. "I presume there are bedrooms through those doors?"

"Yes, that's correct. One room belonged to Mr. Collins and the other to Tony Reid."

"His valet?"

"That's correct."

"Was this arrangement a common thing back then? I would've thought the valet would have a room on a different floor from his employer."

"Someone of Mr. Collins's stature wouldn't share a common room with his valet, but the valet's room would be close by to assist his employer with all his needs." Anh's kind smile grew shrewd. "I think we both know there was nothing common about their relationship though, especially for that era."

"You think they were lovers?" I asked.

"Don't you?" she countered.

"I do," I confirmed. "I also don't believe Denver Collins and Tony Reid were their real names."

"Now we're getting to the good parts," Anh said, rubbing her hands together.

"Can I see the bedrooms?"

"Of course, but I warn you I feel like I need to knock on Denver's door to let him know I'm coming in."

"Well, it is polite." She didn't knock though, she opened the door slowly and stepped aside so I could enter. Denver's bedroom was nothing like the rest of his residence. It was still an elegant space, but it wasn't as ornate and fussy. The focus of the room was a large four poster bed with blue velvet drapes tied back to each post. The bed was both masculine and intimate at the same time. "The carvings on the bedposts are phenomenal."

"It's his beloved horse, Starlight."

"Starlight was the name of his horse?" I asked, although I don't know why I was surprised. Why would he have thought to change the horse's name? Who would've known any different?

Anh nodded. "The property maintenance garage out back used to be the stable where she lived. He loved that horse so much. There are photos of her all throughout the hotel."

"Speaking of pictures," I said, "can you tell me if this is the only known photo of Denver Collins?"

Anh looked at the photo and said, "It's the only photo that's been made public. I have a safe in my office where I keep important documents and artifacts." She studied my face closely, and I could tell something was on her mind.

"I'm not detecting his presence right now if that's what you're wondering."

"It is," she admitted. "Are you looking for anything specific for your investigation, Lyric?"

"A specific item? No," I told her. "Evidence that proves Denver's true identity and that of his lover? Yes."

Anh looked at her watch and grimaced. "I have about fifteen more minutes before I have another meeting. Do you want to take a quick look at Mr. Reid's room? If you'd like, I have more time available tomorrow to answer questions for you, and I can show you some of the personal items in the safe in my office. There have been many stories passed through the generations of Yangs. Maybe I can help you find the answers you seek."

"That would be amazing, Anh."

Tony Reid's room was stark and bare in contrast to Denver's. In fact, it didn't give the appearance anyone had lived there. It seemed like the room was there for appearances only. Anh and I exchanged smug smiles.

"What time tomorrow?" I asked.

"Does noon work for you?"

"Perfect," I replied. "Thank you so much for the tour this afternoon. I appreciate it so much."

"It was my pleasure. I hope you enjoy your seafood trio platter."

Enjoy was an understatement. I made an absolute pig of myself and was grateful I had time afterward to get cleaned up and read the story Memphis wrote before I Skyped him. He answered on the first ring, and his beauty took my breath away. Then I saw the shirt he wore, and I couldn't keep the grin off my face.

"That's a cute Rainbow Brite shirt, Firecracker."

"Thank you, Ric. It's one of my favorites."

"Now lose it. I want to see all of you." Memphis immediately complied, and I saw the love bite I left on his chest in the early hours of the morning. God, how I loved marking him. "Mmmmm, you are so fucking hot. Just a few more days until we act out your paranormal porn."

"Adjust your ancient laptop, I can't see your cock," Memphis growled.

"Better?" I asked after rearranging my computer.

"Much. You're so hard for me."

"That story was the hottest thing I've ever read. I want to see you too."

Memphis moved his laptop and got to his knees on his bed. His dick was eagerly poking through the front opening of his Superman boxer shorts. Superman and Rainbow Brite. Did it get any cuter than that?

"Now what?" Memphis asked when stripped bare and repositioned himself in front of his laptop. "Something like this?" He spread his legs and circled his pucker with his middle finger.

"Hell yes."

As sexy as it was getting off with Memphis over Skype, I adored the heart-to-heart chat that followed because it let me get to know Memphis better. He told me all about his family and his secret passion for creating comics. I encouraged him to follow his dream because his talent was off the fucking charts.

"Is there a market for X-rated comics?" I asked him.

"You see a lot of it on Deviant Art and Tumblr, but I don't know if there's an actual market to produce and sell adult-themed comic books. It isn't something I've looked into for myself, and I've never had a client ask about them."

"Have you considered creating an LGBTQ superhero who fights bigotry and homophobia? Or maybe a series for teens who are struggling with their identities?"

"I have thought about those things, but I have no idea where I would begin."

"I would think you write a complete comic book first then worry about selling and marketing it," I answered him. "I know a few people you could probably talk to when the time arrives."

I was ready to open up more to Memphis about my past but doing it over a video call didn't feel right, so we talked about Wallace's private residence in the hotel. "It couldn't have been more obvious that the valet's room wasn't used. There wasn't a personal item to be found."

"Did you find out from Anh when the *valet* arrived in San Fran and when he died?"

"Not yet because she had another appointment she needed to get to, but I'm meeting her at noon tomorrow."

"Man, I wish I was there," Memphis said wistfully. "You're going to blow it wide open tomorrow."

"I wish you were here too, Memphis."

"Lyric, I've been thinking about the humidor with the cremated ashes inside. My grandpa's urn is much bigger than it, so do you think it's possible that only some of his ashes were sent to Melanie? Perhaps, Wallace kept some too."

"Anything is possible," I replied. "Maybe that's why Anthony's spirit is so unsettled."

"Could it also be that his heart and soul were in San Francisco, but the item that kept him tethered to this world was sent to Blissville?"

"You're getting very good at this, Firecracker."

"Well, I had a great teacher," he replied. "I can't wait to see what else he teaches me."

"A few more days, Firecracker."

"It gives me time to do some shopping and planning."

Just like that, we were ready to go again.

CHAPTER
TWENTY-ONE

Memphis

T HE MIRACLE TWINS AND THEIR SIGNIFICANT OTHERS INVITED
me to the movies with them on Friday night, but I politely
declined. I would've felt like a fifth wheel, and it would've made
me feel Lyric's absence more acutely. Damn, I had it bad if I was
already moping after only two days apart. I think I would've pouted
less if I'd talked to him throughout the day, but we were both busy.
I always had a customer in the store when he texted me, and by the
time I got back to him, he was conducting an interview with the hotel
staff or talking to the networks about how they wanted to proceed
with what he discovered.

I was dying to know why Lyric was so excited, but he insisted on
telling me in person. *Just one more night*, I kept telling myself. His
flight was scheduled to land at CVG at noon, and Emory offered to
cover the store for me so I could pick Lyric up. To stay busy, I started
working on another illustration I titled *Afterglow*. Instead of whining
because Lyric was away, I put my energy into making the image of us
cuddling in bed as lifelike as I could. The adoration of the characters
as they looked into each other's eyes was a tangible thing; they wanted to grab onto each other and never let go.

Like always, I lost track of time when I started to draw. Gigi and
Daisy let me know when they needed to go outside. I would take that
time to give them cuddles and make sure they had food and water

before I got lost in creating again. I had no idea what time it was when the doorbell rang; I only knew it was dark outside.

I figured it had to be the Miracle twins and crew, or maybe even the Matrons coming around to check on me. My jaw practically hit the floor when I saw who stood on my porch.

"I received your email about possible paranormal activity in your home," Lyric said before a wry grin spread across his face. I recognized those words as ones I wrote, but I wasn't ready to follow the script yet. I launched myself at him, and Lyric caught me in his strong arms. He backed me up against the side of the house and kissed me as if he'd just returned home from serving a year overseas. Fuck me; I was ready to salute his soldier.

"Wait," he said, stepping back from me. "You're not following the script." Lyric caressed my damp lips with his thumb. "Go back inside and let's start over."

"You can't be serious?" I asked. "How are you even here? Did I lose an entire day while drawing?"

"I took an early flight home and hired a driver to bring me here so I could surprise you. Surprise!" I was surprised all right. Lyric dropped one last kiss on my lips and stood back. "Mmm, you taste so good. And did I hear you admit you're drawing more naughty pictures?"

"This is more on the sweet side. It might give you a toothache."

"You know how much I love sweets," Lyric said. "Speaking of which, are you wearing a Josie and the Pussycats T-shirt? Can you get any fucking cuter, Firecracker?"

"I can put on my Pussycat ears that came with the shirt, or I can get naked."

"Close the door, and don't forget your lines this time. I've stayed semi-hard all damn day long just thinking about this moment. Do you have everything set up for our reenactment?"

"No, because I didn't think you'd be home until tomorrow." I slipped and said home instead of here, but Lyric didn't seem upset about it.

"Close the door, get everything set up, and be ready. Have you heard that song 'Like a Wrecking Ball' by Eric Church?" Lyric asked.

"Oh yeah."

"I hope this house was built well, Firecracker. I've missed you like crazy."

My knees almost buckled. I would've stripped down and offered up my ass right then and there, but that wasn't a show the Matrons needed to witness. "Give me five minutes."

"Two," Lyric countered. "Don't trip running up those steps either. I have big plans for you, and they don't include a trip to the ER."

I practically slammed the front door in his face in my hurry to get everything arranged upstairs. I decided to ad lib a bit by stripping down until I wore nothing but my rainbow-colored bikini briefs. I reached the front door just as Lyric rang the doorbell again.

I opened the door as if I didn't have a care in the world. Lyric repeated his line from earlier and added, "I was in the neighborhood, and thought I'd drop by."

"Oh, that's great," I told him. I couldn't remember a fucking thing I'd written in the story when he looked at me with smoldering gray eyes. "I was just about to take a shower, but you can look around if you want."

"Oh, I want," Lyric replied, shutting the door behind him. "I want it more than I ever knew I could."

"Well, I'll just be upstairs if you need me," I told him, backing away.

The wicked smile on Lyric's lips told me what he needed and how much he needed it. I tried to casually walk up the steps but that act only lasted until I was midway up. I prayed the water would heat fast because I wanted to give him an eyeful when he opened the door. I heard the heavy tread of his boots on the wooden stairs as I pushed my underwear down my legs and stepped into the shower, closing the curtain three-quarters of the way. I wanted Lyric to be able to see me fucking myself on Big Bob 2.

I shook with lust when I lubed the dildo and positioned it against my ass. Just like in the story, Lyric opened the bathroom door just as I worked the large, round head of the dildo past the first ring of muscles. I cried out because the excitement from Lyric watching me pleasure myself was hotter than anything I'd ever done. Of course, I knew what would happen next would far surpass the fantasy that I wrote.

I wasn't playing up the moaning and whimpering as I continued to work Big Bob's massive girth inside me. I heard Lyric undressing inside the bathroom, and it took everything I had not to turn and look. I gasped in mock surprise and genuine pleasure when a hungry-looking Lyric Willows whipped back the curtain and stepped inside the steamy shower.

"You're the hottest fucking thing I've ever seen in my life, Firecracker," Lyric said, casting aside the storyline to live in the moment with me. He took my face in his hands and kissed me while I continued to fuck myself for both of our pleasure. I reached out to stroke his flushed cock, but he blocked my attempt. "That's not how the story went."

"How did it go then?" I asked.

Lyric dropped to his knees in front of me and placed his hands on my hips to hold me still at the perfect spot where the dildo pressed against my prostate. He looked up at me as the water drenched his hair and body. "Something like this," he replied then placed his flattened tongue against the base of my cock.

I braced myself on his broad shoulders as he licked the length of my erection, sucked the swollen head inside his hot, wet mouth, then took me to the back of his throat.

"Fuck," I moaned. My wildest fantasy couldn't compare with the reality of being penetrated and sucked at the same fucking time. Lyric moved my hands up to his hair, encouraging me to fist the strands and fuck his face just as I wrote in my fantasy. I rocked my hips forward just a bit to experiment, fucking myself at both ends. "Nirvana,"

I said while staring into Lyric's eyes.

Lyric gripped an ass cheek with his right hand and slid his left hand up to take turns pinching my nipples. It was sensory overload, and I fucked myself faster, chasing my pleasure while trying not to brutalize his mouth. Lyric released my ass to jack his cock just like in the illustration I drew for him. Real-life Lyric looked at me in ways I could never dream up for cartoon Lyric.

I gripped his head and tried to pull out of his mouth when my balls retracted tighter against my body, but Lyric sucked harder. My orgasm just kept building until I felt like a rubber band stretched to its breaking point. Instead of snapping in half, I shattered into a million pieces when I came. Lyric swallowed all he could, but some of my release spilled down his chin as he let my cock slip from his mouth. His fists worked furiously up and down the hard length of his cock. I eased off my dildo and dropped to my knees in front of him. He kissed me hungrily while I tugged his nipple piercing until he grunted into my mouth and shot his load all over my stomach. We continued to kiss and run our hands all over each other's bodies as if we couldn't get enough.

"I'm so glad you came back a day early," I admitted. "I was worried when I hadn't heard from you in several hours."

"I only wanted to surprise you, Firecracker."

We stood up once our legs were strong enough to support our weight and quickly washed before we ran out of hot water. After we dressed, I led Lyric downstairs so I could reheat some leftover spaghetti I'd made before I allowed myself to start drawing. Lyric dug in like he was half-starved. I was eager to hear about his trip, but it was obvious he needed to eat.

"This is incredible," Lyric said with a mouthful of food.

"Thank you."

Lyric took a large drink of milk then wiped his mouth. "What brand of spaghetti sauce do you buy, because I've never tasted anything this good from a store? In fact, I think it rivals most of the sauces I ate in Italy."

The pleasure I got from his praise for my sauce was almost as good as the sex we'd just shared. "I made the sauce myself."

"Get out of here," Lyric said. "Are you being serious right now? I'm not kidding you, Memphis. This sauce is incredible."

"It's an old recipe handed down through the family," I told him. "I usually make the sauce in large batches and can them, so I have a jar whenever I need one."

"My grandmother used to can everything, but even she didn't make her own meat sauce." Lyric got quiet suddenly. "I miss her so much, Memphis. I thought not talking about her would make the pain go away, but I think it's made it so much worse."

I reached over and placed my hand on his thigh. "Would you like to talk about her now? I'll listen."

Lyric didn't respond right away; he just kept twirling his fork in the spaghetti like he wasn't even present with me. He finally set his fork down and looked at me. "You're probably aware that I took two sudden breaks from filming my show in the last year." I nodded. "The first break was when my grandfather passed away after battling Alzheimer's disease for five years, and the second was when my grandmother succumbed to her battle with cancer. She fought so damn hard to prove that she wasn't giving up. Grammy didn't want to leave me all alone in the world, Memphis. She was in so much pain every day, and it was fucking cruel for me to be selfish. She meant the world to me, and I couldn't stand to see her suffering anymore, so I set her free. I promised her I wouldn't live a lonely life, and that I wouldn't let my cynicism ruin my potential happiness when I found it. I might've said *when* but meant *if*, because I couldn't see a future beyond my current life experiences as an adult. It turns out I didn't know jack about living. I only knew death, and the restlessness that unsettled spirits left behind because helping them made me feel less hopeless and helpless."

"That makes sense to me," I told him before kissing his lips which tasted salty from his tears. "At the same time, I understand why you've been gun shy about romance and love. Other than your grandparents, it sounds like all you've witnessed is the toxic side of relationships. I get why you thought love was an illusion or an excuse to act wildly."

"Smoke in the mirror," Lyric whispered, repeating the phrase used to describe him. "It turned out that I didn't know all that much about life and l-l-like." His stuttering over the word made me smile.

"It's never too late to learn about life and *like*," I told Lyric. "You're not the only one who had the wrong impression about relationships. Of course, I just thought they were boring and tedious."

"Is that why you were attracted to bad boys? You were seeking thrills?"

"It turns out that people aren't that linear. They have depth and layers. Take, for instance, this smoking-hot, tatted and pierced guy I met. Beneath the ink and piercings lives a kind and caring heart that I find far more attractive than his outside appearance."

Lyric snorted. "Your bad boy with a heart of gold?"

"Hooker is overused."

"Not to mention it doesn't apply," Lyric teased.

"That too," I admitted. "What I'm trying to say is finding out you are compassionate and caring doesn't detract from your attractive-ness. It makes you even more beautiful to me, and I can tell you one thing I've learned this week."

"Just one?"

"Several, actually, but you only get to pull out my pearls of wis-dom slowly." I leaned forward and pressed my lips to his ears. "Sort of like a string of Ben Wa balls."

"God, I don't know how it's possible after I came so hard, but I'm getting hard again. Quick. Tell me what you learned."

"That nothing about you is remotely boring."

"You got that right, Firecracker. I'm about to prove it too."

Normally, I wasn't one who appreciated a naked ass and nut sack on my kitchen table but having my legs propped up on his shoulders while Lyric fucked me like a man possessed helped me get over it.

After the intense round of sex, Lyric asked to see what I was working on. I was much more nervous about showing the tender, intimate picture I drew that day than I was when I emailed the sexy one. I knew he would recognize how hard I was falling for him when he saw the way cartoon Memphis looked at cartoon Lyric. There was no walking it back once it was out there but denying him anything was impossible for me.

"Oh, wow," Lyric breathlessly said when he looked at the illustration of me lying against his chest with his arms wrapped around my waist. My arms were crossed over his chest, and my chin was resting on my forearm so I could look into his eyes. The blankets were pushed down beneath my butt cheeks, and Lyric's legs were spread so I could nestle against him. "There's so much detail here." He traced his finger over the folded blanket before trailing it over the curve of my ass, the dip in my lower back, and up my spine. My skin pebbled with goose bumps like he was touching me instead of the illustration. "This is fucking beautiful, Memphis. Can I keep it?"

"Sure," I said huskily. I hoped someday Lyric would ask to keep me, but the look of awe in his eyes was enough for me right then.

CHAPTER
TWENTY-TWO

Lyric

"I'M MORE NERVOUS THAN A WHORE IN CHURCH," MAEGAN SAID when I stopped at Curious Things the next morning. "Tell me everything."

"The good news is I had enough evidence to convince the network executives I've solved the mystery of Anthony Bliss. They want to air the mystery as a documentary on the network."

"That's great news," Maegan said. "What's the bad news?"

"I wouldn't say it's bad news, but it puts a damper on the excitement." Then I explained to her that the network would need to obtain permission from the management company in charge of The Golden Gate Bridge Inn and the law firm that acts as trustee for Denver's irrevocable trust before we could film. "The concierge showed me photos that proved Denver Collins and Tony Reid were the new identities of Wallace Bennington III and Anthony Bliss. The proof was irrefutable."

"But it might be for nothing if we can't get the permission to film," Maegan said softly. "If they say no, what will you do?"

"I will privately do what I hope to do on camera for the show."

"Which is?"

"Take Anthony's remains back to San Francisco so I can reunite his spirit with Wallace's."

"Wallace's ghost is still ambling around?" she asked.

"He is. I didn't feel him on my first visit to his private rooms, but he was there the following day. He's lonely, and he misses Anthony. The only way to set these ghosts free is to reunite them. Memphis gave me an idea the other night on the phone when he mentioned the humidor was too small for all of Anthony's remains to fit inside it. I asked Anh about it, and she showed me a matching humidor that contained the other half of Anthony's ashes."

"Why would Wallace send part of his ashes to Blissville?"

"Anh's great-great-great-grandfather said Wallace knew Anthony's ghost was present. He thought his lover was unsettled because he would've preferred his final resting place to be at his beloved Bliss House. Wallace also felt guilty for taking Anthony away from his children, even though Melanie helped her husband safely leave for San Francisco."

"What?" Maegan asked in disbelief. "What about locking him in the attic and sending him to the asylum?"

"Anthony was never sent to the asylum because Melanie thwarted her mother-in-law's plans. According to Wallace's private journals that are locked in the hotel safe, Anthony's mother showed up for a surprise visit the summer Wallace and Anthony had planned to run away together. Mommy dearest must've figured out something other than friendship was going on between the two men because she drugged her son and locked him up in the attic. She was determined that the sickness Anthony's father suffered wouldn't infect her only remaining child. She was the one who arranged for Anthony's commitment, but it would take months for everything to work out."

"What a sweetheart," Mae said sarcastically. "I'm trying really hard to accept it was different times, but how could anyone do that to their child?" She shook her head sadly. "Then what happened?"

"Melanie sent a telegraph to Wallace, and he came back for the love of his life. Melanie used the same potion Hilda Bliss used on her son to drug her tea. Wallace and Anthony left, and Melanie reported his absence. With Anthony gone, Hilda returned to New York.

Melanie hid inside her home to avoid public scrutiny until she died."

"I hate that she was lonely and sad," Maegan said. "She must've really cared about Anthony to put his love for Wallace before her own happiness and her children's."

"It sounds like Melanie knew all along Anthony and Wallace were lovers. I believe their marriage was one of convenience so she could provide him with heirs to his estate. Who knows? Maybe Anthony tried to be a husband to her but just couldn't deny who he really was."

"Speaking of heirs," Maegan said. "Will the network insist on obtaining approval from any of Anthony and Melanie's descendants?"

"They will reach out to them to see if they're interested in participating in the documentary, but they can't lay claim to any of his possessions since they were legally sold along with the house. They could probably get a temporary cease and desist order, but it won't hold up in court."

"Wow," Maegan said softly. "This is a bit overwhelming. If the network can't make it work out between all the parties, are you going to sneak the ashes to San Francisco?"

"Well, I'm hoping you'll come with me."

"Seriously?" Maegan covered her mouth as tears leaked out of her eyes. "You can't imagine how happy that makes me."

"I know how much solving this mystery meant to you, Maegan. I wouldn't dream of excluding you. Whether we do this on film or Anh aids us privately, you and I will do our absolute best to reunite their spirits and set them free."

"I-I don't know what to say other than thank you, Lyric." Maegan gave me a big hug.

"I should be thanking you," I told her. "Without Bliss House, I wouldn't have met Memphis."

"Oh, yes, you would have," Maegan replied. "I have a feeling Emory would've gotten tired of waiting for you and Memphis to find one another and forced your hands eventually."

"What's that mean?"

"Uh oh," Maegan said then looked at her watch. "Would you look at the time? I have a phone call to make in my office. It's very important and private. Urgent even. See you around, Lyric."

What did Memphis share with Maegan but not me? There was only one way to find out. I made a quick stop at Books and Brew for a second round of coffee and pastries for two before I went to Vinyl and Villains. Earlier that morning, I caught Milo eying the vintage Rolling Stones T-shirt I borrowed from Memphis. I was sorely in need of clean laundry, and he said the shirt was too big for him. It fit me great, and I liked the looks of it.

I would best describe Milo's smile as smug when I approached the counter to order. I expected him to say something about my borrowed shirt. Instead, he said, "I am so glad you're here." Then he slid a Books and Brew rewards card across the counter to me. "I think this will come in handy now that you're sticking around." How would he know that? I didn't discuss my long-term plans with anyone. "Honey, I don't need special abilities to recognize a man who is completely smitten."

"I didn't know people used that word anymore," I teased.

"Call it what you want, but you have the look of the man who has finally solved life's biggest mystery."

"Jack the Ripper? The Zodiac Killer? Bigfoot?"

"Love," Milo replied with a wry smile. "You're wondering how it's possible you've only known Memphis Sullivan for a week. Am I right?" Okay, he had me there, so I nodded. "There's a part of you that is eager to learn everything about him, but the other part feels like you've known him forever." I nodded again. Hell, maybe Milo needed his own show. "It's serendipity, Lyric. If you can believe in your psychic abilities, then why is it so hard to accept that you and Memphis were written in the stars?" Milo's eyes widened like he was surprised those words came from his mouth. "Written in the stars," he whispered.

"Gonna jot that down so you can use it on Andy?" I teased.

"Hell yeah," he said. "We have an anniversary of sorts coming up, so it would be a great time to use it."

"First date?"

"First time for something else," Milo said then winked. "I vividly remember the stars in the sky that night, so it's very appropriate."

"Well, it seems that you've helped us both this morning. Thank you," I said, picking up my rewards card. "At this rate, I'll earn my free coffee and pastry by the end of the week."

Memphis was in his office talking on the phone when I knocked on his open door. It had only been a few hours since I last kissed him, but I wanted to jerk that phone out of his hand and hang it up, so I could taste him again.

"Sonny, that's great news. Thank you so much for working around mine and Maegan's schedule. Are you sure we're not interrupting your Sunday plans?" Memphis listened to whatever Sonny had to say then thanked him again and said he'd see him the next day at one o'clock.

"Looks like we're going on our first pick together," I said when he hung up. "If you're okay with me tagging along, that is."

"Of course, it's okay." Memphis rose from his chair, took the coffee and pastries from me, and set them on his desk. "I *really* like spending time with you." Plus, I needed to prove that I didn't only want to spend time with him when we were naked. I wanted to show him he mattered to me. He mattered very much.

"I can't wait to see you geek out over vinyl albums, comics, and toys."

"How'd your visit with Maegan go?" Memphis asked, slipping his arms around my waist. "Is she excited about solving the mystery."

I repeated the conversation I had with Maegan, including the little bomb she dropped. "What did she mean about Emory?"

"I learned while you were away that Emory saw the two of us together in a vision at some point. He wouldn't tell me anything about the vision, not even when he had it. He just said you weren't a serial killer."

"That was a concern you had about me?" I asked Memphis. He laughed and told me about past conversations Memphis had with Emory about his psychic ability and knowing things before they happen.

"I once told him I only wanted to know if the guy I was interested in was a serial killer or something. Other than that, I wanted to experience the journey on my own."

"Firecracker, your standards are probably way too low."

"Not when it comes to sexy, bad boy paranormal investigators. I've set the bar just right." He emphasized the word bar by tugging the new barbell piercing through my nipple. "And I better knock it off before we get caught fucking in here."

"Okay, I need to get to my haircut appointment anyway."

"Haircut appointment," Memphis asked. "When did you schedule that?"

"This morning after you left for work. The guy who answered the phone said Josh had an opening, and he acted like it was a miraculous thing."

"It is," Memphis told me. He ran his fingers through my hair. "You're not going to cut it too short, are you?"

"Nope, it just needs a trim and some shaping." I cupped my hand around his neck and pulled Memphis even closer. "Do you have plans tonight?"

"No, but I have a wish list."

"I just bet you do." He wasn't the only one dreaming about all the mischief we could get in to together. "I'd like to take you out."

"On a date?"

"Yes."

"With you?"

"Memphis, I'm not asking for a friend. I would like to take you on a date. Dinner and maybe a movie. I saw that Goodville has a drive-in theater. Those are rare as hell these days. We can take my truck so we're forced to park in the back."

"Along with all the other horny teenage kids who plan to do the same thing."

I gasped like I was insulted. "I'm appalled that you think so little of me. I am—"

"Cut the act," Memphis said, cutting me off.

"At least Reaper's windows are tinted," I told him. "No one will be able to see me jerking you off."

Memphis swallowed hard then licked his lips as if he could already feel my hand working his cock. "The fact that we'll have the windows rolled up in summer will give us away."

"Do you care?" I asked.

"Not really. You better get going if you have an appointment with Josh. He runs a tight ship. He's a great guy, and I bet you'll like him. If you want to use him again in the future, you'll want to book your next appointment before you leave Curl Up and Dye." Memphis must've thought he sounded forward or pushy because he blushed and broke eye contact. "*If* you're going to be around."

I slid my hand around to tip his chin up so I could look into eyes the color of melted chocolate. "I'm going to be around." I couldn't promise Memphis forever right then because we barely knew each other. I did know I more than liked him, and I wanted something special with him. "I'll see you later."

The goodbye kiss he gave me lingered long enough to make me question my decision to leave his store, but I forced myself to get going. I wanted a healthy relationship with him which meant we needed to spend time apart to do the things that were important to each of us.

The cute guy behind the counter at Curl Up and Dye greeted me with a happy smile and introduced himself as Dare. "I love your show, Mr. Willows. It's such an honor to have you at our salon while you're visiting." In my heart, I knew I was doing so much more than visiting

Blissville. "You're in luck today because Josh had a rare cancellation. Mrs. Jersey had an emergency appendectomy yesterday. Her husband said she took the news well until they told her she'd have to stay overnight because she knew she'd miss her appointment with Josh." Mrs. Jersey sounded just like my grammy, who'd once told me death was the only valid reason to miss a hair appointment. "Josh is going over to her house tomorrow after she returns from the hospital."

"Oh my God!"

I looked over and saw a blond man staring at me with his hands on his cheeks. "Um, hello. I'm—"

"Lyric Willows," the man said. "Oh, lord. Please don't tell me you're here to investigate my salon or my home. If I have ghosts, I want to leave them alone because they add character to a home. Besides, I can't always blame my kids and crazy birds every time I do something stupid at home."

"I'm just here to get a haircut."

"He's your first appointment for the day, Jazz."

"Oh. I'm so honored. My name is Josh Roman-Wyatt, but my staff and clients call me Jazz. I'm the owner of Curl Up and Dye." Jazz placed a finger to his lips and hummed while he studied my hair. "Follow me to the wash room and let's get you started."

The places I usually visited just gave me a dry cut, or sometimes they'd wet it down with a squirt bottle. I could tell Jazz would be highly insulted if I suggested he do either of those things. It was just strange to recline in the chair and wait for someone else to wash my hair. I think my mom was the last person, other than myself, who washed my hair.

I got over my aversion when Josh started massaging my scalp while working shampoo into my hair. Holy fuck! It felt *amazing*. No wonder Grammy never missed an appointment.

"Are you staying in town long?" Josh asked, making polite conversation.

"I'm planning on moving here," I admitted. Making Blissville my home was the only way to see if my feelings for Memphis were real.

The only question was where I would live. As much as I hated to move out of the house on Maple Lane, I figured it would be best for our young relationship. I wanted to do things right with Memphis so he'd know how much I valued him.

"I know a real estate agent who could probably help you find a rental home, or even a place to buy if you're planning on moving to town permanently."

"I'm not sure if I want to rent or buy, but I'd love his number."

"Sure," Josh said as he rinsed the shampoo from my hair. "Dare has some of Becker's business cards at his desk. The guy might smile like a used car salesman, but he's very earnest and sincere." Josh rubbed some coconut-smelling concoction in my hair for a few minutes before he rinsed me again. "Do you just want me to trim your hair, or would you like to try a new style?"

"I want to try something new as long as you promise not to laugh."

"Would I be in business if I laughed at my clients? Sugar, we're going to be just fine as long as you don't ask me to set your hair on fire or cut it with torches, swords, or gloves that look like Edward Scissorhands."

The Edward Scissorhands comment made me laugh. "Nothing like that, but I want to be clear that I don't want my hair to resemble this guy's exactly. Maybe cut it short on the sides and keep it longer on the top so I can have this style on a smaller scale."

"Let me see it."

I pulled out my phone and showed him the picture of Daken I found on Google. "I don't want you to shave my head and give me a real mohawk though."

"Of course not. That's so 1980." Josh handed my phone back to me and tilted his head to the side to study my hair. Then he took the center of my wet hair and spiked it up in the small but fashionable fauxhawk I'd seen on television a lot. "Scissor cut here," he asked, looking at the hair above my ear, "or razor cut? To be clear, when I say razor, I don't mean that we have to buzz it down to your scalp. Here, let me find the look I'm thinking about for you. I know you can pull it off with your amazing bone structure."

Josh left the salon area for a brief second and returned with a magazine that specialized in men's haircuts. "What do you think about this one?"

"That's exactly what I had in mind."

"The stylist used a razor on the sides, nape, and partway up the crown, and scissor cut the top. Are you comfortable with this length for a fauxhawk or would you like something shorter or longer? Right now, your hair is longer than the model's in the picture."

"Can you do the sides and nape first, so I can see how it looks with my current length?" I asked.

"Absolutely. Are you ready?"

"Let's do it." I worried that the length on top was too much of a contrast to the shorter sides, so Jazz cut about two inches off the top. When he finished, he showed me how to style it myself and the products I needed to do it. "Thank you, Jazz. This is perfect." I hoped Memphis thought so too. Just thinking Firecracker's name made me want to run my fingers through his soft curls. "Jazz, can we make a deal?"

"Why do I feel like this is a trap?" he asked suspiciously.

"I won't ever tell you if the salon or your home is haunted as long as you promise me no one in this salon will ever cut off Memphis's curls."

"You got yourself a deal, Lyric," Jazz said.

I purchased the products I needed from Dare at the counter and scheduled my next appointment for six weeks. I also remembered to grab Becker's business card but still wasn't sure what I'd ask him to look for once I called him.

One day at a time, I reminded myself. Today was all about taking Memphis out on a real date.

CHAPTER TWENTY-THREE

Memphis

OUR FIRST OFFICIAL DATE STARTED WITH DINNER AT THE DINER before we drove to Goodville to watch a movie at the drive-in. Lyric pulled into a spot in the back of the parking lot and spread a blanket in the bed of his truck so we could stretch our legs and watch the movie in comfort. We didn't make it through the first half of the movie before the need to get naked overpowered any other desires. Instead of going back home, I directed Lyric to a secluded spot in the countryside where we could have sex and not worry about anyone seeing us.

"How'd you even know about this place?" he asked me.

"I came out here to watch the Fourth of July fireworks." Lyric narrowed his eyes like he was trying to figure out if it was one of the spots where I hooked up with Joey. "I came with a group of friends, not a date. You're the first guy I brought here to do wicked things with." The starlit sky made an excellent backdrop as Lyric made slow and tender love to me, and the fireworks he ignited inside me were more explosive than the ones that had burst across the sky in vivid color not long before he showed up on my doorstep.

"Do you believe in serendipity?" Lyric whispered in my ear as he trailed his fingers up and down my spine. The night air wasn't cool on my bare skin, but I shivered anyway. "Do you believe our lives are written in the stars, and our paths are a foregone conclusion?"

"Is this about Emory's vision?" I had asked him.

"Partly, but that's not the only reason I'm wondering why holding you like this feels so right and so familiar. I just met you this week, but the deepest part of my soul already recognized you, Memphis. How is that possible?"

"I'm sure you questioned the ability that allows you to communicate with the dead before you accepted it, right?"

"Absolutely, and I even questioned my sanity on many occasions. I'm not sure I'm drawing a connection though."

"Believing in your ability and destiny both require having faith in things you can't explain. I think certain things are easier to accept as children because kids are usually more open to experiences. We're more jaded as adults and less likely to readily accept the unexplainable."

"You don't sound like a jaded adult who can't accept the unexplainable," Lyric said.

"I collect comic books, Ric. It's quite possible I'm a twelve-year-old boy trapped in an adult's body."

"There's nothing childish about you, Firecracker. I think your exuberance for life is endearing." He got quiet for a few seconds while he continued bumping his fingertips along my spine. "I think you made a valid point about kids being more open to experiences though."

"How young were you when you realized you could see ghosts?" I asked Lyric.

"Ten," he replied after a pause. "My mother was the first ghost I encountered.

"Oh, Lyric. I'm so sorry," I said, snuggling even closer to him. I hated that my questions stirred up such a painful memory.

"It's okay, Memphis. I'm learning that repressing things isn't healthy." He kissed my forehead and slid one of his hands up into the curls he loved so much. "My grandparents didn't know right away that my mother had died. They thought she needed some time to grieve privately and tucked me into bed with assurances she would be back the next day. I had a tough time falling asleep because the world just felt off to me, but I didn't know why. My rest was fitful when I finally drifted off, and I don't know how long I slept before I felt someone softly touching my face. It reminded me of when my mom would touch the back of her hands against my cheeks or forehead when I had a fever, so I jerked awake expecting to see her. And I did, but it took me a few seconds to realize I was also looking through her.

"I screamed bloody murder, and my grammy rushed into the room. She saw my mom's spirit and started sobbing. She kept saying, 'Why, Elizabeth? How could you leave him?' Then I heard my mother's voice in my head just as clear as I had that morning. She said, 'I love you so much, Lyric. I'm sorry I couldn't be stronger for you. I failed you as a mother. There will be days when you'll want to blame yourself. Don't, my beautiful boy. You were the greatest gift your father ever gave to me. My treasure. I love you, Son.'

"My ten-year-old brain couldn't comprehend everything that transpired that night, but reality set in the next morning when the state police arrived to inform my grandparents their only child had drowned in the ocean. Witnesses saw her go in and never come out, but there was nothing the police could do until her body washed up on shore the following morning. They identified her by the driver's license she left in her abandoned car. I probably always could see ghosts, but it was the tragedy of losing my mom that triggered my awareness. From that day forward, it grew stronger. Thank God I had Grammy to help guide me. She taught me how to tap into my psychic power and when to turn down the volume to preserve my sanity. There were many days I thought my ability was a curse, but others where I could only be grateful. I would never have met you without it," Lyric told me. "I must sound fucking crazy."

"You ought to know by now that I like crazy," I assured him.

"But can you love crazy?" he asked.

I rose up so I could see Lyric's face. He nervously chewed his bottom lip while he waited for me to answer. "How about crazy love?" I asked. "As in, I am crazy in love with you."

A slow grin spread across his face then he rolled me so I was beneath him once more. "I crazy love you too. I guess it doesn't matter how or why; it only matters that it's real and true."

Lyric and I made love once more and talked until the sun came up. We fell into bed as soon as we got home, slept through brunch, and barely woke up before Maegan picked us up on Sunday afternoon to head north for our treasure hunt. The sunlight was brilliantly bright on a perfect summer day with low humidity, but I was still lying on a blanket in the bed of Lyric's truck staring at the blanket of stars above us.

"Good morning, fellas," Maegan whispered when we got in her SUV.

I snorted and leaned over to kiss her cheek. "We're not hungover, Mae."

"Drunk on love, my dear. Same difference. You fellas look like you need a damn nap. You'll want to be sharp for our hunt this afternoon, Memphis. I have a good feeling about this one."

I was exhausted, and the drive would take nearly ninety minutes, so resting our eyes was a logical thing to do. Lyric stretched out across the back seat, and I reclined my seat. Next thing I knew, Maegan was gently shaking me awake and handing me a piece of gum to freshen my breath.

Sonny Gambini was as friendly in person as he was over the phone. He seemed overwhelmed by the sheer amount of stuff his parents had collected over the years and sad to let it go. Luckily, he was willing to at least show us around and entertain any offers we wanted to make. Maegan was blown away by the dishes and things his mother had owned. There must've been at least three completed sets of fine china. I knew nothing about plates, cups, and gravy boats, but Maegan was in heaven. Maegan pulled out her iPad and was showing Sonny how rare one of the sets was, so I headed to the den where

Sonny said I would find his father's vinyl record collection.

"These values are inflated so the seller makes money, but it helps us come up with an idea of the value," I heard Maegan tell him.

If Maegan was excited about the dishes, you could say I was over the moon with the vinyl record collection. It was the most eclectic selection I had ever seen. Then I found two that stole my breath.

"You're not breathing," Lyric whispered. "Must be something amazing."

I carefully lifted Bob Dylan's "The FreeWheelin'" from 1963 from the storage crate. It was still wrapped and had never been opened. I was starting to feel dizzy.

"Breathe, Firecracker. I have big plans for you later."

I flipped the album over to look at the track list. My heart raced even faster when I realized that I held the Holy Grail of vinyl albums. "Sonny!" I called out.

He must've heard the excitement in my voice because he rushed into the room. "Did you find something valuable?"

I went over and sat down on the sofa and placed my head between my knees because it felt like I was going to pass out. I still held onto the album with a firm but gentle grip though. I raised my head when the dizzy spell passed. Lyric smiled and looked at me like I was both the dorkiest and most beautiful thing he'd ever seen.

"This album is worth a small fortune."

"Bob Dylan?" Sonny and Lyric both asked.

"There's something unique about this album, guys. This record in mint condition was sold for thirty-five thousand dollars at an auction. This album has never been opened. I can't imagine how your dad even got his hands on it, Sonny."

"My dad had a good friend who worked for a couple of different record labels. That's why my dad had so many albums. He wasn't really into music much but felt they might be valuable someday. That's why it has never been opened."

"What's so special about this Bob Dylan record, Firecracker?"

"They replaced four songs on the track right before it was scheduled to release, but someone at the pressing facility used the wrong master to press albums. No one knows how many of the original tracks are out there, but only a few have surfaced. Sonny, I have no idea how much this album is actually worth, and it is way outside my price range anyway, but I will help you find someone trustworthy who would either know a private collector or can help you find the right auction house."

"Wow, that's amazing," Sonny said.

"What about the Bowie album you gasped over before you found this one?" Lyric asked. I carefully put the Bob Dylan record down and picked up the album cover that depicted David Bowie as half man and half dog.

"That's a fun story," I told them. "This particular copy of David Bowie's 'Diamond Dogs' is rare. This is the original cover artwork that RCA worried was too vulgar because of the dog's genitals in the painting. The artwork was airbrushed to cover the genitals for the final production, but some employees squirreled away the original album covers. The last one sold for almost five thousand dollars, and that was before he passed away."

I found several albums more in my price range because they were popular but not rare. Sonny got a decent chunk of money, and I would be able to turn a nice profit. As excited as I was over the albums I bought, nothing prepared me for when Sonny opened the door to a spare bedroom that was filled with the most incredible toys and collectibles.

"Oh my God. That's a 1970's Holly Hobbie Easy Bake Oven. And look at those metal lunchboxes. The Dukes of Hazzard one looks brand new." That thing would bring at least three hundred dollars, if not more. "My sister had this one with Strawberry Shortcake and her friends on it." I looked up to find Lyric watching me with that same goofy grin as before. "Still find my 'exuberance' endearing or are you trying to find a polite way to pack your bags and get the hell out of Blissville?"

"I'm doubling down on your adorability," Lyric said. Maegan called Sonny's name from somewhere in the house, and the man left us alone. "In fact, I would love to strip you down and show you just how much I love you."

"The aftermath would lessen the value of the items that ended up with my 'exuberance' on them."

"Fine, I'll wait, but I'm going to remember the joyful grin on your face for the rest of my life. Everyone should love their work as much as you do."

"Not everyone is as fortunate enough to figure out what their passion is, let alone make money doing it," I told him as I turned my attention back to looking through the toys. "I think we're both lucky in that regard." I expected Lyric to respond, but he didn't. I looked over my shoulder and saw he appeared to be lost in thought, so I couldn't be sure he even heard me.

"My career hasn't felt like a passion for a long time now," he said a few minutes later. "I've felt like I was just going through the motions these past few years."

Lyric walked up behind me and wrapped his arms around my waist. "Thank you for opening up my eyes to so many things."

I set the boxed He-Man toy down and turned around to face him. "It's never too late for a fresh start."

"A new love, a new town, and a new career?" Lyric asked. "That's a lot of new stuff to adjust to."

"Well, the new love and new town aren't giving you up, but maybe you ease out of one career and into another. Maybe start on a small scale. I do believe the lady downstairs made you an offer once upon a time."

"How do you know I was thinking about baking."

"Other than me, it's what you're most passionate about," I replied.

"Nothing and no one will ever surpass the passion I have for you," Lyric said, melting me into a puddle of goo. "I didn't know I was even capable of saying these sorts of things."

"Let's get serious about picking through these toys so we can get back home to see what else you're capable of. I might've bought a few more things when I went shopping for Big Bob 2."

"Tell me what I'm looking for?" Lyric asked eagerly.

I rattled off the most popular types of toys, and he started his search in the corner farthest from me. By the time we finished, Maegan and I had her SUV packed down with some amazing finds. Like me, Maegan promised to put Sonny in touch with someone who could help him get the best price for his mother's rare china. It was a great afternoon, but the sly grin Lyric wore on his face promised the night would be even better.

CHAPTER TWENTY-FOUR

Lyric

"**H**EY, LYRIC," MAEGAN BREATHLESSLY SAID WHEN SHE walked into the kitchen at Books and Brew that I'd taken over for the last four months. "What's the ETA on the next batch of strawberry cheesecake muffins?"

"They just need to cool a few more minutes," I assured her. "The final batch just went into the oven. Do you want me to make more?"

"Nah," Maegan said. "The early birds get the muffins. There's no way for us to predict the demand each day. You have a dozen other delicious goodies to choose from out there. You're better off switching your focus to the afternoon and dinner crowds."

"Turtle brownies are going in next."

"I hope you're putting together a business plan because the demand for your baked goods is quickly outgrowing the kitchen here," Maegan told me. "Blissville needs a good bakery, Lyric."

I was surprised to learn that Books and Brew purchased their baked goods from a commercial bakery in Cincinnati when I approached Maegan to see if her offer to hire me as a baker was still on the table. I was able to provide better quality pastries, muffins, and cookies to Maegan and Milo at a fraction of the cost they were paying the company in Cincinnati. There is a bakery in Goodville and a small one inside the grocery store in Blissville, but neither of them seemed like much in the way of competition compared to what

I could make. I was giving serious thought to starting my own bakery. I had the startup capital from my grandparents' estate, and they would approve of me pursuing whatever dreams made me happiest.

I was happier making pastries, muffins, brownies, cakes, and cookies than I ever dreamed possible. I knew a lot of that had to do with the man I was sharing a life with, but baking fulfilled something inside me paranormal investigating couldn't. It felt like passion versus obligation, and anyone who'd experienced the difference would know how much lighter my soul felt.

"I have given it a lot of thought, Mae. If the right storefront came along, I'd jump on it."

"I'll keep an eye out," she said then shot me a playful wink.

"The crowd is getting restless," Milo said, rushing into the kitchen. "Are the muffins ready?"

"They've cooled enough," I answered then carried the tray over to him.

"I could probably charge fifty cents more because they're still warm," Milo said before he scurried off.

"I better go help Milo with the morning rush, or I'll never hear the end of it."

"See you later," I called out then got to work making brownies and cookies for the afternoon and evening crowds. I lost all track of time until Memphis showed up with lunch.

"Chicken salad sandwich on rye, barbecue chips, coleslaw, and a dill pickle," he said before greeting me with a long, sweet kiss. How was it each kiss tasted sweeter than the one before, and I felt luckier every time I looked into his warm, brown eyes?

"What did you get?" I asked, taking the takeout carton from him.

"Same as you minus the dill pickle." Memphis shuddered at the thought of eating a pickle. He didn't even want pickle juice anywhere near his bread.

"Are you nervous about heading to West Virginia to meet my family tomorrow?" he asked me. "They love you already, so you have nothing to worry about, Ric."

"I'm more excited than nervous," I replied. "I feel like I already know your family really well. I talk to your mom a lot on the phone, your sister and I text back and forth, and your dad forwards me funny emails."

"They're not that funny," Memphis said.

"They're hilarious," I countered. "Anyway, I'm looking forward to seeing the Blue Ridge Mountains and the Shenandoah Valley in the fall."

"I hate to sound like John Denver, but it's heaven on earth," Memphis said. "I know some beautiful locations where we can wrap up in a blanket and—"

"Drink hot cocoa," I finished for him. "I have too many hours of baking left for you to distract me. I want to leave Maegan and Milo in a good place since I'll be gone all weekend."

"Don't work too late," Memphis said. "I have a surprise for you."

"Oh," I said, perking up. "I love your surprises."

"This one didn't come from Kim's Toys. I hope you won't be disappointed."

"Fat chance of that, Firecracker. I'll be done around six."

"I put a roast in the crockpot before I left, so dinner will be ready to eat when you get home."

Home. I never did move out of the rental house on Maple Lane. I thought about it, and we even talked about it, but neither one of us were eager to live separately. I kept telling myself it was crazy to fall in love so soon, let alone move in together, but the thought of sleeping somewhere other than beside Memphis every night left me feeling cold inside. Why fight what felt right and natural to us, and to please whom? His family seemed thrilled that Memphis finally fell in love, his friends accepted me into their lives with open arms, so who'd that leave? Joey? I didn't care what that arrogant prick thought about me. He disrupted my life every chance he got, but he sure ate my cinnamon toffee chip muffins like they were going out of style.

Other than my small circle of friends, I stopped caring about what other people thought a long time ago. I worried that Jerry, Mack, and Drew were going to be upset when I decided I no longer wanted to film *The Paranormal Whisperer*, but they confessed they knew the day was coming. They were genuinely happy for me and loved Memphis when they came to Blissville to film the Bliss House portion of the documentary. It took the network two months to get all the proper parties on board with creating the show. The cast and crew showed up in Blissville a month later to a warm welcome from the town and all our friends. I kept the portions of the investigation I did with Memphis then added more segments with my castmates.

We all flew out to San Francisco a week after the Blissville taping wrapped up to reunite Anthony and Wallace once more. Anh, Maegan, and Memphis joined my crew up in Wallace's private suite to say goodbye and wish the men a peaceful journey. Outwardly, not much of anything happened. No dramatic wind blew through the room, and no paintings were knocked to the floor. But internally, I felt every second of their reunion. The chill in my soul warmed as sorrowful loneliness faded and their spirits recognized what could never be taken from them in any life; true love. I could hear faint whispers of adoration and echoes of laughter before still silence settled over me.

Of course, I had to play it up for the camera, especially since it would be my last show. I asked the questions I prepared in advance, and we even did an EVP session and set up cameras to see if we could catch any spectral activity. I wasn't expecting anything to show up on any recordings, but the EVP picked up two words that warmed my heart. "Thank you." One camera picked up two shadows moving toward one another and the other picked up activity on the thermal imaging camera. To date, it was the strongest evidence of paranormal activity I ever found.

There was so much excitement for the documentary that the network was flying us all out to San Francisco for a special viewing of the show at The Golden Gate Bridge Inn in December. They were turning it into a red-carpet-type event and held contests so viewers could win VIP packages that included dinner, a meet and greet with the cast and crew, a tour of Wallace and Anthony's residence, and a private screening with us before the show aired. If God truly existed, none of the freak shows that ran *Willows Whisperers* would win the fucking sweepstakes. It was a real dick move to sic the cyberstalkers on my friends, but I got NerdBoy88 to "leak" the news that the network was planning a new series that would include everyone from the original cast except me. NerdBoy88 also said he'd heard the rumor Drew would be taking over as lead investigator. It worked like a charm too, because Myla, Elvie, and Steven shut down the *Willows Whisperers* site and turned their attention to poor Drew, the quietest and sweetest on the crew.

Memphis vowed to remain vigilant on the new site so the wicked threesome never really tracked Drew and the crew down, but the guilt got the best of me. I confessed my sins to Drew over the phone one night, and he laughed harder than I had ever heard him.

"You've seen my husband, right?" Drew said. "They won't get close enough to give me problems." Then he got quiet for a few seconds. "So, Memphis is NerdBoy88, huh? He sure as hell can write paranormal porn like no one's business. Is he just as good at acting it out?"

"I'm hanging up now."

"See you in San Francisco," Drew had said before he hung up.

I was looking forward to going to San Francisco next month to celebrate the end of a big chapter in my life, but not as excited as I was to learn what Memphis had in store for me when I got home.

I was disappointed he was dressed when I came through the kitchen door. I greeted the girls with ear scratches and belly rubs before I moved on to my man. I told him hello with my kisses and seeking hands that traveled south.

"Nope," he said, breaking our kiss and pulling away quickly. "Not until after you eat dinner, and I take you to see your surprise."

"You mean my surprise isn't here?"

"Wash your hands and get ready to eat."

"Yes, dear," I said, earning a sharp smack on the ass. "This roast is very tender," I told Memphis after the first bite melted in my mouth.

"The acid in the tomatoes tenderize the meat as it cooks."

"I've never had a tomato-based roast, but it's delicious. And the potatoes and carrots…" I trailed off so I could eat another bite.

"Do you want to save the leftover roast to make sandwiches for lunch tomorrow? We can pack a cooler and eat them on the trip to my folks' house."

"Sure, if the leftovers last through the night." I did dishes while Memphis neatly stacked the containers of roast, potatoes, and carrots in the refrigerator. We took turns cooking and cleaning, so everything felt balanced. "We're so damn domesticated now," I said when we were through.

"I love us," Memphis said. "Grab your jacket and let's go check out your surprise."

Memphis drove us across town to a vacant storefront next to Marabel's shop, Essential Grace, where she sells goat milk soaps, lotions, bubble bath, and bath bombs. "I saw that this place is available for sale or lease."

"And you're looking to expand Vinyl and Villains?" I teased.

"I think this would be a wonderful place for a new bakery in Blissville. The most convenient part is that the back door of this storefront is across the alleyway from the back door of Books and Brew. It would be easy for you to keep supplying them with your baked goods."

"Why would anyone want to have baked goods so close together? Wouldn't I negatively impact their sales?"

"Not if you work out a plan together. Maybe you focus your bakery more on cupcakes and special-order cakes and leave the muffins and pastries to Maegan and Milo. You'll sell the muffins and pastries to them, so you'll still have a share of the income they bring in."

"You've given this a lot of thought," I told Memphis.

"Ric, you encouraged me to follow my passion, and I'm a few chapters short of realizing my dream of publishing a comic book. None of that would've happened if you didn't show your friend a sample of the comics I drew."

"I didn't show him the intimate ones you create just for me."

"Do you want to see the next installment of Captain Firecracker and Ric?"

"Of course," I told him.

"Then you need to follow me inside." Memphis got out of his car, and I followed him.

"You have a key? Memphis, please don't tell me you put a deposit down. What if I don't like the space?"

"Relax, Ric. I only borrowed the key from Becker. No money exchanged hands." He smiled up at me as he stood next to the front door. "Ready?"

"Yeah," I said softly.

Memphis unlocked the front door and flipped the switch for the overhead lighting. The dingy plastered walls were cracked and in bad need of repair, and the black and white checkered linoleum was peeling away from the walls. "It needs a lot of work, but we know an excellent carpenter who could rehab this space in no time. Come check out the area I think would make the best kitchen."

I was too stunned to say anything as I followed behind him. The place was in too much disarray for me to picture it as anything other than a dump.

"I know you're too overwhelmed to envision what I see when I look at this place, so I enlisted some help. Do you remember Dare from Curl Up and Dye? The snarky receptionist?" I nodded. "Well, he's a gifted interior designer who is also looking to get his own business off the ground. I asked him to look at this place and come up with some drawings to show you what kind of potential this location had." Memphis gestured to a series of drawings that were printed and glued to poster boards. "This is how I see the kitchen." It was big, clean, and filled with commercial equipment that would help me turn my passion into a career. "I wasn't sure what kind of look you would want for your bakery, so I kind of went for fifties retro look." Memphis went over all the minute details in the picture from the tile floor, the seating area, and the display cases. "There are so many more options to choose from, but I just went with the black, white, and chrome design so you could see beyond the ugliness that exists right now."

I picked up each picture and studied it before moving on to the next. When I got to the last one, there was a sketch hidden behind it. Memphis had drawn the two of us holding hands and gazing into one another's eyes while smiling like the lovesick fools we were. I was so busy looking at the adoration he so rightly captured it took me a minute to realize that cartoon Captain Firecracker and Ric stood beneath a striped canopy awning. Beside them was a large storefront window with dozens of colorful cupcakes on display. In the center of the window was a large logo that read: Serendipity.

"What do you think?" Memphis asked.

"I think Captain Firecracker is the most amazing superhero of all time," I said. I glanced away from the drawing in time to catch Memphis's cheeks turn pink. "He's sexy, intuitive, and I love the way his costume molds to his bulge. Is he happy to see Ric or eager to sample the baked goods?"

"Both," Memphis said. "About the bakery…"

"I think it's a brilliant idea, and I'd love to hear how long Andy thinks it would take to make this," I circled the disastrous room I stood in, "look like this," I said, pointing to the photo of the pristine kitchen Dare created.

"He's on standby. You want him to come over tonight and start looking?"

"No way," I said. "I have big plans for Captain Firecracker

tonight. We'll talk to Andy when he comes over to pick up the girls in the morning."

"Big plans for me, huh?"

"It's an anniversary of sorts," I told him as we backtracked through the dirt and debris to find the front door.

"I know," Memphis said softly, locking the door behind us. "That's why I brought you here tonight."

"Four months ago today, I showed up at your home unannounced. I had no idea I would fall crazy in love with you, uproot my life, and quit my job to follow my passion for baking. Four months ago today, I met the man who taught me love isn't a sickness, an illusion, or smoke in the mirror. Four months ago today, I began a journey that focused on life instead of loss, beauty instead of pain, and endurance instead of a temporary fix. You are my serendipity."

"Oh my God. That's so beautiful. I think my serendipity sketch pales in comparison to your beautiful words."

"It was a thoughtful thing for you to do, Memphis. I love it. Especially the drawing of us."

Then we both realized that we stood gazing into each other's eyes while sappily smiling just like in the drawing. "Hmmm," Memphis hummed. "I might have another drawing for you at home you'll want to recreate with me to celebrate the special occasion."

I snorted. "Like I need an excuse to mount you."

"Oh, baby, I'm the one doing the mounting tonight."

"To the sex cave, Captain Firecracker. Don't get pulled over for speeding either." Memphis fired up his Beetle and gunned the engine. "I'd have to bend you over Officer Hard-Up's cruiser to show him just how taken you are, and how bad I can be."

"Christ," Memphis said as he nearly ran up over the curb.

In all my life, nothing prepared me for the awesomeness that was Memphis Sullivan. I vowed to show him how much he meant to me every single day for the rest of my life and beyond.

EPILOGUE

Memphis

One month later...

"THIS IS THE COOLEST THING I'VE EVER DONE," MY MOM SAID from her seat on the railroad car that was part of the mining and prospecting excursion Lyric set up for all of us while he and the crew were having a private lunch with the executives from the network. "The weather is just perfect, and the sun will be setting soon. Do you think we'll get to role-play since we're all wearing period costumes?"

"The brochure said there would be interactive activities throughout the mining town," I told her. "I'm not exactly sure who I'm supposed to be though."

"You're James Handley, the banker," Emory said from beside me. "Didn't you read the packet of information that came with your costume?"

"Only that we would wear them on our railroad trip from one pretend depot to another before we got on stagecoaches that would take us the rest of the way to the pretend mining town."

"What kind of interactive activities?" Elijah asked, eyeing Maegan's rounded cleavage rising above the bodice of her saloon girl costume. He ran his finger over his clergy collar while he smiled lecherously at his now fiancé. "How much for a tumble, Mistress Ruby?"

Maegan slapped him with her fan and said, "More than you can afford, Father Andrew."

Elijah leaned over and whispered something in Maegan's ear that made her giggle and blush before she elbowed him in the ribs. I was willing to bet money those costumes got some serious role-playing action before they returned them.

My mom and sister both wore schoolmarm outfits while admiring Maegan's emerald-green, satiny dress. Andy and Milo looked like shady gunslingers. Dad and Emory both looked like prosperous ranchers, while Jon wore a clergymen outfit similar to Elijah's. The stark black suit and pristine, white collar made Jon look even more dark and dangerous. Emory looked at his husband like he was picturing him wearing nothing but his collar.

"Ladies and gentlemen," the conductor dramatically said as he traveled up the aisle. "This part of the journey is the most dangerous, so we need to be on the lookout for bandits."

Bandits? I guess that was the word they would've used back then.

"Oh no," my mom said theatrically.

I glanced over at Emory who was grinning like a fucking lunatic. I suspected he was getting a kick out of my mom enjoying herself so much until I saw a group of men sitting on horseback on top of the slight hill. A lone rider broke off from the group of other actors and galloped toward our railroad car. The closer he came, the wider my eyes got. I mean, I knew it was all part of the experience, but the rifle in front of him on the saddle looked lethal.

"I hope these actors put blanks in those guns," I whispered to Emory.

"Oh darn," the conductor said as if on cue as the rider neared the railroad car. "It's the ruthless leader of The Death Valley Gang."

"Why is the train slowing down?" Maegan asked, looking out the window as the bandit drew nearer. "Not sure it's smart to make it easier for the bandits to rob us blind."

"It's better to give them our money than to be killed, miss," the conductor said. "Everyone needs to remain calm and do what he says. Our possessions can be replaced, but we can't."

My mother fanned herself nervously while my father chuckled beside her. Everyone else focused their attention out the window to watch the bandit who had stopped his horse and climbed down. There was something familiar about the cool drink of water, but the black cowboy hat he wore and the black bandana pulled up to his nose effectively hid his face from view. We'd have a fun time trying to give a description of the fake bandit to the fake sheriff. I wondered if he was some former actor who fell off the Hollywood "It" list and was getting his acting thrills wherever he could. I was mentally preparing myself to hear some ridiculous lines, and I would do my best not to ruin my mom's experience by laughing.

The bandit ambled to the steps with a rifle in hand. I got my first good look at his eyes once he boarded the train. I'd know that beautiful gray hue anywhere. My heart raced as the bandit slowly made his way down the aisle toward me.

"I hear you've got something really valuable on this train," Lyric said in a slow, raspy drawl. "I think it's something I want really bad."

"Right here? In front of our friends and family?"

Emory chuckled softly, and I turned and looked at him. He looked ridiculously smug in the seat beside me. "*This* is what you saw, Emory?" My cousin didn't confirm or deny, he just kept grinning.

I looked up at the man who I fell deeper in love with every day. "I think you must be mistaken, mister."

"No, I don't think I am. There are two things I want from you, and I will throw you over my shoulder and carry you off this railroad car to get them."

"What might those things be?"

"Your heart," Lyric said.

The same heart that pounded erratically in my chest? The one that threatened to rise into my throat and choke me? I felt tears of joy burning the back of my eyes. "Too late," I replied dramatically. "I've already given it away to another fella. What's the other thing?"

Lyric dropped to one knee and pulled out a golden band from his pocket. "Your hand in marriage."

"Awww," my mom said tearfully. "That's so beautiful."

"Did you make that yourself?" I teased. *Holy hell, dumbass. The bad boy of your dreams drops to one knee and asks you to marry him and you reply with a smart-ass question?*

The laughter I saw in Lyric's eyes told me he expected nothing less. "Yep, I mined the gold this morning then melted it down this afternoon to make a ring for you. Nothing but the best for my guy. What do you say? Will you be my husband?"

"Yes!" I would've yelled fuck yes, but my parents probably wouldn't appreciate it very much. I laughed as those tears of joys finally won the battle and slid down my face.

Lyric slid the ring on my finger then pressed his lips to mine for a long, but fairly chaste kiss considering the audience we had. There was no doubt that he had a celebratory night of debauchery planned for when were alone again. Lyric swiftly rose to his feet then hoisted me out of my seat and over his shoulder.

"Where are you taking me?" I asked as he carried me off the railroad car.

"We're going to ride off into the sunset on that horse," my bad boy with the heart of gold said.

And so, we did.

THE END!

Want to be the first to know about my book releases and have access to extra content? You can sign up for my newsletter here: *eepurl.com/dlhPYj*

My favorite place to hang out and chat with my readers is my Facebook group. Would you like to be a member of Aimee's Dye Hards? We'd love to have you! Click here: *www.facebook.com/groups/AimeesDyeHards*

ACKNOWLEDGMENTS

First, I need to thank my husband and children for their constant support and encouragement. It's not easy living with a writer who often disappears into a fictional world for long periods of time. They do so many things to help me out so that I can realize my dream. I love you guys more than words can ever express.

I want to thank Nicholas Bella for helping me name Memphis's store and Michael Bailey for helping me find the perfect villain for Memphis to love. I appreciate you both so much.

To my creative dream team, thanks seem hardly enough for all that you do. Miranda Vescio of V8 Editing and Proofreading, thank you for your tireless work, feedback, and many laughs while editing. Jay Aheer of Simply Defined art is an incredible artist, and I love how she brings my words to life. Stacey Blake of Champagne Formats is also an amazing artist who does incredible interior formatting, illustrating, and designing for e-books and paperbacks. Let's not forget Judy Zweifel of Judy's' Proofreading. She does an amazing job of finding the tiniest details that make a book shine.

To my lovely PA, Michelle Slagan. I'm not sure how I ever did this without you. I love you to the moon and back!

Lastly, I am so grateful for my beta readers and the honest feedback they provide me. Thank you for all that you do, Racheal, Kim, Laurel, Michael, Brittany, Dana, Michelle, and Jodie.

ABOUT THE AUTHOR

Ever since she was a little girl, Aimee Nicole Walker entertained herself with stories that popped into her head. Now she gets paid to tell those stories to other people. She wears many titles—wife, mom, and animal lover are just a few of them. Her absolute favorite title is champion of the happily ever after. Love inspires everything she does, music keeps her sane, and coffee is the magic elixir that fuels her day.

I'd love to hear from you.

You can reach me at:

Twitter— twitter.com/AimeeNWalker

Facebook—www.facebook.com/aimeenicole.walker

Blog—AimeeNicoleWalker.blogspot.com

OTHER BOOKS BY
Aimee Nicole Walker

Only You

The Fated Hearts Series

Chasing Mr. Wright, Book 1
Rhythm of Us, Book 2
Surrender Your Heart, Book 3
Perfect Fit, Book 4
Return to Me, Book 5
Always You, Book 6
Any Means Necessary, Book 7

Curl Up and Dye Mysteries

Dyeing to be Loved
Something to Dye For
Dyed and Gone to Heaven
I Do, or Dye Trying
A Dye Hard Holiday

Road to Blissville Series

Unscripted Love
Someone to Call My Own
Nobody's Prince Charming
This Time Around

The Lady is Mine Series

The Lady is a Thief

Coauthored with Nicholas Bella

Undisputed
Circle of Darkness (Genesis Circle, Book 1)

Standalone Novels

Second Wind

www.ingramcontent.com/pod-product-compliance
Lightning Source LLC
Chambersburg PA
CBHW020729210626
46807CB00016B/527

* 9 781948 273060 *